KEEPING UP

MIA FOX

Evatopia Press

This book is for every woman who has ever stared at a closet full of clothes, but felt like she had nothing to wear.

It's for every woman who plastered on a smile and pretended to enjoy the party, when in truth, she'd rather be home with one of her book boyfriends.

This book is a reminder that women should bond, not compete.

Embrace your friendships and never covet someone else's life.

Know in your heart of hearts that you are strong, beautiful, witty and "keeping up" with the Jones' (or that woman who cut you off in her Escalade) belongs in a farcical book, not real life.

Prologue

Since first grade, basically as long as Katie Pettigrew could remember, she had always wanted to be like Amanda. Amanda was the prettiest girl in school with long, blonde hair, blue eyes and porcelain skin. She was also graceful with the ability to jump rope for what seemed like forever without missing a step. In chorus, Amanda was always given the solo not just because she had what the teacher referred to as perfect pitch, but also because she was the only soprano. This was yet another God-given talent that Amanda possessed, making Katie believe that she was assigned to the front of the line not only in school, but before life even began.

In a word, she was perfect...and everything Katie was not.

Katie admired Amanda's easy way of breezing through life. She wanted Amanda to like her, but more than anything she wanted to be like Amanda. But friendship with Amanda wasn't to be.

Although they attended the same elementary school and then the local middle school together, they did not move in the same circles. In elementary school, Katie was relegated to the lunch tables at the back of the cafeteria with her friends, Chloe

1

and Natalie. Chloe had chronic eczema causing her inner arms and backs of her knees to appear angry with red welts and scabs. Natalie's head was covered in unruly, red curls that defied gravity and matched the myriad of freckles that were splattered across her cheeks as if God decided to sneeze on her. Katie was neither pretty nor ugly, just nondescript with mousy brown hair that hung limply at her shoulders, a frame that was slightly too big, and a nose that turned up more so than the girls with 'turned up' noses, who were deemed adorable.

The three became friends initially out of necessity, a need to have a group to belong to, and then remained so due to their mutual admiration of Amanda. They even had a scrapbook filled with descriptions of the clothes that Amanda wore in the hopes that they would remember this bit of coolness when they were taken back to school shopping.

As the years passed, the scrapbook was shared among the three friends' homes, but eventually Chloe and Natalie tired of Amanda's superior demeanor and decided they no longer wanted the scrapbook. Katie hadn't achieved this same enlightenment, and when Amanda was sent to a prestigious Beverly Hills private school and the others remained in public high school, Katie continued to admire her from afar. Even though they were now miles apart, Katie stayed informed of Amanda's activities and honors for there were so many, each one well documented in the press due to Amanda's father's good fortune in business, making her a media darling.

Katie kept every single clipping and carefully pasted it into her scrapbook, hoping that one day, she would achieve similar status. The creme de la creme of Amanda's good fortune occurred after her graduation from Wellesley College, widely acknowledged as the nation's top college for women, and not just any women, but privileged women. Following her receiving a Bachelor of Arts degree, naturally with honors, it was announced that Amanda would marry Steve Exeter, the founder and CEO of Exeter Computers, one of the latest in a series of

.com companies to hit it big with the development of a new app. This one became especially lucrative after the press estimated it would find its way into nine out of ten homes. Subsequently, the company launched an initial public offering and Amanda's role as fiancee to a millionaire became fodder for every girl's dream.

For the six months leading up to the wedding, an event that was of royal standard, Amanda and Steve were photographed at restaurant openings, theater events, and charity balls. Because of Amanda's role as a leading lady of charity functions and Steve's innate business sense, reporters of all sorts--from the financial section to the society pages--wanted to interview and photograph the happy couple. In nearly every image Amanda and Steve stood side by side, her left hand joined with his right, forming a heart with their fingers in a pose that had become known as the Exeter Engagement.

These photos would take Katie's breath away every time she saw them. Amanda seemed to be the epitome of a romantic and privileged fairytale. Katie hadn't spoken to her in years, but never gave up hope that one day, she would finally be invited into Amanda's inner circle. Until that day came, she saved every clipping and carefully taped it within her book using the latest acid free linen tape so as to preserve her precious dreams for a lifetime...or until she could replace Amanda at the top of the social ladder.

Chapter 1

The moving truck was still in the driveway of their dream home, a spacious two-story Mediterranean complete with built-in bookshelves, Sub-Zero appliances, sunk-in tub, and walk-in closets; yet, as Katie looked out the window she decided that something was missing.

She had yet to spend the night in her new home, but already she was aware of its inadequacies. The home across the street was larger, and in spite of popular rhetoric indicating otherwise, larger was better. A sign tucked in a discreet corner of its front lawn indicated its landscaping was "Conceived by Dwight Designs...Beverly Hills...New York...London." Even the driveway was born to impress, its length accentuated by tall palm trees, erected every few feet like soldiers guarding Buckingham Palace. A hammock cradled a tanned and muscular man who turned at the sound of his wife, maneuvering their Mercedes convertible up the drive. She was pretty enough to be a model or even an actress, but the Pettigrew's real estate agent casually let it slip that she wasn't a "real" actress. Apparently, the couple's money had been made in the porn industry, and as if she still favored public displays, she got out of the car and promptly planted a juicy kiss on her husband's mouth.

"They seem nice enough," noted Katie's husband, Rich. "A bit showy, but that's to be expected in these gated communities." He stood behind Katie and nuzzled her neck as she continued to stare out the window. "Well, we're finally here. It sure beats the Valley."

Katie and Rich had scrimped and saved to get out of the San Fernando Valley, but their real break came when a developer wanted to buy ten house plots adjacent to a shopping mall to create a new luxury office complex complete with restaurants, state-of-the art fitness center, and amenities such as a dry cleaners and health spa. Every one of the homes except the Pettigrews' had been occupied by the original owners who had purchased their homes a good thirty years ago at a price that was a fraction, more adequately described as not even in the same stratosphere as what the developer was offering. Each one of these homeowners settled within a week, but not the Pettigrews'.

Negotiations went on for months until the developer started to realize that his dreams were disappearing at the hands of one couple living in a ratty, downtrodden home that was better off bulldozed into oblivion. And the only way that would happen was if he paid a cool million for the privilege.

"I bet they never lived in the Valley," Katie said absently, her mind on the couple across the street. "They seem kind of nouveau riche, if you ask me." She turned suddenly to look at Rich and declared in a voice that was an odd mixture caught between pride and resentment. "We're not like that. We worked hard to get here."

Although it was Saturday and neighbors from both sides bustled about, nobody showed signs of doing what Katie and Rich had come to view as typical weekend activities. Not a tool box was in sight. No ladders were propped against these homes. Every car was pristine, making the need to pull out a garden hose non-existent. Nobody even dared bend down to pull a weed. Katie watched and waited and soon discovered the reason.

A red pick-up truck with a broken tail light pulled up in front of their next door neighbor's home, causing two joggers to pick up their pace before any offensive noise ensued. The driver and passenger exited the truck and took their new positions, one behind a lawn mower, the other holding a leaf blower. They stopped for a moment to admire two women departing from another house. The women piled mops, pails, rags, and a vacuum into a car of similarly dubious origins, which Katie hadn't noticed until now as it had been completely covered by a tarp. Katie wondered if the homeowners insisted that such care be taken in order to preserve the "street appeal."

The neighbors themselves had seemingly no chores to accomplish. With the exception of a lone dog walker, nobody seemed to exert any effort. Katie turned at the sound of one of the movers' voices.

"Where do you want this one?" he asked indicating a box marked "fragile" that teetered precariously on top of many others that he hauled on a dolly.

"Yipes..." she said rushing to retrieve it. "Don't worry, I'll handle this one." The large box made walking a bit awkward since she could just barely fit her arms around it, her head perched on top to hold it in place. While awkwardly shuffling across the room, a sight outside the window caught her eye. The dog walker had stopped in front of their house. Katie shuffled the box onto one hip, waiting expectantly for the doorbell to ring. She halfway hoped that the dog's owner was stopping by with a welcome basket. Nothing fancy, just a few cookies, maybe some brownies...a box of herbal tea? But no. The woman hadn't paused in front of Katie and Rich's home to greet them, only to let her dog take a quick pee on the rose bushes.

"Rich? Can you give me a hand?" she called, hoping she could go back to her window perch and people watching. When no answer came, she continued her struggle and carried the box into the kitchen. A nagging realization dawned on her -- in this neighborhood, weekends were for lounging, not heavy lifting. This was a different type of crowd. Not unfriendly, Katie decided, as the dog walker had caught her staring out the window and no sooner gave a friendly wave before departing with her poodle. But, Katie was fooling herself if she didn't recognize the truth. It was more like a beauty pageant wave, very practiced and slightly aloof. This was not a come-over-and-meet-the-wife-and-kids type of crowd. It was, Katie decided, the IT crowd.

The jewel studded, luxury car laden, perfectly coifed neighbors across the street had yet to tire of the hammock or each other. They laughed loudly as they tried mercilessly to heave the other off the side with each undulation. Katie couldn't remember the last time she and Rich had the time to not actually do anything.

Rich joined Katie, who had now deposited the box and returned to her window seat. "What's going on out there now?"

"Just the neighbors...still..." she responded absorbed in their antics. She wanted to turn away, but somehow just couldn't. It was like watching a network television show -- they were so beautiful and happy. Katie shook her head, never having seen real people that were quite so...perfect.

"Noisy, huh?"

Katie didn't answer, mesmerized by the sight of them toppling from the hammock and onto each other, right there on the front lawn for everyone to see. "Downright, irritating," she finally replied as a most disturbing thought entered her mind...She wanted to be just like them.

Chapter 2

W hat struck Katie was not the opulence of their neighbors' homes, but rather, that each owner had managed to make so many improvements and upgrades to their homes so that each one no longer looked like the cookie-cutter mold that was conceived by the developer.

"Just look at that one with the fancy front door," Katie said pointing. "And they even added bay windows. It doesn't even look like a 'Plan 1' anymore."

In spite of their payoff, Katie and Rich struggled to afford the smallest of the model homes in the Briarwood gated community. They purchased in what insiders of the community called the "Lowlands." It was a term that the realtor, a resident of the neighborhood herself, struggled to keep silent. The super rich lived in the Briarwood hills, where every home was custom designed, sat on a minimum of one acre with another acre separating it from the house next door, and every home was at least 10,000-square-feet. Katie knew that it was in this privileged part of Briarwood that Amanda resided.

But her own realtor had insisted that owning the smallest among larger homes, even in the Lowlands region of the neighborhood, was a far better investment than had they done things the other way around. "You have something to aspire to," she had told the Pettigrews. "And there's so much you can do to make this place more individual."

However, even though they conserved their finances, there still wasn't much left for improvements. And, as Katie glanced at the other homes on her street...each one larger, each more impressive than theirs...she felt the inkling of buyers' remorse. Whereas the other houses on the cul-de-sac exhibited a certain signature style, Katie and Rich's home bore an assembly line like quality. "Remember when we turned down all those upgrades?" Katie asked, her voice wistful.

"Yeah..." Rich hedged, knowing what was coming. "We agreed that it was too much money to spend all at once...we said we could always do those things later on."

Katie nodded, thinking that 'later on' just couldn't come soon enough.

Rich approached Katie's perch in front of the window. "Hey, shove over."

"This is my spot," she playfully complained, but moved over.

"We'll get there. Don't you worry."

"I know," she said and rested her head on his shoulder. "It's just that this spot would be more cozy and comfortable if it were a bay window and not just a window."

He kissed her forehead. "I could always take a sledge hammer and..."

"No!"

Laughing, Rich pulled her in close. "You always know how to spot the best things...must be how you found me."

Katie smiled and rolled her eyes. "Okay, but don't get any ideas about turning this into your reading nook." The two of them continued to sit in comfortable silence, watching the street and taking a welcome break from unpacking. That is, for as long as Katie could keep her mind off its current track.

Katie jutted her chin at another house, unable to stop her

thoughts. "See the place next door? I like that one," Katie noted.

"Ehh, it's nothing special. Certainly not better than our place. Besides, what's that play house thingie?"

Katie made a noise that half resembled a horse's snort. "That's not a play house. It's a gazebo."

"What's it doing on the front lawn?"

"It's pretty. It's an O.A.A.," she said knowingly.

Rich gave her a blank stare.

"Remember? Stacey, the realtor told us that *this*," she said indicating their own rather bare and nondescript front yard, "was what comes with the house. Everything you see around the neighborhood...those are O.A.A.'s -- Owner Added Attributes."

Rich took it all in--the news and the neighborhood. In addition to the gazebo on the front lawn, the home next door and to the left of the Pettigrew's featured white iceberg roses, planted precisely twelve inches apart and leading from the sidewalk, up the path, and all the way to the front door. The house to their right featured an Italian-designed fountain depicting a Phoenix rising out of the water and a hand-carved swinging bench swaying on the front porch.

As they each made mental notes about the have's of their neighbors and the have-not's of their own existence, a few more residents made appearances and it became apparent that each home's attributes were matched by inhabitants with similar qualities. This was a neighborhood where impressions were carefully manufactured.

An immaculately dressed woman carrying a toddler outfitted in a chic Baby Lulu dress emerged from the home with the roses and approached her gazebo carrying a tray of lemonade and biscotti to where her husband sat reading the paper.

"What do you think he does?" Katie gestured toward the man, who appeared oblivious to the child who pulled on its mother's pearls or her feeble attempt to transfer interest to a sterling silver rattle. He merely sipped his drink and read intently from his iPad.

"What they all do," Rich answered with a shrug.

"Who?"

"Those types. The financial planners, investment bankers, stock brokers, computer software designers. They're the type that make it big...or lose it big," he said thoughtfully.

"Wouldn't be so bad..." Katie mused. "You know...to have it for awhile and lose it, rather than never...," but Katie let her voice trail off.

"Talk about types," Rich continued, not wanting to address his wife's fears. "Those two," he said pointing to the couple that emerged from the house with the two-seated swing, "Are professionals."

"Professional what and how can you tell?"

"I'm guessing doctors. They're getting into an expensive, but sensible car. She's carrying a brief case and is kinda lesbo," he added. "And him? He's multi-tasking more than a porn star in a threesome."

Katie rolled her eyes, but immediately looked more carefully in their direction.

"See? He's checking texts, drinking his coffee, and tying his tie. Talented," Rich added with obvious envy while nodding his head.

"How can she be a lesbian? She's married," Katie argued in defense of the neighbor she had yet to meet. "And what's so great about being able to drink and check a text?"

"Without spillage?"

Katie shrugged her shoulders, an admission that Rich had a point.

"Anyway, I didn't mean that she was a lesbian, just that she dresses like one--and not the good kind. Not the...you know, lipstick lesbians," he said, lowering his voice. "Nah, she's the type who dresses that way so she can compete with men in the workplace. God, I hate men's suits on women. Very unfeminine."

"Alright, Mr. Armani," Katie teased.

"Actually, Armani designs those awful suits. Jodi Foster wore one once to the Oscars. I prefer to think of myself more like Christian Dior, bringing a bit of quiet elegance to the fashion world."

Katie surveyed Rich. Quiet maybe; elegant never. Like the furniture that was being paraded into their new house, Rich was a little worn around the edges. His job as a bio-chemist in charge of researching alternative energy sources, made him a news junkie. He didn't just read the techie section; he kept up with everything from who wore what to the Oscars to the latest in missile defense systems. Yet, when it came to his personal life, he rarely conformed to the information he gathered. He fancied himself a worldly savant, but emerged an average suburban as comfort would prevail.

"Come with me," requested Rich, leading the way to the backyard.

"I don't have time. The boxes..."

"Just for a minute," he said leading her outside and to a wrought iron bench with splintered wooden planks that always threatened to lodge themselves into Katie's backside. It was a feature from their old garden that she had hoped wouldn't find its way to the new one, but Rich wasn't one to throw away "a perfectly good piece of furniture." He patted a spot next to him. "The boxes can wait. This is important."

Katie took her seat beside her husband. He gave a perfectly contented smile and moved closer to put his arm around her, but Katie didn't feel inclined to admire the mountain view from the back of their home. Besides, these mountains were more like hills -- even if it was the Hollywood Hills. Still, to her, the mountains of the Hollywood Hills were second-class views to the ocean views of Malibu.

Mountains. Steady. Unmoving. Never-changing. An ocean

view was dynamic and interesting. It was what the celebrities were always after. Location was what it was all about. Having morning coffee on a veranda with windswept hair, not a patio where morning fog threatened to produce frizz. Certainly the view would warrant respect from visitors of their old neighborhood, if they ever felt inclined to invite them around. But Katie wanted to leave the days of Woodland Hills and the San Fernando Valley behind her.

She inhaled deeply and closed her eyes, resting her head in her hands, arms crossed behind her. They were really here...Hollywood...over-the-hill, all those cool phrases that people from the Valley would speak when they ventured thirty miles south for a big night out on the town. Now, she and Rich could hobnob in the hot spots every day of the week, if they chose to do so. Yes, this was nice, she thought with a sigh...especially when they settled in and fixed up this fixer upper. Yesiree, a cool mil didn't buy you much these days, at least not in Hollywood. Katie knew what she had to do. If she and Rich were to really be happy, their house...hell, their entire lives, would have to turn it up a notch.

Rich sighed with equal contentment. "Picture perfect."

"Yeah, I think we can really make something of it," replied Katie.

"What do you mean? It's 'move-in' condition," corrected Rich, reciting once again from the real estate agent's mantra.

But Katie wanted to scream that for a 'move-in condition' house it was suspiciously void of wood or terrazzo tiled floors, a built-in barbecue, french doors, and other expensive, designer features. A mover walked by with a box labeled "objet d'arts," but with her new mindset, Katie barely flinched. She knew the box contained a myriad of vases, but in spite of the fact that they were balanced precariously on the man's shoulder, it no longer bothered her as now they seemed more like useless nicknacks. The "Shabby Chic" fabrics on their furniture could no longer wear that moniker as they appeared shabby, not chic. Not to mention that their driveway was the only one without a luxury vehicle. It was bad enough that their compact Camry littered the drive, but now the unpacked boxes deposited by the moving crew had accumulated there as well.

"I have to get back to the boxes. The neighbors are sure to notice the mess." It wasn't the type of first impression that Katie had in mind.

"WHERE DO YOU WANT THIS ONE?"

The same question over and over.

Katie looked up at the moving man with a beer-stained t-shirt. He was carrying a supposed antique wing chair that once belonged to Rich's grandmother, but had seen better days and now looked as if it should join her in the old age home. Katie had once even gone as far to suggest the Salvation Army, but was quickly reminded that it held sentimental value. The moving man was beginning to drip with sweat. Rather than have him leak on her furniture, regardless of how shabby it was, she merely pointed a polished finger to a remote corner of the living room, hoping that he got the chair there before he deposited any more of his DNA on it.

"Garbage!" Rich yelled from where he still sat in the garden.

Katie hoped Rich had seen the light, deciding to part with his cluttered odds and ends. Finally, they were on the same page. She beamed happily as her husband approached and stretched her arms toward him, only to stop mid-hug. "That smell," she said horrified, pushing Rich away.

"That...is the smell of success," he replied.

Katie remembered reading in Rolling Stone magazine that actress Pamela Anderson had fallen for rocker Tommy Lee's bad boy image, complete with body odor. In recent years, Matthew McConaughey also admitted to forgoing the use of deodorant because he preferred his natural smell. Well, that was one aspect of Hollywood and celebrities that Katie did not want to experience. In fact, she found the idea repulsive. "What have you been doing out there?" she asked, surveying the yard, now newly cultivated. A row of shovels and rakes stood suspiciously at attention. "I've been working on this in the garage at the old place...couldn't wait to get it here where it belongs."

"It smells like the city dump."

"Nah, it's my new compost invention, one I'm taking straight to the top people at work. Might even get myself a patent and government funding," Rich said proudly.

"Maybe dump was too forgiving of a word. How about, 'it smells like cow dung?'"

"Katie, dear," he chuckled. "You just leave the bio-chemistry to me...cow dung," he started to laugh harder and shake his head. "An experienced nose would recognize the slightly acidic odor of rabbit feces delicately blended with a mixture of egg shells and flash frozen flies. Now look over here," he said taking her to a similarly smelly and now barren area, which used to be a tulip garden.

Katie looked at the area with her mouth agape. "Why would you do such a thing?"

"Mark my words, Katie, this..." he said with a sweep of his hand, "will be all the talk."

"That kind of talk I don't want!"

"Don't be silly. This is the most environmentally sound growth mixture available. No chemicals, just pure manure, and a few other biodegradable compounds. Just get a load of it. Catch."

Much to her horror, Katie instinctively held out her hands. "Gross it touched me!" she said indicating her arm. Just look."

"Let me see," he said gently, and then grabbed Katie in close for a bear hug.

"Rich, let go," she pleaded, but was then surprised when he obliged without warning and sent Katie flying into a pile of the freshly cultivated concoction. Katie looked up forlornly, covered in brown filth. In a tentative almost feeble movement, she reached her hand to Rich.

"I'm sorry. I thought I heard a car pull up," he said gallantly taking her hand only to find himself pulled atop the heap in one swift movement. Katie was a woman of considerable bulk, who had no trouble asserting herself against Rich's lean frame when she chose to do so. "I didn't hear anything, but if you'll excuse me..." she said in a hoity-toity voice and left the garden to retrieve her decapitated tulips.

Katie was in the process of testing the odor margin of one tulip when Stacey Simon of Simon Says Realty and the agent who sold the Pettigrews their new house, approached. From Katie's vantage point on the ground, the first thing she saw of Stacey was her fawn colored stiletto heels, whose minute circumference implied that the less touching the Pettigrew property, the better. Stacey gingerly stepped around the spilled slop.

"I rang the bell, but then thought I heard voices back here. And look, here you are. Already making yourselves at home."

"Sorry...we thought we heard a car, but didn't realize...anyway, we're just doing some gardening," Katie lied.

"That's so suburban," Stacey noted.

Knowing that he and Katie were a sight, Rich bristled over Stacey's comment. He had grown to distrust real estate agents, particularly since discovering that Stacey had a brief affair with the seller of their new home. Yet, while Rich went on about it being a conflict of interest, Katie chose to ignore the indiscretion because Stacey had promised to introduce them to the neighbors once they got settled in.

Stacey was someone that Katie could imagine herself emulating -- not the sleeping around stuff, but her style. Katie was in awe of Stacey's fine tailored, albeit revealing clothing, her flashy car, and even the Channel lipstick and perfume she doused herself with each time she and Katie would arrive at a potential home. Katie had made a mental note to dispose of all drug store lipsticks and treat herself to the $21 type that would surely make her lips look fuller.

Katie was also impressed with Stacey's California native status. She was the first person who was born and raised in Los Angeles that Katie had ever met. So although Katie was well aware that Stacey's antics with the seller of the house could cause the entire deal to fall through, Katie merely hoped that Stacey was darn good in bed and would be able to convince the seller to accept a lower offer. Unfortunately, the affair ended just one week before they were supposed to enter escrow. It was touch and go for awhile with the seller suggesting that he felt the Pettigrews repair requests were out of line.

Rich had confronted Stacey, asking if every agent in Los Angeles beds their client's house prospects, but Stacey merely shook her head and said she didn't see what the problem was. "I gave him head and bam...right afterwards, he signed off on your request to fix that back fence."

But in the end, the back fence never did get fixed. Stacey got dumped, and the Pettigrews had to accept the whole fiasco or risk losing the house to another couple. Stacey showed up one morning in tears, complaining that the seller was a total douche, and Katie found herself offering a shoulder for her to cry on. It didn't matter about the fence, she reasoned. Stacey had officially become her first Briarwood friend and she hoped the relationship would extend beyond that of agent and client. The fact that Stacey was now paying them a visit was a good sign in Katie's book, maybe even solidifying the fact that they really were friends and not mere business associates.

"Rich is conducting some very important environmental research and he graciously allowed me to participate," she beamed while displaying her manure covered arms. "It's also all the rage in the Paris spas," she added.

"You're kidding?" Stacey looked on with unmasked disgust.

"I would never kid about a beauty *regime*," Katie answered, accentuating the word in an overly french accent that she thought sounded sophisticated.

Stacey blocked the idea of wearing manure out of her mind and concentrated on the potential of the Pettigrews hitting it rich and perhaps buying an even bigger house. It was the L.A. thing to do, after all. Every relationship had to serve a purpose.

"What type of research?" she asked politely, trying to breathe through her mouth in order to not gag from the smell.

Katie could see Rich on the verge of telling the truth and quickly stepped in. "Oh, it's all very top-secret. Going for venture capital funding...mergers, acquisitions, I.P.O.s, you know," she said in an effort to drop as many catch phrases as possible.

"Well, I'll leave you to it then," Stacey offered. "Still, it's a pity about those tulips," she said retreating from the carnage.

"Wait. Wasn't there something you wanted to ask us?" Katie inquired.

Stacey seemed determined to think up a quick fib, but the horrendous sight of a discolored Rich and Katie left her tongue-tied and lie-impaired. "Oh, right," she said sounding defeated. "I'm helping Rachel plan a block party," she said gesturing to the house next door. "You'll love Rachel. She and her husband, Paul, are to die for. Anyway, mark your calendars for this Saturday."

Chapter 3

Stacey was barely out of earshot when Katie jumped for joy. "This is our chance. Our first Hollywood party where we get to make The. First. Impression!" she squealed.

"We're not actually going," said Rich horrified.

"Of course we're going. Why wouldn't we? You want to meet the neighbors," responded Katie more as a statement than a question.

"The neighbors didn't even bother to invite us. Stacey did, and not very politely I might add. Where's the invitation?"

"Don't be so old-fashioned, Rich. It's just a casual block party. You don't need an invitation," she said following Rich through their non-existent flower garden.

Rich was now busy moving the patio furniture that had once looked bright and cheery, but was now dismal thanks to too many hot San Fernando Valley summers. "Stacey is a phony," he declared while struggling with an oversized umbrella.

"That's not true. I can see us becoming real friends."

"She just wanted to sell our house and now she probably wants to sell us our next one too," he puffed. "Besides, I never heard of going to a party where the host can't be bothered to send or at least call with an invitation. I mean, we do live right next door," he said shaking his head while still struggling with the umbrella. "Hey, can you give me a hand?"

"Will you go to the party?"

"Katie, just help me."

"I think I hear the telephone," she said and hurried to the house.

"Fine, be that way," Rich said to himself and determinedly picked up the umbrella again. The shaft was at least seven feet tall and when the umbrella was fully erected, its diameter was another six feet. The task was straight-forward. Rich merely had to place the umbrella into its hole. Unfortunately, Rich had little experience in getting large items into small spaces. A considerable breeze made his job even more difficult. He tried running and thrusting the pole like a javelin, but couldn't get enough leverage to lift it. Next, he straddled the pole, trying in vain to close the umbrella's outstretched prongs. But after inching forward, Rich only succeeded in jabbing a sharp point into his eye. Katie ran from the house upon hearing Rich screams and found him lying defeated on the ground with the umbrella sprawled out next to him.

"What have you done?" she asked.

"Never mind. But, I think I've made that important first impression."

Dean and Ireland Alexander, from across the street, had poked their heads over the Pettigrew's fence and were watching the scene intently.

"Can we come in?" the woman asked although her husband was already working the latch on the fence.

Wearing matching jogging clothes that could only be described as minimalist, the couple smiled and waved as they made their way through the gate. "We heard the screams," the man explained. "Need a hand? An ambulance?" he shouted from across the yard.

"Get up! Get up get up," Katie whispered in a panic.

Katie lent Rich a hand, which he gladly accepted and the two stood side-by-side, watching their new neighbors approach with the eerie slow motion quality of a movie in which the beautiful people waltz onto the scene. It wasn't really that much of a stretch considering that Dean and Ireland originally met while filming "Single in Paradise" a reality dating show where ex-porn stars find out if they can have a relationship with a "normal" person. Dean and Ireland found that they couldn't and ended up going off with each other, once the show aired and they were cleared to be seen together in public.

"Wow," Katie uttered.

"Wow is right," Rich agreed.

Katie immediately thanked her lucky stars for having Rich in her life as she could never be comfortable with a man like Dean, whose bottom was twice as small as her own. She looked up at him in his jogging shorts and waved. Ireland was also on full display in a teensy jog bra with matching leggings. Both had washboard abs, legs and arms without the decency to produce even the slightest wiggle, and ample pectoral muscles.

When they finally made their way to where the Pettigrews awkwardly stood, they didn't merely stand; they posed. Dean looked as if he halfway expected the Pettigrews to snap his picture as he crossed his arms across his chest, puffing it out and flexing his biceps. Ireland seemed bored waiting for the introductions to begin and started to stretch, and not just in an extend your leg fashion, but in a languorously cat-like manner. She seductively bent at the waist, arched her back so that her bottom tilted upward, and leaned forward allowing her cleavage to spill over her top. Rich watched intently.

Katie crouched behind the umbrella, now fully extended and becoming airborne with the sudden breeze. "Duck!"

The umbrella took flight and smacked Rich upside the head, while Katie dodged out of the way of its flight pattern.

"Just smile," advised Katie.

"I'm trying," Rich mumbled through gritted teeth.

Either it was the sight of his new neighbor or the smack he got on the side of his head, but Rich was mesmerized by the image of Ireland, as she migrated toward him. He was lost in the sight of firm breasts, the kind that he knew were probably purchased, but seemed the way God intended nonetheless.

Katie thanked the heavens that she was clad in a long dress, which admirably hid her family thighs. Like Rich, she couldn't help but stare at the woman's long legs, which allowed her to glide rather than walk. Ireland and Dean hadn't merely arrived at their house; they landed. Too beautiful to be mere mortals, they awoke Rich and Katie from their hypnotic stares with a barrage of small talk that neither Katie nor Rich were accustomed to taking part in, particularly so early in the morning with strangers.

"You must be Rich," the man said and extended his hand while using the other to deliver a friendly, manly-styled punch to Rich's left arm. "I'm Dean and this..." he said while waving his hand over the length of his wife as if unveiling a statue, "...is Ireland. Stacey told us you moved in. No kids, right?"

"Just the fifteen," said a straight-faced Katie.

"You're kidding," Ireland responded in horror.

"Sort of. I'm a nursery school teacher."

"How noble. Taking care of other people's children."

"Actually, I do more than look after them. I initiate their developmental awareness," said Katie.

"That's great. We needed another set of DINKS around here," Ireland piped in. "We're both in sales," she added, although Katie and Rich seemed unable to make the connection.

Dean nodded his agreement and then explained, "Dual income, no kids."

Ireland took her turn at bat. "Not that kids aren't a good idea...in case you're, you know, are you?"

"Are we what?" asked Rich.

"Pregnant," responded Ireland.

"Well, I'm certainly not," said Rich. "Never understood all that talk about the couple being pregnant. By the way, Katie isn't either," he said, patting Katie's stomach, to which she inhaled and pulled it in as tightly as possible.

"Great," beamed Ireland. "Like I said, not that it's a problem. It's just that we want our freedom right now. Don't we honey?"

"Absolutely. Couldn't go out for a leisurely run if little bambinos were underfoot. Couldn't do all sorts of things, come to think of it," he laughed and gave Ireland a pinch on the bottom, to which she squealed with delight.

"Although, I hear that pregnant sex can be unbelievable. I'm talking major O," she said under her breath to Katie.

"Oh?" asked Katie.

"Dean, aren't they cute?" Ireland said, who now reached up to playfully tickle Rich under the chin like one would do to a puppy. "Or-gas-mmmm," she said in a slow, deliberate way, accenting each syllable as if speaking to children.

"Katie," Dean said taking her into a friendly hug, "welcome to the neighborhood."

"Yes, welcome," agreed Ireland who then kissed Rich's cheek while leaning her ample breasts against his arm.

"You're coming to the party at Rachel and Paul's on Saturday?" Dean asked.

Experiencing a sudden change of heart, Rich piped up, "We wouldn't miss it."

Chapter 4

Katie tried to convince herself that there was no reason to
be concerned over Rich's sudden willingness to attend
the Cox's party. She reasoned that even if Ireland were the cata-
lyst for his wanting to go, the end result worked to her benefit --
she was attending her first Hollywood Hills party. Still, Katie
never expected Rich to actually look forward to the evening.
And, when she caught him stealing glances at Ireland during the
week, Katie secretly began a new sit-up regime. She also
promptly telephoned Stacey for some much needed shopping
advice prior to the fated gathering.

Unfortunately, shopping with Stacey was less fun than Katie
had imagined. She pictured a typical female bonding experience, complete with ice cream to commemorate an afternoon of
successfully avoiding unforgiving mirrors and snooty sales
women. But, instead of empowerment, Katie discovered uncer-
tainty and humiliation.

Forget about ice cream, Stacey never put more than an iced
tea to her lips, and it was diet! When it came time for lunch,
Katie had decided on a plentiful plate of lasagna, but immediately thought better of it when Stacey ordered first.

"The Santa Barbara Salad, please," Stacy told the waitress. "But can you hold the onions, the corn -- corn is truly evil," she said shaking her head and whispering to Katie before turning back to the waitress to continue, "no cheese and of course, no croutons."

"So just lettuce," the waitress confirmed.

Stacy wrinkled her brow and checked the menu. "Hmm, can you add a chicken breast? Skinless, naturally. And grilled, no basting of any sort, please. Oh, and one more thing, dressing on the side."

The waitress stopped writing and leaned over Stacy to point to the menu. "Why don't you just order the 'Every Woman' salad, sweetie? It's all organic spinach and kale with just a plain chicken breast, no seasoning, no dressing, no added anything. And, it's our special of the week."

"Perfect!" Stacy exclaimed. "Thank you!"

Katie wanted to scream. Not because of the litany of requests Stacey had made, but because she couldn't fathom asking for a salad without croutons. To her, the fried little devils were the only redeeming part. Katie saw a plate of the lasagna being taken to the next table, noticed the woman who ordered it could have also afforded to lose a few pounds, and then made her one, simple request of the waitress. "I'll have the caesar salad." Smiling broadly and trying her best to make the right impression, she added, "No croutons."

KATIE WONDERED IF STACEY'S IDEA TO EAT FIRST AND SHOP later was some type of cruel joke. Even though she had only eaten a salad, Katie's stomach had sufficiently expanded making trying on clothes in her normal size ten an impossibility. Her stomach growled in loud protest due to the lack of calories and the contortions that Katie was placing it under to fit into a pair of trousers. She jumped up and down while holding onto the waistband, willing the pants onwards and upwards.

Stacey watched Katie's aerobic moment. "Once during a really big Thanksgiving meal I casually unbuttoned my top button, just so my tummy could expand. When it came time to zip up, I had to do just what you're doing now."

"I do that after every meal," Katie said evenly.

"Well, we all have our bloated moments."

Katie was sure that Stacey's 'bloated moments' were infrequent and quickly passing. She doubted that Stacey, a size six at best, ever mooned herself in a dressing room due to bending over and then having one's own backside slap the mirror. And, she was sure that Stacey never experienced the panic of not having anything to wear because thus far, every outfit she tried looked like it was meant for her.

Katie had tried on three pairs of trousers to no success, but still, she was determined to find one that fit above her thighs. This time, she decided to lie down on the floor in the small cubicle--an effort to get her stomach as flat as possible so she could wedge the zipper up. As she lay wriggling on the floor with her feet propped against the mirror in front and her head extending out from underneath the partition, a sales woman walked past, nearly stepping on Katie's face.

"Is everything alright?" she asked bending down.

"Just fine, thanks," Katie responded.

"Can I get you anything?"

Katie mused aloud, "Maybe an appointment for lipo."

"How about another size?" the woman suggested sweetly.

"No, but you can take these," Katie said, feeling defeated as she struggled to rise to her feet with the trousers falling around her ankles.

"Katie, don't give up. They're bound to have something. Just let the sales girl in to get a better look at you," Stacey suggested and then opened the door before Katie could object. "Miss, will you come in here for a minute?"

The woman walked in and Katie was immediately transported to when she was thirteen-years-old and went shopping with her mother for her first bra. Her mother had opened the dressing room to a sales woman, inviting her to look over Katie's nearly non-existent bosoms to figure out how to further hide them. Today, the horror of that experience not only came flooding back, but her humiliation was even surpassed.

"We're both looking for something that would be appropriate to wear to a casual party," Stacey explained. "Can you just take a look?" she said pointing to Katie, who was trying her best to suck in her stomach and clench her butt cheeks, "maybe you have something suitable?"

"I've got just the thing," said the salesgirl. Katie was momentarily elated, until, that is, the woman finished her thought, "You and your mother will be the hit of the party."

As they walked away, Stacey put her arm around Katie's shoulders. "Don't let her upset you."

For a moment, Katie relaxed and thought that yes, she had found a new friend in a city that was known for its superficial people. But Stacey wasn't like that, was she? Sure, they had initially met for business reasons, but wasn't that the norm with Hollywood? After all, she had read that Sandra Bullock and Reese Witherspoon both went shopping and jogging with their 'people.' Heck, Reese had even married her agent. If it worked for Sandra and Reese, then why couldn't Katie find a best friend in her real estate agent?

Stacey droned on and Katie suddenly realized that she hadn't been listening. "What did you say?"

"Oh, I was just telling you not to let that little twit get to you. Remember Katie, there are people who matter and those who don't."

Stacey looked over her shoulder at the sales girl, who up until the time that she inadvertently called Katie middle-aged, had actually seemed quite pleasant. "She doesn't matter," Stacey said aloud and ushered Katie from the department.

Chapter 5

Something was wrong. Rich had been at the bottle again. Katie could smell the strong cologne from the moment she stepped in the house.

"Where have you been? We're supposed to be at the party in fifteen minutes," said an eager Rich, who had been waiting for Katie at the front door like a devoted pup, but not nearly as cute in his party dress wear.

"Why are you in such a hurry?" asked Katie suspiciously.

"It doesn't matter," said Rich, his eyes traveling to Katie's overstuffed shopping bags and his mind now distracted with fear of even more expenses beyond the closing costs of their new home. "You know we're supposed to be going easy on our expenses. What's all that?" he asked, a worried tone now gracing his voice.

"Don't worry. You'll love it. I'll only be a minute. Stacey says it's the new me."

"There was nothing wrong with the old you," Rich grumbled, but Katie had already dodged out of the room.

KATIE TWIRLED IN FRONT OF RICH SHOWING THAT SHE WAS more of a recycled, rather than new version of herself. Her top was completely see-through, but thankfully Katie had decided not to totally go for the free love sixties revival look as she wore a bra underneath, even if it was rainbow patterned. To her delight, hip hugging pants were now in style as Katie usually had trouble getting pants not to grab her. The tightness of the black velvet pants on her hips were contrasted by the loose flowing bell bottoms around her ankles.

"That's some get-up," Rich commented, not knowing what to say in response to Katie's inquiring stare.

"Stacey says it's totally hip," said Katie proudly. "She even bought a similar outfit, but no bra."

"Figures. Trying to attract attention and potential clients no doubt," said Rich. "The woman has no morals. Did you see this?" he said holding up the weekly newspaper that the city distributed to homes in the area for free. Katie had usually found it first and thrown it out. Typically the city tossed it onto their front lawn where it started to decompose after being watered by the sprinklers.

"So?" asked Katie.

"So? It says the city wants to build a dam. Here!" he pointed excitedly at their new surroundings. "If that happens you can kiss our view and our property value goodbye."

Katie had turned her attention to putting the final touches on her contribution to the party. As she carefully placed mini marshmallows along the edge of her double-layer jello mold, Rich continued to rant.

"I'm going to have a word with Stacey. You can be sure of it," he said with force.

"Don't you dare," exploded Katie with even more conviction. "This is our first public appearance in the neighborhood. Look at the trouble I've gone to in order to make a good first impression," she said indicating her outfit and jello mold. "Rich, you can't talk about boring things like politics. And no compost talk either," she said nervously. "I don't want to hear any shit talk, just classy conversations."

"Such as?" he said more out of curiosity for what his wife considered class as opposed to a general interest in her conversational skills.

"Honestly, Rich. You read the papers. Something current."

Rich merely responded by holding up the same newspaper and pointing to the article about the proposed dam.

"No, Rich. Something current *and trendy*. Alternative protein sources, for instance. Tofu, soy...stuff like that. Or...," she added excitedly, "how 'bout yoga?" Suddenly Katie became sidetracked. "You're not wearing that, are you?" she said referring to Rich's jeans and alligator emblem top.

"If you can be a sixties throw-back why can't I be from the seventies?"

"Because my outfit has made a comeback and was purchased today from a boutique. Your shirt really is from the seventies."

Rich smiled at Katie and led her out the door. "I won't tell if you won't. Besides, it's comfortable."

As Katie stood beside the buffet table she couldn't help but feel self-conscious. Her feelings didn't stem from her clothing, but rather, her jello. This wasn't the type of pot-luck get together she was used to. There wasn't a macaroni salad in sight. The table was void of mini weenies. And, try as she might, Katie could not locate the ever present ketchup bottle that had always graced the tables of her friends' homes.

"Katie...I know you must be Katie," the woman she recognized as Rachel Cox called out to her. Rachel was even prettier close up. Now that Katie wasn't spying at her through the window she could see that her dark hair perfectly framed her porcelain complexion, just as her clothes lightly draped over her figure, showing off the tiniest waist Katie had ever seen.

"I'm Rachel. So nice to meet you. Now, let's see where can we put this?" she said taking the jello from Katie's hands.

Katie spied the table just as Rachel was doing. Only Katie had the urge to crawl underneath it. Just herself, a fork, and her jello. It didn't seem right for jello to share the same table with duck a l'orange, crabmeat stuffed mushrooms, and sun-dried tomato couscous.

"Here," Rachel announced triumphantly. "Your jello will sit right next to Janet's goat cheese on endive. It's sweetness will be the perfect accompaniment." Then, conspiratorially, Rachel leaned toward Katie and whispered, "I happen to know that Janet buys English goat cheese."

"Oh?" replied Katie at a loss for words.

"Yes. She says it's all the rage in Europe, but I find it a touch bitter."

"As do I," said Katie in her most affected manner.

"Way to go on the whole retro theme," added Rachel. "From bell bottoms to jello. You must throw a mean theme party. I know where the next neighborhood barbecue should be," she added with a wink. "Anyway, make yourself at home; just introduce yourself around. Everyone's friendly so I know you'll be looked after."

Katie took a deep breath, preparing herself to mingle when she noticed that things had already started heating up for Rich. Despite her insistence, Rich had sought out Stacey. However, Katie couldn't help but notice that Rich did not seem to be accusing Stacey of non-disclosure over the dam issue. Rather than feel pleased that Rich had listened to her about not discussing politics, a nervousness flowed over Katie. Rich could not take his eyes off Stacey's blouse and her exposed bosom beneath its see-through material.

"May I offer you a drink?" a man of about forty with salt

and pepper hair and an English accent suggested while handing Katie a blue concoction in a tall glass.

"Oh, thank you," said Katie, relishing the opportunity to turn her attention away from Rich. "It's very pretty," said Katie struggling for conversation.

"It's called a Blue Hawaiian. Great party drink, but be careful," he warned. "It packs a punch that hits you from behind," and with that, he slapped Katie's own behind.

"Thanks for the warning, but I can hold my liquor," said Katie taking a long drag from the straw, and giving him a pointed look, a warning in its own.

"Just look at that," the man said pointing in Rich's direction. It figured. Already Rich was bringing the wrong kind of attention to himself. "That poor guy doesn't stand a chance against Stacey the Slut."

"Excuse me?" asked Katie, surprised at the man's observation.

"That's how she gets her business," he gestured toward his chest, making a show at pretending to stick out non-existent breasts. "She uses her natural assets, although frankly, I doubt that they're real. You don't see me wearing crotchless jeans."

"Well, technically her blouse is just see-through, not actually missing fabric," Katie corrected.

"It's still indecent," he said, but quickly recovered when he saw Katie was wearing the same top. "You, on the other hand, have the sense of style to wear that lovely undergarment." Then, unable to keep his attention from those without underwear, he added, "Yeah, that Stacey just gets the men to roll over and play house."

"Oh there won't be any playing going on over there," said Katie now slurping the last trickle of liquid through her straw. "That's my husband, Rich."

"Oh! Right...I must have gotten the wrong impression. Let me make it up to you. I'm Harry Greene, one of Stacey's colleagues. I'm from a different real estate agency, of course, one that doesn't believe in taking advantage of people's weaknesses."

Katie held out her hand. "I'm Katie. I'm sure they're just talking about our new house. We just moved in next door. By the way, I love your accent," she said leaning in closer. If Rich could play the game, so could she.

"Ah, you enjoy the sound of our mother tongue, do you? Well, Katie, I could talk to you all night. Say, your drink is nearly finished. Let me bring you another one," Harry said taking her glass. "I'll just be a minute, my lovely Katie."

Katie blushed in response and then waited for Harry to return. She wished Rich could be as suave. But while watching him out of the corner of her eye, making eyes at Stacey, she was relieved that he couldn't.

KATIE WASN'T THE ONLY ONE WHO HAD NOTICED RICH. IT was ending up to be more than a neighborhood barbecue. It was a flirtatious fest, a haven for impropriety, and in one woman's mind, a business opportunity.

Janet Boyer sidled up to Katie, noting her closed stance, the arms crossed over her chest, her eyes downcast.

"Are you okay?" she asked.

"Oh fine, thanks. Lovely party, huh?"

"Is it?" Janet gestured to Rich. "You can talk to me; I'm a doctor," she said, gently placing a hand on Katie's shoulder.

"But I'm not sick," replied a confused Katie.

"I'm a psychiatrist," Janet said presenting her card.

"But I'm not sick," repeated Katie, this time more urgently.

"Of course, dear. But I would keep an eye on your husband. This neighborhood...this entire city, well..." she let her voice drift off.

"What?" Katie asked, now more interested. "What could possibly be wrong about this place? Everyone's so..."

"Beautiful? Sophisticated? Rich?"

"Yes!"

"Well, Hollywood isn't an easy city to live in. Those kind will take you in and spit you out. One minute you're in and the next," Janet snapped her fingers near Katie's ear.

"Wow," Katie said, more to herself than Janet.

"And, you might want to consider this," she said handing Katie a flyer.

MARRIAGE IS LIKE ICE CREAM

If they say sex is like chocolate, than marriage is like ice cream. This seminar is perfect if you're on a Rocky Road. Gain insight if your mate is a Tutti-Frutti. Take comfort from others if you're living with a Nut Crunch.

Esteemed marriage and family psychologist, Janet Boyer, will conduct this two-day workshop designed to return the excitement to your marriage and eliminate Vanilla blandness.

Sign up today and receive a special two-for-one offer. David Boyer, M.D., teams with his wife to provide free plastic surgery consultations. Think the honeymoon is over? Remind your spouse what you used to look like.

Katie hated the idea of being viewed as a victim. She and Rich were happily married and she was determined to show Janet. She excused herself, after assuring the doctor that neither her services, nor those of her husband's would be needed at this time.

"Denial is the first step toward the road to recovery," Janet shouted after Katie, who was now galloping toward Rich.

"I'm fine. I mean, *we're* fine," Katie called over her shoulder, not realizing that another party-goer, carrying a plateful of Katie's jello, had crossed her path. In one motion, Katie and the party-goer landed on the ground, and the jello became air bound. Rich helplessly watched his wife and the other woman, a mid-thirties brunette wearing a halter top, stumble on jello slicked floor.

"Can someone help me up?" the brunette called out.

"Here," Katie held out her hand.

"You...you've done enough."

"That's not really fair," Rich said, coming to his wife's rescue. "Her balance has been impaired ever since the brain surgery last year."

"Oh, I'm sorry," the woman looked at Katie with pity. Finally, both women successfully navigated the sticky mess and were safely back on their feet. One glance at Katie's face and Rich knew his attempt to save her reputation had failed. Seeing his wife's angry stare resulted in his own frozen horror, but he recovered with misplaced chivalry as he began to dab at the other woman's halter with a napkin.

"Let me help. I don't want it to stain and I think some of that jello is trying to slip down there," he pointed toward her cleavage while waving the white linen napkin as if to say he approaches her breasts in peace.

"Thanks, but I can handle it," the woman said and left for the restroom.

"What about me?" hissed Katie.

Suddenly a voice of an angel reached Katie's ears. Under normal circumstances, heavenly intervention might be helpful in a circumstance such as this one, but this was no such angel.

"Katie? Katie Pettigrew is that you?"

"Amanda," Katie said, her heart plummeting, her entire being wishing with all its might that this was not the moment that she would come face to face with Amanda after all these years. "Yes, it's moi. In all my glory."

"Well just look at you. You...you haven't changed a bit."

"You hear that, Katie? Just like I'm always telling ya...you're as beautiful as the day I laid eyes on you."

"And who's this charmer?"

"Rich, this is Amanda Exeter. Amanda...my husband, Rich, who was just helping me up."

"Right...here you go," Rich said while offering Katie the use of his napkin. "That wasn't what it looked like, I was just..." he started to explain.

"Shh. People are watching. They're listening, too! Just smile and let's get out of here," Katie hissed in his ear before turning to Amanda.

"Lovely seeing you Amanda. We live here now so I'm sure we'll run into each other again," Katie said trying to sound casual and indifferent.

"Oh, I don't get to the Lowlands very often, but sure..." and with that, Amanda turned on her heel, looking just as beautiful as Katie remembered.

"Oh my God!" Katie looked toward the ceiling, rolled her eyes and then turned back to Rich. "Could it get any worse? Do you think anyone else saw all that?"

"It was nothing. You ready to leave?"

"Definitely. Let's go before people notice my jello stain. I think it's starting to spread."

But people were indeed watching and noticing the Pettigrew's first predicament.

"Did you see that?" Ireland asked of her husband, Dean.

"Looks like the Pettigrews are swingers," he answered.

"You think?"

"Are you kidding? She didn't even flinch when he started feeling up that other woman."

"She's going to get her coat. I'm going to check it out before they leave. This is too good to be true," Ireland said and breezed past her husband. Ireland got across the room and took Katie by the arm. "Are you okay?"

"I wish everyone would stop asking me that. I'm fine. It was just..."

"The brain surgery? I heard," Ireland said worriedly.

"No! I was..." Katie struggled for a new lie that was an improvement over the old one. "It must have been my sciatica acting up. It was just a little tumble. Thank goodness for my Rich being here," she grinned as Rich approached, and linked her arm in his.

"Katie, can I help?" asked Janet with concern. "Do you want to, you know...talk," she said motioning to Rich.

Katie tossed her head back and gave a loud, false laugh. "Oh Janet, Ireland, you two didn't think...no, you couldn't have known. You see, Rich has a nervous muscle twitch. Causes his arms to flail out in front of him," she said while throwing her own arms in front of her chest. "I admit, sometimes he grabs at the most interesting objects, but it's really nothing to be concerned of. Is it, Rich?" she said and elbowed Rich in the ribs.

"No, no. It comes on without any...," and then he flailed his arms out toward Janet's neck and just as quickly recoiled. "Comes on without any warning."

The Pettigrews finally made it to the door and waved their final goodbyes. Rich, of course, used both arms, and together they left their first Hollywood party having made quite an impression.

Chapter 6

R ich came inside from the garden to find Katie, donned in
yellow, plastic gloves, scrubbing the sink. Earlier, he had
discarded a rather unruly rhododendron down the disposal. Not
wanting its unpleasant aphid infestation to spread throughout
the garden, he had deemed the kitchen sink a more suitable
burial ground than the recycling bin outdoors. If more people
were like him, he reasoned, the need for multiple garbage cans
would cease. What the average family deemed garbage, such as
leftovers from previous dinners, Rich found perfectly acceptable.
He was quite willing, one might even say...pleased, to take
discarded food and turn it into compost when his appetite failed
him. This was often the case after "Monday night surprise," a
weekly casserole comprised of everything leftover from the
weekend. The fact that Rich was a rather finicky eater was often
a subject of discussion as Rich would remind Katie not to
overeat. Today, he spotted discord in Katie's mood and decided
to be agreeable at any cost.

"How could this happen?" Katie wailed as she scrubbed
even more feverishly. Katie was in the habit of cleaning whenever stress struck. Feeling guilty over the extra work the rhodo-

dendron had caused his wife, Rich reviewed the sanitation engineer's manual, which outlined preferred garbage can etiquette as outlined by their city. The whole business of suburban garbage cans still confused Rich. There was one can for trash, which seemed self-explanatory, one for garden refuge, one for plastic and paper recycling labeled #2-#7 with the exception of #4, and the last for plastic and paper recycling as well as wood and wood by-products, or items labeled #1, #4, or #8-#12. Rich was moved by Katie's stress, but still deemed it easier to simply decapitate the aphid infested plant and force it down the disposal rather than call on his degree in mathematics, which was obviously needed to decipher this foreign code of garbage.

"Destructive monsters," he said referring to the aphids.

Katie held up her plastic sheaved hands. "I had such expectations, that's all," she said while actually referring to last night's party.

"Well, we won't have to see them again," said Rich with satisfaction as the plant stalks washed down the drain.

"What are you saying?" said Katie with growing concern. "We live here. Of course we have to see them."

"Not necessarily. I'll keep them under control. Nasty little buggers."

"You've done enough already," said Katie, shuddering while she remembered Rich, albeit accidentally, fondling the jello-clad woman's breasts and Amanda seeing every horrifying moment.

Rich looked down the sink and smiled with satisfaction, "It was nothing, really."

"I'm not convinced. We need to correct this situation. We need...," she halted, searching her mind for the right word, while still talking at cross purposes with Rich. "Status! That's it!"

"Katie, be patient. I've got big plans," said Rich with a wave to the garden. "Over there," he said motioning to the site where an angel-minding fountain waited to be installed, "will be our conservatory. Now, hand me those magazines," he pointed to the kitchen table.

Katie picked up the copies of *Compost Quarterly* and *Better Bugs* as well as the city's local paper where she flipped to an article about the dam proposal slated to be built in the ravine behind their home. While reading the opposing arguments for and against the dam Rich's voice triggered an idea. "You see, Katie, if we can cultivate this particular strain of lady bug, the aphids will be kept under control. We can virtually put our mark in this place."

Katie thought about the party again. She was surrounded by other potential household pests: neighbors that were too beautiful, flirtatious realtors, an assuming psychoanalyst. Forget lady bugs or any other small and virtually unnoticed entity. She needed to become a regular praying mantis, something that commanded respect.

"Look at this Rich," she interrupted, showing him the article on the dam.

"I told you. Stacey knew about this. That's a lawsuit, that is. She should have disclosed it. Her and those see-through tops. I've got a mind to..."

"Rich, there's a better way to deal with this," said Katie calmly. "Why don't you run for city council?"

"Don't be ridiculous," he said glancing across the street.

Katie followed his gaze. Dean and Ireland had just returned from someplace where the need to wear a bikini top had once again presented itself.

"You know," Katie said reaching to put her arms around Rich. "Politicians are very sexy."

"Are you sure?" asked Rich.

"Of course. Think about all the action Bill Clinton got." Katie then waved to the neighbors, causing Ireland to bound toward them like a lost puppy.

"You know, Rich, you could make quite an impression on people," Katie commented.

"You think?" he said staring dreamily at the approaching Ireland. "Okay then. What the hell? What do I do next? Buy a couple of new shirts?"

"You just leave it to me," responded Katie, who had turned her attention to their first possible constituent. "Ireland, so glad you could stop by. I've got the most exciting news."

Chapter 7

Katie was determined to erase any negative impression she and Rich may have given while at the Cox's party. Jump starting Rich's campaign and letting everyone know that he was on his way...into the sophisticated world of politics, even if it was just a bid for local city council, was just the ticket. All she had to do was devise an appealing campaign platform, one that was easy for people to get behind.

Rich, she decided, would stand for all of the usual hot topics: slow growth, preservation of open spaces, better teachers and schools, more police. For the first time in his life, Rich would appeal to everyone.

The next step was to start her own grassroots effort by going door to door and inviting the neighborhood women to her version of Rich's coming out party. Before heading out, Katie put on another outfit she purchased while with Stacey. Again, the ensemble, which consisted of a white, lycra top and capri pants, looked better on Stacey than Katie. Rich took one look at Katie and stopped her.

"You're not going campaigning for me in that," he said pointing to her outfit.

"What's wrong with it? Stacey got one too," Katie said defensively. "Besides, I'm the campaign manager. I know what's current, and that," she said pointing to the red Hawaiian shirt and orange bathing suit trunks he paired with them, "That is a fashion disaster."

Rich looked down at his shorts and shrugged. "Maybe, but I'm not going out. You can't go out with those like that."

"With what like what?"

"Your boobs! They're braless and very exposed," he said knowingly.

"It's all the rage."

"Well, it may be okay for Stacey, someone with little kiwi cuties, but you're more of a grapefruit gal."

"I resent that," she said sticking out her chest proudly.

"Don't misunderstand, my little kumquat, I love your grape-fruits. I just don't think the neighbors are ready for them."

Katie thought it over. "I'll wear a blazer over them," she said and left for Rachel's house next door.

THE COX'S CAR WAS IN THE DRIVE SO KATIE RANG THE BELL and waited. The sound of a vacuum running explained why nobody had come to the door so Katie peered into the window facing the stoop. She could see a petite woman in a maid's uniform pushing the vacuum over thick carpet that already looked perfectly clean. From her vantage point, Katie could also see the entire layout of the living room. Unlike Katie's furniture, which was a lively mixture of primary colors including a sofa in red plaid with denim blue throw pillows and an over-stuffed arm chair upholstered in a lively yellow, which the store tag referred to as "Ripened Squash," Rachel's living room was a heavenly expanse of soft white. Everything was a shade of pale -- from the carpet, which didn't have a footprint mark on it, to the love seat and sofa with matching throw pillows. When

Katie first chose their furniture all the catalogs were touting primary colors as country casual, a look that would always be in fashion. It figured that just two years later, Katie's interior seemed garish in comparison to Rachel's sense of style and elegance.

With her nose still pressed to the glass, Katie suddenly became the victim of a dive-bombing fly, buzzing so close to her ear that she mistook its friendly advances for that of a bee and swatted frantically. She stepped backwards and then lost her balance, never noticing the potted azalea nestled under the window sill. The vacuum stopped as the plant crashed, echoing Katie's arrival.

Rachel forced open the door in a huff and then stared at Katie in surprise. "Oh, I thought it was vandals. I heard a crash."

Katie had quickly scooped up the few pieces of the pot that remained intact and helplessly handed them to Rachel. "No, I'm afraid it's just clumsy ol' me. I'm terribly sorry," she said extending a hand that clutched the broken pottery. "I'll replace it."

"Don't worry about it. It was a foolish place to put a pot. I never consider the curiosity factor when I decorate."

Normally, Katie would have tried a quick retort, but remembering her initial reason for spying, she decided better of it. According to Stacey, Rachel was a decorating genius and if Katie could gleam even a few tidbits from her, she should consider herself lucky. With that knowledge, Katie let the insult go and delved ahead with the business at hand.

"Rich is running for city council and would like to share his views at a ladies tea at our home next Sunday," she said crisply. "We hope you will be able to make it."

"Well, I usually spend Sundays with the family."

"If you could make just one exception. So many others from the neighborhood have already responded," she easily fibbed.

"Oh? Who?"

Katie never expected to be called on her lie. The only thing to do was lie even more. "Stacey, Janet..." she rambled.

"Really? That's funny. Stacey never mentioned it to me before."

"She probably didn't get the chance. I just spoke to her." Katie was already backing down the walk, anxious to get to Stacey's house before Rachel could pick up the phone.

"Alright," Rachel answered hesitantly. "I'll come but I'm not promising my vote, yet."

KATIE MAY NOT HAVE BEEN BUILT LIKE AN ATHLETE, BUT SHE found the motivation to run like an Olympic medalist. When she arrived at Stacey's door, she was panting and beads of sweat had formed on her nose and forehead. Trusting that Stacey would not lead her wrong, she decided to ignore Rich's fashion advice and remove her blazer. She was sure that the top looked just as good on her as it did Stacey, grapefruit-sized breasts or not.

She was just about to ring the bell when she felt a trickle of sweat drip from between the mounds in question and looked down to see a suspicious wet mass spreading from underneath both breasts. Katie cursed herself for listening to Rich. Surely this would not have happened if it hadn't been for the blasted blazer. As she looked down at herself, she knew that this was not the look Stacey had in mind when they went shopping. She didn't even have a tissue with her, not that a single square would help her overactive sweat glands.

She could hear Stacey on the phone through an open window and knew from the cooing and flirting that she was not talking to Rachel.

"That would be simply to die for, but only if you're with me."

Katie was thankful that Stacey was occupied with a caller

other than Rachel and decided to take the time to fix her appearance or die of embarrassment.

"Don't tease me," Stacey laughed. "I could never stand to be left in such a precarious position...unless you're there to rescue me."

Katie spied a large flowering plant, a calla lilly, and decided to rob it of one of its paddle-shaped leaves. She successfully grabbed a hold of the stalk and pulled. The first leaf was nearing the end of its life cycle and came off easily in her hands.

Stacey murmured, "I love your touch, too."

Katie moved into the shade of a nearby tree, away from view of the street, and started to mop up under her bosoms with the plant leaf. Unfortunately, despite the plant's large size it was no match for Katie's breasts. Katie reached out for the plant again since one leaf was just not enough. She pulled and tugged finding the second leaf not as interested in becoming a partner to her new grooming regime. To her dismay, a trickle of wetness was now moving south toward her stomach. What progress she had made in controlling her overheating with the first leaf was counteracted by the second leaf's insistence on living. She looked around, and satisfied that nobody was about, stripped herself of the shirt that was causing the offending problem. Then, standing topless next to Stacey's front porch, she went to wrestle the plant again and this time was successful in causing a sufficient tear in the stalk.

"Oh, I wouldn't like to feel any pain, lover," Stacey's voice continued.

The plant put up a valiant fight, leaking sap all over Katie's hands and arms, until she bled the last drop from it. Then, with a feeling of accomplishment, she blotted her breasts with the leaves. She had just decided that the grass would be a suitable surface to wipe the sticky sap from her hands when she heard words to turn her overheated system ice cold.

"Oops, hang on lover, that's my call waiting." A pause and then, "Rachel, honey, let me get off the other line. On second thought," Stacey said noticing Katie crouched outside her window, "I'll call you back. I seem to have company."

Bent over at the waist, without a top, and rubbing the grass feverishly was how Katie was discovered. There was nothing left for her to do, but act natural, or at least as natural as one could act when caught au naturale.

Katie checked the lycra top, but found that it was still too wet for wear. Rather than commit a fashion blunder with a wet top or wilted calla lilly leaves, she reached for the flowering portion of the plant and proceeded to cover her breasts with them feeling satisfied that the white flowers complimented her pants.

Stacey opened her door, Katie took a deep breath, and thrust the invitation in front of her. "We're holding Rich's political coming out party next weekend. Hope you'll be able to make it."

"Katie, you're a campaign genius!" Stacey cooed. "Leave it to you to come all out for a coming out party. Maybe I should try it when recruiting for new clients. I could just hear Harry Greene complain now. Wait 'til I tell Rachel. I was just talking to her," she said reaching to redial the phone.

Katie instinctively made a move to grab the phone away, but nearly lost one of her flowers in the process. She readjusted her thoughts and flowers. "Oh, Rachel knows about the party and is looking forward to it. You will come, too?" she asked worriedly, knowing that if word got back to Rachel that Stacey hadn't officially committed then she would lose her as well.

"Oh I'll be there," Stacey answered. "But, where can I get some of those?" she said pointing to Katie's breasts.

Katie wasn't sure if she should direct Stacey to a qualified plastic surgeon or a garden center. She just turned down the walk with her shoulders proudly thrust out and called back, "You know, sometimes natural beauty is lurking right in our own backyard."

"WHERE DID YOU FIND THAT OUTFIT?" KATIE ASKED surveying Rich, who stood before her in lime green slacks, a shirt that could only be described as spumoni-colored, and a belt with silver and turquoise studs.

"Nice, huh? Good thing I found it. Can you believe the movers must have put these things into the donation pile," he said smoothing down the creases in his shirt.

"I put it there. You can't wear those. They're positively suburban."

"We live in suburbia."

"No, we live in a gated community, which is nothing like the burbs," said Katie in a decidedly snobby tone. "That outfit belongs on a retiree golf course in Palm Springs."

"I like it. It's comfortable...and colorful."

"I'll say, but that isn't exactly a testament to its being appropriate fashion material. It's more of a fashion foible."

"You're one to talk. Look at you gallivanting around in not much more than your birthday suit."

"Rich, I told you not to mention that incident again. It was just an unfortunate case of sweat glands gone hey wire. Anyway, Stacey actually liked my flowers."

"How come you can wear pasties, but I can't wear this?"

Katie decided to take another tact. "Rich, I've been wondering if it's really wise to invite Ireland."

Rich looked crushed. "Why not?"

"Well, we have space constraints. And, let's face it, Ireland is not the most influential woman in the neighborhood what with her, well, to use one of your phrases, gallivanting around the neighborhood in bikinis."

"I hadn't noticed," he started to say, but seeing Katie's raised eyebrows quickly added, "recently."

Trying to not look too pleased, since after all, Rich's concession only meant that he was ogling their neighbor, Katie responded, "I'm sure that if you were to wear something, er, less bold, the room would appear bigger. We'd probably even be able to invite another person or so."

"How's navy blue?"

"Perfect."

ON THE DAY OF THE TEA PARTY, KATIE BUZZED ABOUT nervously in her bathrobe, trying to make sure that everything looked perfect and ensuring that her own outfit didn't once again get damaged by overactive sweat glands. She had selected a dress that Rich once said brought out the color of her eyes and accented the curve of her hips. She knew that Rich would never try anything with Ireland. After all, skinny types weren't his thing, but one could never be too careful. So, she paid extra attention to her hair and makeup and even applied the false eyelashes that she believed gave her an Audrey Hepburn look. She gave herself the once over in the mirror and, deciding that she looked as good as she could, went downstairs to where Rich was waiting in the kitchen.

"These look terrific," he said enthusiastically pointing to the mini chicken drumettes that were arranged on a plate. "Can I try just one?"

"Don't be silly. They're for the guests."

"I have to eat too. I'll need my strength to talk about politics and other important stuff, like..."

"No compost talk!" Katie warned.

"Of course not," said Rich, but then thought for a minute and replied, "You will save me the chicken bones, won't you? They make a hell of a mulch."

"You wouldn't..."

"No, I'm not suggesting you steal them off people's plates while they're munching. Just put them aside once they're in the kitchen."

"That's the bell. Be good. Be...presidential."

"I thought I was running for..."

"Never mind," added Katie as she made her way to the front door.

The first of the women arrived in impeccable tea attire. Janet wore a peach-colored silk suit paired with an Hermes bag and as Katie took it from her to put in the guest bedroom where it would be safe, she casually checked the label to see if it were the real thing. Rachel was dressed in a chiffon skirt and crepe blouse embellished by an enormous flowing collar that Katie thought looked quite clown-like, but overheard that it was the newest from Donna Karan and decided that she would have to get one herself. But the real kicker was when Ireland showed up with *the shoes*.

To think that Katie almost hadn't invited her. How would she have known that Ireland had the where with all to own a pair of Manola Blahnik shoes? She was in the midst of thinking that she would have to do lunch with Ireland when a potential party faux pas occurred. Rich was slouched on her new sofa, his bottom resting comfortably on one of the throw pillows that she had so painstakingly fluffed. She could only hope that Rich wouldn't stand up before she could get across the room. It would be just like him to lounge around when he should be mingling and then get up when he should be sitting.

To Katie's horror, she heard Janet question Rich. Please be an inept slob, Katie prayed. Don't show your manners now. Please stay seated. But no matter how much Katie tried to tele-pathically warn Rich about the danger to come, it was to no avail. He stood, leaving a distinct butt impression on the pillow.

"Rich, do tell us your thoughts about this dam proposal."

Rich started to relax believing that maybe these women weren't as stuffy as they appeared. "I'd be happy to. Now which damned proposal are you referring to?" he asked.

Janet huffed and replied stiffly. "I didn't mean damn proposal as in an obscenity. I was referring to dam, d-a-m."

"Oh that!" The light went on within Rich. "Well, I believe it's a complete atrocity," said Rich to the group who had now gathered around him.

"It will ruin our views," Rachel declared.

"Well, if elected to our council, I'll make it my top priority."

"We certainly don't need our property values decreasing as a result of some dam," concurred Janet.

Katie watched the scene and began to relax. Rich seemed to have the crowd motivated and thus far, the butt fiasco had not been discovered.

"Look!" Stacey screeched, pointing to Rich's indented cushion.

"Katie, are you responsible for this?" asked Rachel, queen of interior decorating that she was.

"Well, I can explain," stammered Katie who didn't quite know how to explain without implicating Rich in the entire mess.

"It's fabulous," Rachel declared. "How ever did you think of this new indentation? To think that I was still doing the karate chop," she said, the epitome of self-deprecation.

"Just something that popped up one day," responded Katie.

"Oh Katie, do show us how you do it," insisted Stacey.

Katie stared nervously at Rich. Maybe he was right about Stacey. "Stacey, I can't give away all my secrets. You already have my jello recipe," she said.

To Katie's amazement, Rich's blundering had once again managed to put them in good standing. Naturally, she was convinced that her influence must have had something to do with it. She breathed a sigh of relief while listening to the women coo about Rich's ideas. Stacey was concerned about the dam because it might affect her real estate business. Rachel also had home values to consider especially since she had spent a small fortune on "improvements" that she promised her husband would be sure to increase the value. But Katie felt that acceptance among this inner circle was most imminent when Amanda moved closer to the group.

"Say something impressive," Katie whispered to Rich. "This is our big chance."

"Like what?"

An uncomfortable lull hit the crowd that Katie had to fill.

"As a nursery school teacher, I must say that I believe children are our future," she piped up.

Amanda studied her carefully. "Yes, what's your point?"

"Well, as a teacher I feel we should teach them the beauty they possess."

"Do you always recite Whitney Houston songs?"

Katie couldn't stop herself. Once the lies started, the attention factor also grew. All eyes were on her and rather than be mortified, she found that she loved every minute of it. She leaned in closer, "Actually, Amanda, I'm the inspiration for that song. Years ago, I had lunch with Whitney...Whit, as she liked me to call her, and I told her my teaching philosophy. The rest is music and recording history."

Amanda gave Katie a disbelieving smile. "You mean to tell me that you wrote Whitney Houston's hit song? Because if that's not what you're saying than I think speaking of someone who has passed and is so revered...well, that's just..."

"No, no! That's not what I meant," Katie interjected nervously, the lie taking on dragon wings and being close to spouting fire.

"I didn't think so," said Amanda with a snooty air.

And that's when Katie lost it and decided not to retract her statement.

"I didn't *write* her song. She stole the key lines from me," Katie responded.

"What?" Amanda shrieked, but Katie wouldn't entertain any more.

"Anyway, if my ideas were good enough for Whitney, I'm

sure you can embrace them as well. If Rich is elected, our schools will become number one in the country."

"How can you be so sure?"

"We'll put immense pressure on the testing board to make sure that our children score highest," answered Katie with tremendous self-assurance.

"You can't do that," argued Amanda. "It's illegal."

"Honey, maybe you should refill the lemonade," Rich suggested in Katie's ear.

"Shhh, I'm on a roll."

"More like a runaway train," he muttered.

"Amanda, what you don't realize, probably because you aren't networked the way that Rich and I are, is that politicians always do things like that. Fudging test scores, bribing school boards...They just don't tell you. If you think about it, Rich is actually an honest politician because he is fully disclosing his planned indiscretions. Anyway, don't you just think Winter White is the newest color craze?"

"What are you talking about?" Amanda asked. "Now, back to our local schools. Katie, I'm very concerned..."

"Schools, schmools," said Katie. "Back to Winter White. I hear it's the ideal feng shui color," Katie quoted from her recent issue of *House Beautiful* in an attempt to get off the persnickity topic of politics. "Rachel," she said recruiting decorating salvation, "is Winter White or Creme Brulee the white to have on walls this fall?"

"Oh well that's an important question," answered Rachel in a serious tone while Amanda rolled her eyes skyward. "Of course it depends on if you're decorating bedrooms or family living spaces. In my opinion...," she droned on.

And with that simple digression, the talk left the political fairground and Katie considered her party's mission to be a success.

Chapter 8

If there was any concept more foreign to Katie than creating the perfect home interior it was working with her hands in the garden. This was a chore she felt better suited for other people and perhaps the only thing she innately had in common with her more affluent neighbors.

"I don't understand how you can actually like pulling weeds and planting flowers," she said in amazement over the breakfast table. "Pass the coffee, dear. Oh, and another danish, please."

"It's relaxing. Don't you think you've had enough of the carbs?"

"No, I don't," Katie said between mouthfuls. "What's it to you, anyway?"

"Just worried about your health, that's all."

"If you want me to look like that Skinny Minnie across the street, it won't happen. I tried sit-ups and didn't like them."

Rich knew that it was perhaps the truest statement to come out of Katie. "No, I don't want you to be skinny. But svelte might be nice. Or at least an athletic build. You know, the type of woman who would get on her hands and knees in the garden."

"Rich, svelte would never be found in a garden unless it was sitting posed on a bench. Honestly, what would our neighbors think if they saw me digging in dirt? You wouldn't catch Amanda beating away worms."

Rich took a mouthful of the granola he had made from scratch over the weekend. Katie never enjoyed granola mornings since the mixture that Rich prepared was so chewy it was as if she were eating alone because Rich could never speak after taking a bite. The granola contained almonds, oats, and an assortment of dried fruits including cranberries, apples, apricots, and anything else Rich thought could withstand his new dehydration machine, his favorite Christmas present of last year. Rich insisted that the chewier the fruit, the more vitamin-laden it became. Katie never knew if this fact were true, she just knew that the stuff was so tough she wouldn't dare eat a bowl for fear of losing a filling.

Finally, he swallowed. "I need help with my chicken bone mulch. What if we buried the bones at night? Nobody would see you and it would be romantic."

The thought of Ireland making eyes at Rich still brewed in Katie's mind. "Romantic?"

"Very. I can imagine you wearing those cute gardening gloves by the light of the moon."

"Alright then. I'll meet you tonight."

"WHERE HAVE YOU BEEN AND WHY ARE YOU WEARING THAT?" Rich asked pointing to Katie who had emerged from the house wearing a tattered, powder-blue, terry cloth robe. "It's nearly midnight; I've been waiting."

"Sorry, I fell asleep. I had a hell of a day. It was show and tell at school and Amanda's daughter, Brooke, brought her rabbit, which poo'd everywhere. Damn rodent. Anyway, your pounding woke me up."

"You did say you would help."

"That I did. Anyway, what is all that noise? Flowers don't make noise. Speaking of which...Did you know that Rachel has a separate gardener just for her flowers? The regular guy won't even touch them."

"Can you blame him? With someone like Rachel, all it would take to get fired is the death of one dahlia. She's scary."

Katie beamed in spite of feeling so tired. "You mean that? You don't find her...attractive?"

"Are you kidding me? Too high maintenance. Katie, come here," Rich urged, holding his hand out to her. "I was digging a trench for the chicken bones when I hit something."

"Probably a pipe from the sound of it. You know, this job really should be done by a gardener. I can call Rachel..."

"Katie, shhh!"

"If you're not going to talk to me, I should just go back to bed. Honestly, the day I've had. People like the Exeters would have an incontinent rabbit. Probably brought it to school so that I could play maid to it. People just don't respect nursery school teachers, if that's what I am. Half the time, I'm a maid, toilet monitor, babysitter. I'm so busy cleaning up vomit and other bodily fluids that I don't even get to shape their young minds. And then, to make matters worse, I got a message when I returned home that the damned rabbit is missing. Can you imagine the trouble I'm in? The Exeter's rabbit is missing."

"Who are the Exeters?"

"Oh my God, Rich. Where have you been? Amanda Exeter. The Amanda from my childhood?" she prompted, only to get a blank stare in return.

"She lives in the big house that looms on the top of the hill?" Katie prompted, but still received another vacuous stare from Rich. "You know...when you enter the gates and look up?"

"That house? The big one?"

Katie nodded. "Amanda Exeter, wife of Steve, head of

Exeter Computers. He created some app or other techie thingie and made a fortune."

"And now we live in the same neighborhood with them," Rich said proudly.

"Please. They live on top of the neighborhood. We just happened to get a house on the outskirts. People like Amanda don't even consider our part of the neighborhood to be included in the neighborhood."

"But we're behind the gates," Rich pointed out.

"Barely. She's behind the gates and up the hill."

Rich shrugged his shoulders. "Well, our homeowners associate fees say Briarwood."

Katie shook her head, traces of jealousy threatening to emerge. "You know that I'm happy to be here, but since arriving I've learned that even in here there's a hierarchy."

Rich sat down and patted the bench next to him. "What do you mean?"

"This part of the neighborhood..." Katie said motioning her head to the front of the house and the street, "is called the Lowlands."

"By whom?!" Rich shouted outraged.

Katie patted his arm, reminding him that they were outside and well past when normal people would be awake. "By the people who live on the streets called Upper Lake, Queen's Garden, and of course, any house that's been given it's own name."

"We can name our house. What about...," Rich searched his imagination.

"We can't just name our house ourselves. It's like a child. We didn't give birth to it. Only the developer can name a house and he chose not to name these."

"I thought you said that Stacey, Ireland, Rachel...this group is what you aspire to become?"

"Stepping stones. You can't learn to run until you know how to walk" Katie said by way of an answer. "We'll get there. But for now, I've got to find out what happened to the Exeter's daughter's pet rabbit. Or, we can forget about ever living in La Fontaine."

"La what?"

"The last house of Plan 3. It was just released."

"You sound like a spy. What is Plan 3 and why was it just released."

"There's one man who owns all of Briarwood real estate and in order for it to maintain its value, he only releases homes a few at a time. For that matter, those houses aren't even houses. They're *estates*. Let me break it down for you."

"Before you do...how did you learn all of this?" Rich asked, squinting at Katie in the moonlight.

"Stacey told me. She's been trying to sell in the Plan 3 area for years, but even she has a ladder to climb. There's only one real estate agent who has gotten in with the developer and been given a contract to sell his premier estates. Stacey thinks one more will be added and it's between she and Harry Greene."

"So we're just stepping stones for her?"

"Not exactly," Katie said, knowing she had dug a hole for herself. "I know what you're thinking."

"That you aren't friends with her and just another potential client?"

"Shades of grey, Rich. Even if you were right. People do business with those they like and respect. I'm just trying to get us into the top echelon...just like everyone else who lives here."

"But Katie...why is that so important?"

A single tear dripped down Katie's cheek.

"Ahh, why are you crying?" Rich asked and reached an arm around her shoulder.

"I don't know. Maybe it was the day. I'm just tired. Can we talk about this tomorrow? I'm too worried about that stupid rabbit."

"Sure. I'm sure it just got out of its cage and will turn up under one of the desks. Can you give me a quick hand before you turn in?"

Katie stood up. "What if it doesn't turn up?" asked Katie worriedly. "The Exeters are pretty powerful. They could ruin all we've worked for."

"What are you talking about?"

Katie looked at Rich as if he were out of his mind only to find her expression of exasperation being thrown right back at her. "Your campaign," she said simply. "It could make a huge difference to our lives."

Rich chuckled. "Don't worry about things like that."

"Are you talking about the rabbit or the campaign?" Katie paused, thinking. "It means a lot to me, Rich."

"Okay...If it doesn't turn up, just buy them another rabbit, or trap one of the ones that's been eating my vegetables, better yet," he said picking up a spade and shoveling it deep into the earth.

"But what if..."

"Hey, I think I've found something," Rich said mysteriously.

"Honey, wake up," Paul bounced the bed when he got not response from his wife. "Rachel..."

"What? Why are you waking me? You know I have an early pilates class."

"Listen!"

Rachel suddenly bolted upright, hearing sounds of banging from next door.

"The Pettigrew place," Paul answered his wife's unspoken question. "Let's take a look," he said jumping out of bed and turning on the light. Rachel joined him by the window and was surprised to see Katie in her bathrobe and Rich holding a large spade.

"Quick! Turn off the light. They'll see us!" she ordered.

"What difference does it make?"

"Paul, there's something weird about the Pettigrews."

"Rich, I'm tired. Let's call it a night. Whatever you thought you felt, isn't there."

"I tell you, I'm getting closer. Listen to this." Again, Rich pounded the spade deep into the hole he was digging and his effort was rewarded with a definite thud.

"Katie, who did Stacey say used to live here?" Rich asked.

"She didn't. Why?"

"Because of this," he said, triumphantly, lifting a metal box from the earth. He laid down the spade and started to loosen the dirt around the small, black box, lovingly dusting the lid in preparation to open it.

"Eww. Put it back, Rich. It's probably someone's pet, may it rest in peace."

"It's too small. Nobody would bury something this small. If a fish or bird dies it gets flushed."

"Don't be gross. It could be a rabbit."

"You've got bunnies on the brain. Now give me a hand."

"Did you hear that?" Rachel whispered to Paul.

"No, I gave up listening...half an hour ago! Come back to bed. You've had your head hanging out the window for long enough."

"You're the one who woke me up," Rachel reminded him.

"It was a mistake. Come on, Rach. They were just talking about gardening."

"Paul, you said yourself that it's weird to be outside at this hour. Do you actually believe they're planting a vegetable garden in their bathrobes at midnight? Besides, nobody gardens around here. We have *people* to do that sort of thing."

"I don't care what they do as long as it doesn't affect me and right now it's affecting me because you're talking about it."

Rachel looked at her husband. "You don't really mean that."

"I do. Now come back to bed."

Rachel yawned in spite of herself and contemplated doing just as Paul wanted, until she made the mistake of taking one last glance behind her curtains. "Paul, look!" Rachel said suddenly. "They're knee keep inside some sort of shallow grave and I heard them say the word rabbit."

"So? Their pet probably died."

"They don't have a pet, but Amanda's daughter, Brooke did. Until...well, Amanda said that Katie made a comment."

"A comment?"

"Apparently, she's one nursery school teacher who doesn't like bunnies. Actually suggested the bunny wear diapers. Did you ever hear of such a thing? Maybe we should keep Emily home?"

"Don't be ridiculous," Paul answered.

"Well something's going on over there," Rachel said, continuing to spy out the window.

Chapter 9

With children in school and husbands at work, the neighborhood mothers were indulging in tea at Amanda's estate. It was something that occurred approximately once a month, never more because Amanda's husband didn't like the intrusion and never less because Amanda felt it was her duty to give back by giving her friends a few moments in luxury.

Although Amanda had a driver, a maid, and a cook, she tried to fit in with the others by discussing the pre-dawn frenzied activities of preparing lunches, laying out clothes, and finding homework. She insisted that it wasn't much easier for her since she had to "manage" the staff. The women only had three hours to spend before it would be time to retrieve their pre-schoolers and start the routine of afternoon snack making along with helping these toddlers with homework that was too demanding for even the most precocious of children.

"Who ever heard of children this age being given homework?" Rachel complained. "Emily can't possibly know her family tree, so Paul and I had to both call our parents to quiz them about Uncle What's-His-Name and Aunt Who's-It. Thank goodness you invited us over today. Being here is such a respite from the difficulties of my life," Rachel cooed.

"Definitely. It's so appreciated." Janet spoke up quickly for she had learned that to not praise Amanda could result in one's invitation to the monthly gathering being revoked.

"So good of you, Amanda," Stacey added, just as fast.

"It's my pleasure," Amanda demurred, pouring more hot water into Rachel's china tea cup. "Anyone else?" When none of the other women accepted, Amanda continued, "When you called me about your day, Rachel, it just didn't seem right to let you sit alone in your everyday existence when I knew you could be here and escape."

Rachel looked around the room that they occupied. It was a home theater complete with wide screen, plush velvet curtains that cut out any and all light, reclining chairs and massive ottomans that nobody's feet were allowed to rest upon unless shoes were removed.

The sound of Amanda's lilting voice brought Rachel back. "I'm not immune from everyday tasks either, though. Just last week, I spent five hours trying to make a fort out of bow-tie pasta for Brooke's native American lesson."

"You two don't know how lucky you are to have so much time on your hands," Rachel said to the childless Stacey and Janet.

"But we work!" the two chimed in together.

"We work too!" Amanda and Rachel said in unison.

"Yesterday, I showed this guy five houses and when we got to the last one, you know what he said?" Before the others could answer, Stacey continued, "How 'bout we try out the bedroom? Did you ever hear of anything so gross?"

"My clients aren't any better," Janet responded. "Married guy cheating on his wife. She doesn't understand him in spite of everything he does for her. Blah blah. He works late and finds out that his secretary is more supportive of his needs, especially in the bedroom."

"Well, it still sounds like a piece of cake compared to what I'm dealing with at the moment with Brooke."

The three women immediately leaned forward, fascinated at the prospect that something...anything might not be quite perfect in Amanda's life.

"Brooke hasn't been sleeping since her bunny disappeared. How could it possibly have gotten out of its cage at her school? That's never happened at home," Amanda sighed. "I've got a mind to speak to Katie Pettigrew about it."

"I don't know if I should say anything," Rachel started.

"What is it?" Amanda asked. "Now you've got to say."

"Well, I like Katie. I mean, she seems to have a real sense of style...for a nursery school teacher, that is," Rachel quickly added in order to hedge her bets with the other women. "But, last night Paul and I heard them in their garden and they were talking about rabbits."

"I knew it. She was weird as a child and nothing's changed. I'm telling you all, there's something not right about those people. Did you see the way he was ogling Ireland at that campaign luncheon they held?"

"Amanda, every man ogles Ireland," Rachel said. "That's why she does so well in her new career...sales. Pharmaceutical sales," she added. "She can network with the other beautiful girls who once appeared on reality shows."

"Poor dear," Amanda offered. "All that beauty and she still has to work for a living."

"What do you mean?" asked Janet taking offense.

"I mean, she's not like you two," Amanda said to Stacey and Janet. "Women who have their own business, and can set their own hours. The true sign of success."

"True. Speaking of business," continued Janet. "Maybe I should drop another hint to Katie and Rich about the couple's retreat that David and I are holding. Do you think they're having marital problems," she asked hopefully.

"She's worried about Rich straying," Stacy confirmed. "Told me so when we went shopping."

"And, she was wearing terry cloth," Rachel added.

"Oh my stars...," Amanda exclaimed. "She really has no clue."

Rachel continued, "Not exactly the attire of a Briarwood resident."

"At least not the ones who hold onto their husbands," Amanda snorted.

"Paul and I saw them in the garden together, though...at midnight," Rachel said conspiratorially.

"That is just so weird," Janet said, with a distinctively hopeful tone in her words. "Marriages in Briarwood...well, let's just say the women that I counsel certainly have to do a lot to keep their husbands faithful."

"And terry cloth is so separate bedroom," Amanda reported. "I just knew there was something off about them. And now Brooke's bunny!"

"Now, now, Amanda...don't be too rash. They do have good ideas about the dam," Stacey interjected.

"True," Amanda concurred. "We don't want our property value going down. Then, none of you Lowlanders will ever be able to move into Plan 3."

The other women bristled momentarily over Amanda's derogatory label of where their homes were located. Each gave the other sideways glances, but none dared say a word knowing that to be friends with Amanda was at least a step in the upwardly mobile direction that they all coveted. The women simply nodded their agreement, accepting their place in Amanda's eyes. They may have been part of the "Lowlands," but at least their homes were larger models than the Pettigrew's.

"Ladies, let's make a pact. Before voting day, we must get to know more about the Pettigrews. It'll be easy...people like that are happy to have people like us around them," Amanda said and then downed the last of her cappuccino.

Chapter 10

K atie had never been much of a morning person and staying up late in the garden did nothing to improve her mood. She had looked forward to sleeping in, but a barking dog from another neighbor's house had put an end to any delusions of a restful morning. At least Rich was already busy in the kitchen. She could hear him clamoring away, hopefully making french toast or scrambled eggs with half-and-half, just the way she liked them. But when she went downstairs, Rich was far from making breakfast. He hadn't even put a pod into their new coffee brewer. Instead, he sat at the kitchen table staring intently at the metal box.

"I think I've nearly got it," he said taking another swipe at the rusted fastener with a kitchen knife. "Nearly there...," he said banging a spoon over the lid.

"Have you been at it all night?" Katie asked noticing that he was sporting a five o'clock shadow that looked closer to ten, along with the same, grubby gardening attire.

"How could you sleep after we found this?" he said lovingly patting the box.

"It's probably just left over from the people who lived here before us. Kids playing buried treasure or something. Certainly not worth getting dirty over," Katie said wrinkling her nose.

"Maybe not," said Rich with enthusiasm. "Look at this."

Once he pried open the box, Rich took out what appeared to Katie to be a bunch of stones and a dirty piece of paper. "There, you see?" she said.

"I can't believe it," Rich responded.

"Believe it. It's just junk."

"No, you don't understand. These are Indian artifacts," he said holding up the chiseled pieces. "Arrowheads and some kind of tools. I'm sure of it. And this, this must be the map to even more," he said holding up the parchment.

Katie suddenly took an interest. "You're sure about this?"

"Of course I am," said Rich.

Truth be told, Katie had never taken much of an interest in Rich's interests. After all, most of them required one to get dirt under the fingernails and this occurrence was in direct opposition to Katie's quest for living a more beautiful and pampered lifestyle. However, while she tried her best to avoid Rich's compost heap and other feats of nature, she knew that Rich rarely talked a load of rubbish. He was just the type of man to have played Indians as a boy and she was sure that he knew what he was talking about.

"Are they valuable?" Katie asked hopefully.

"Very. And apparently there's more," he said pointing to a series of arrows on the parchment. "You weren't far off in saying we would find buried treasure!" he said with glee. "These arrows indicate the land just beyond our fence."

"You can't dig there. It's against the Homeowner Association rules," Katie reminded him.

"We'll have to come up with a plan. This is too big to ignore."

JANET BOYER'S INVITATION TO JOIN BRIARWOOD'S GARDENING Club couldn't have come at a better time. Katie had no idea that Janet's interest in her was born out of Amanda's directive that all the ladies in the Club keep an eye on the Pettigrews as well as Janet's own desire to entice the Pettigrews to her couple's retreat. She only saw the invitation as a legitimate reason to tear up the backyard in search of more treasure. But like everything surrounding their new life in Hollywood, this one came with the need to prove oneself.

"How am I ever going to remember the difference between a begonia and a bouganvilla?" she wailed.

"You'll just have to fake it," said Rich. "Pretend that you specialize in some kind of eclectic zen gardening. Make it all up."

"Make it up...," Katie said, spooning the idea over her brain. "You don't think they'll know? They're supposed to be gardening experts."

"Nah. It's all smoke and mirrors -- just like this politics game. I've never been in politics, but the fact that I've put my hat in the race makes people believe I know what I'm talking about because I exude confidence," he said with an upward tilt of his chin. "And I've got you to thank for that. You told me I could do it and I'm telling you the same.

Katie smiled. "We're a match, aren't we?"

"That we are. It works all the time in the lab," continued Rich. "You see, whenever I need something mixed or boiled that's real smelly I tell the lab assistants that it's an extremely complicated process, but one that is likely to be our missing link. They're so excited to be the one to find this phony link that they put up with just about anything."

"Are you trying to tell me I smell?" asked Katie, concerned once again with her perspiration issues.

"Katie, you're not listening. I'm saying not to worry if it's a begonia or a petunia. Just tell them you are convinced it's an offshoot of...," Rich searched his mind for the right word. "Something like...the Asian Succulent Cactus."

"And they'll believe me?"

"They'll believe you, if you believe you. And Katie," he said holding up the parchment map, "we need your seat on the Gardening Club as much as my seat on the city council."

"I'll do it!" she said with renewed confidence and grabbed a few extra tissues to place inside her bra before setting off into the hot, mid-day sun.

"KATIE PETTIGREW IS MEETING WITH THE BRIARWOOD Gardening Club this afternoon," Janet told the girls. "I've made sure that they'll approve her. It's not really a stretch, after all, their backyard was perfect when they moved in."

"Yes, but to be honest since the Pettigrews moved in...," Stacey hesitated while searching for the right word. "Well..."

"Just spit it out," Janet interjected.

"It's just that The Pettigrews have since put their own unique mark on it."

"So? Maintenance is key to a healthy garden," Janet said like a mantra.

Stacey shook her head politely, not wanting to piss off Janet and lose her own place in the club. "I'd label what they've done more like demolition. Where the roses used to be is now an enormous hole...they're really going to town on the place."

"I don't care," Janet continued. "I want Katie on the committee. David and I think the Pettigrews would be perfect candidates for our upcoming Love Lost and Found retreat."

"Recruiting business at a homeowners function?" asked Rachel with a hint of disapproval in her voice.

"Absolutely not," said Janet quickly. In the hierarchy of neighborhood women, Amanda was queen, but Rachel was a close second in command and Janet knew her place.

"I'm sure that Katie told me she had no interest in gardening," said Stacey, remembering the conversation about Katie's flower pasties.

"That's weird. When I mentioned the committee to Katie yesterday, she seemed really keen," Janet added. "Rachel, it couldn't hurt to invite her just once."

Rachel looked from Stacey to Janet, thoughts rolling in her head. "Hmmm, nursery school teacher, decorator, manager of her husband's second career, and now landscaper...I just don't know how Katie keeps up with it all."

KATIE WAS NEARLY READY TO LEAVE FOR THE MEETING WITH the Gardening Club review board when Rich drove up in a rented and very battered pick-up truck. To Katie, it was the ultimate betrayal.

"You said you were going to have them delivered," she said pointing to the five Oleander trees in the back of the truck.

"They wanted to charge per tree," explained Rich.

"So?"

"So? That's highway robbery. It's not like they have to go to multiple drop-off locations. They've even got us here to do the unloading."

"What do you mean by *us*?"

Katie pirouetted in front of Rich, who for the first time noticed her outfit. She was wearing a pale yellow sundress covered in a pattern of wild roses whose thorns seemed to point toward her abdomen as if to say the dress was not at all for Katie's proportions. A pair of open-toed heels with straps that criss-crossed up her calves were also in yellow. At least, Rich thought, she looked appropriate for a gardening meeting since in his opinion the shoes made Katie's legs look like tree trunks.

"Just help me haul them in the back."

"You've got to be kidding. They probably weigh a ton."

"No, just fifty pounds each. Come on, these trees are our excuse to start more digging."

"Fine," Katie agreed. "But be careful. I don't want to ruin my dress."

They took each step slowly. Not only because of Katie being in heels, but also to avoid losing valuable flower petals, which Rich pointed out would help hide them from the neighbors. Step by step they managed to carry each tree from the truck to the entry of the backyard. Once they passed through the back-yard gate and could relax it seems Rich's nasal passages also began to take it easy. The first drip came innocently enough and Rich could wipe it away with a swift turn of his head and a brush of his collar, but the violent sneezes that followed were another story.

"Serves you right," Katie called over the branches that sepa-rated them. "That's *His* way of telling you not to bring that ugly truck here," she said gazing skyward.

Rich didn't answer and in spite of his sneezes he was able to navigate walking backwards while carrying his share of the tree. "Watch your step, there's a hose somewhere here," Rich managed to peep before his sneezes started again.

The latest fury caused him to lose his grip, sending the full weight of the tree into Katie's arms. A woman of Katie's considerable size might have been able to handle the weight of the tree. With practice, she may have even been able to walk in her new shoes while weight-lifting, but nothing prepared her for the garden hose.

Katie was trying desperately to maneuver the full weight of the tree, weaving back and forth like a clown balancing dishes. Rich had recovered himself, but as if in a dream, was unable to find his voice. He merely stood dumbfounded as he watched the tree go flying as Katie tripped over the hose and then landed herself into a mass of foliage and mud.

"Just look at me!" she shouted in despair. "How can I turn up to a meeting like this?" she said pointing to her clothes, which were now stained in mud and grass. "And Rachel *styled* me."

"It is a gardening gathering," Rich replied helplessly.

"What was that damn hose doing there in the first place? And what's with all this water? The only thing you could possibly be watering is the dirt. We haven't planted this area yet."

"I didn't want to bother you with such details."

"What details?" Katie asked, suspicion growing in her tone.

"I started thinking about the whole political campaign, and politics in general. It made me realize how important it is that I get elected. You were right, Katie. I don't like a select few being given the privilege to make decisions on our behalf. You should see what our homeowners committee is proposing," he said, rolling his eyes.

"They want to charge us extra at the beginning of each season for the 'seasonal flowers' they plant. I say they should plant drought resistant plants. Forget variety, just plant cacti."

Katie had started to blot the mud spots with one of the moist towelettes she kept in her purse. "Hmm," she replied, not really listening.

Rich continued his rant. "Then they want to charge us for putting in speed bumps to protect the children. The little monsters shouldn't even be playing in the street; that's what parks are for."

"Yeah..."

"And the real kicker? They want to charge us for heating the pool year-round. Who needs it? If anyone wants to swim in October they should move to the Bahamas. I tell you, Katie, it doesn't stop with our homeowners association either. One only needs to look at our monthly utility bills to know that the city is just as bad at making decisions. This business about property tax...why it's nearly as much as our mortgage!"

Finally, Katie looked up. "Well, what can we do about any of this?"

"They owe us, Katie. The city owes us so I decided to take their water!"

Katie dropped the towelette. "You what?"

"I'm siphoning water from the creek bed behind our property to use in our garden," he said sticking his chest out in a proud matter.

"You can't do that. It's illegal."

"I am doing it. Every night my hose creeps into the bushes and takes what rightfully belongs to it. You'll see, Katie," he said taking her by the hand, "you can't mess with Rich Pettigrew."

Chapter 11

"They're at it again," Rachel said to Paul.

"You're at it again," Paul responded. "Always eavesdropping on the Pettigrews. I wish these houses weren't so darned close together."

"You didn't want to spring for the extra two million that would buy us a plot on the Highlands, so deal with it."

"Oh, just an extra two million? And the rest...an extra $500 a month in HOA fees!"

"So, this is the house we could afford and I can't help it if I have excellent hearing. I think they're real sexual deviants. He was just being very explicit."

"Oh yeah?" Paul asked with sudden interest.

"Yeah, talking about his hose and her, well, I don't need to repeat it."

"Oh go on," Paul said taking her in his arms and pulling her against him.

"Paul! How can this give you a stiffy. It's disgusting. Besides, I've got a Gardening Club meeting to get to."

"Can't it wait? You're always running off just when I want to..."

"No it can't," she said maneuvering out of Paul's embrace. "Besides, Katie is going to be there. I want to hear the dirt. No pun intended."

"Sheesh, maybe I should go and pay Ireland and Dean a visit."

"Don't you dare!"

"Yes dear. You skip off, but make sure to take notes. If Katie is some kind of sex maniac, the least you could do is tell me the details."

"RICH, YOU CAN'T STEAL WATER. IT COULD RUIN YOUR campaign."

"It's not really stealing. I mean, it's water. You can't even hold it. How can you steal something you can't hold?"

Since Katie was already late for the gardening committee and a reasonable comeback escaped her, she decided it was best to adopt a 'if you can't beat 'em' attitude. "You have a point," she admitted. "Still, I don't think you should go around bragging about it."

"Of course not. Other people might see what a great idea it is and try to get in on it."

"I meant that we should try to hide these hoses," Katie said pointing to the ground. "Besides, as I've already demonstrated, they're dangerous sticking up like this. I'll tell you what. I'll go to the gardening committee and find out about rapid growing plants."

"Why?"

"We can cover the hoses with them. Just plant, they'll spread, and the hoses will be buried, but still functional."

"I love you, Katie."

"I know. Now in the meantime, you start planting those trees. We've got buried treasure to protect and hoses to hide."

KATIE HAD WANTED TO MAKE THE BEST POSSIBLE IMPRESSION at the Gardening Club. Her rose printed dress would have looked better without the addition of mud stains, but Katie decided to make the best of a bad situation as Rachel and Janet led the questioning.

"Katie, what happened to you?" asked Rachel with more than a casual interest in how she got dirty.

"Rich needed some help in the garden and even though I was on my way here, I just can't miss an opportunity to...you know, commune with my husband amidst all this glorious nature," she replied without missing a beat.

Believing that she and Katie were talking at cross-purposes and not wanting to hear any lascivious details, Rachel tread carefully. "You must be a very dedicated gardener to get so, uh...involved."

"Most definitely. We never miss the chance to get dirty."

Katie didn't notice the shared glances of shock that passed between Janet and Rachel as she was too busy flicking some dirt from her heel.

"But Katie, you're covered in scratches. Are you okay?" asked Janet, a note of hopefulness in her voice. "You know you can speak freely with me...in my office. Just you, me, and that warm, inviting couch."

"Oh don't be silly, I'm fine. Rich and I just got a little carried away."

Rachel raised an eyebrow, remembering Paul's inquiry into the sexual habits of Katie Pettigrew. Although she really didn't want the answer to the question on her mind, nor could she stop herself from asking. "What were you two doing?"

"You know, nothing out of the ordinary...for us. It just got rougher than usual," Katie stalled hoping her brain would suddenly remember what gardeners actually did. "Mainly bolting."

"Bolting?" Rachel asked, wondering if this was a new position.

"I think Rachel meant what were you and Rich planting?" prompted Janet. "You know, our committee takes a serious interest in the gardens of our members."

"Yes...vegetables that flower rather than produce are known as bolting. It's usually caused by late planting and too warm of temperatures," added Katie, trying to sound educated about the issue. "Naturally this was not our intention, but you can't fight mother nature."

Then, remembering Rich's advice, Katie added, "Next we'll try a new form of succulent cactus that is simply ingenious."

"You mean indigenous?" asked Janet.

"That too," said Katie recovering. "It's a marvelously ingenious and indigenous little creature."

"Fascinating," said Janet to the other committee members.

"Quite," said Rachel still wondering what Katie and Rich got up to in their garden.

THE GARDENING CLUB GALS TOOK A BREAK FROM questioning Katie to enjoying the annual newcomers luncheon. Katie, who was starving from the exertion of carrying trees, made a beeline to the buffet table with Janet close at her heels.

"Katie, again...I don't mean to pry, but are things okay at home?"

"What do you mean?"

"With Rich. Those cuts and bruises," she said letting her voice trail off.

"Oh Janet, you've got it all wrong." Katie nervously twirled some of her hair, allowing the strands to hide the graze caused earlier. "This was just a gardening accident."

"It's okay to talk about it, dear. Tons of women fall victim to spousal abuse. It doesn't mean you have to stay a victim. Any couple can benefit from therapy."

"Therapy?!"

"Don't be so alarmed. It's kind of fun when you do it as part of a retreat. I mentioned the retreat to you at Rachel's party? David and I host it each year. It's been a tremendous hit for ten years now. I host some communication workshops and he counsels people on their plastic surgery options. You know, it wouldn't hurt for you to see him right away. Those cuts might scar."

"I don't know, Janet. Rich isn't really the communication workshop type."

"Everyone will be there," she said with a wave of her hand to the women gathered by the buffet table. "It's become kind of a chic retreat, if I do say so myself."

Even though Janet had expressed concern that Rich may be an abuser, Katie mulled over the idea of going to the retreat. "It might be a good place for Rich to campaign," she said brightly.

And, although Janet delivered her a weak smile, Katie chose to ignore it. "Chic retreat...I'll definitely talk to him."

Chapter 12

The last thing Katie wanted to do when she returned home was garden, but since she was now an official member of the Gardening Club, she believed it was partly her duty. Ironically, none of the other women on the committee actually gardened.

"We have people for that," Amanda had bluntly pointed out.

"Landscapers plan our gardens," Janet had added.

"Actually...landscape architects," Rachel interjected.

Although the other women all had professional gardeners to do their dirty work, Rich would never pay someone else to do what he was capable of, which brought up another reason for Katie to venture back to the garden. Rich's yet to be buried hoses were an eye sore that had to be hidden, not only from the neighbors, but also the neighborhood help, whom Katie had noticed started speaking rapidly in Spanish whenever she or Rich came outside.

"This is your idea of hiding the evidence?" Katie asked while inspecting the yard.

"What's wrong with it?" Rich retorted.

"Well, these big mounds of dirt for one thing. Honestly

Rich, one would think there's a body underneath, not a little hose. What happened to waiting for the ground cover to...well...cover?"

"I didn't want to wait. Besides, I thought it would be less conspicuous if I coiled it up like a snake rather than stretch it across the entire yard," he explained.

Katie thought about the predicament. It seemed like life with Rich never went smoothly. Maybe Janet was right and the weekend couples' retreat would bring them closer.

"Rich, you know how I hate to garden?"

"Yeah?"

"Well, I'm willing to help you make this look natural. Not like buried bodies, know what I mean?"

"What's the catch?"

"Come with me to Janet and David's couples' retreat. It'll be good for your campaign," she added as an after-thought.

"How so?"

"Uh, well, you'll be seen as a sensitive man that isn't afraid to get in touch with his inner thoughts."

Unconvinced, Rich asked one more question, "You'll help me?"

"Of course. I'll even dig a few extra holes to search for more artifacts."

"Deal."

It was one thing to agree to help Rich to garden, but quite another to actually be seen gardening. In order to avoid scrutiny by the Club who had just accepted her, Katie insisted to Rich that they plant after dark. It was becoming a fetish that Rich was growing to appreciate for not only did Katie take measures so nobody would see them, she also insisted on gardening á naturale to avoid dirt particles being lodged in her new wardrobe. To show his appreciation, Rich penciled in the couples' retreat on the calendar that hung in their kitchen and grabbed a bottle of wine from the cupboard before joining Katie outside.

"It's a good thing there's not a full moon," Rich teased, seeing Katie bent over their new petunia bed. "It wouldn't be able to compete with your own beauty."

"You say the sweetest things," she answered and appreciatively wagged her bottom.

"Katie, I know you have your reasons for coming out here when it's dark, and I do find your gardening attire, or lack thereof, quite fetching, but are you sure you can see what you're doing? The flowers don't look straight from over here."

"I figure the more holes we dig, the greater chance of finding our hidden treasure. If we get lucky and find something, we'll have so much money nobody will mind. And, if we don't get lucky, we'll just pretend the rabbits made the holes."

Katie took a break from her digging to join Rich by their new garden bench. "Rich, I'm pooped, you take over." With that, Katie plopped down on the bench only to yelp and immediately jump back up.

"What's wrong?"

"Splinter," Katie complained.

"Serves you right," Rich chuckled. "Right cheek or left?"

"PAUL, TAKE A LOOK AT THIS!"

"Spying again? If you're going to stay up late, we might as well...you know," he pleaded.

"Not now Paul! Not when our neighbors are shining lights in the yard at half past midnight."

Rachel continued to look out the window, giving a blow by blow description of the Pettigrew's activities. To think that she once thought they were upstanding citizens. Now, the only thing Rachel knew for sure was that her neighbors had the most peculiar night time habits. She pressed her nose to the glass, hardly believing her eyes. "She's undressed!" Rachel exclaimed.

"Who?" asked Paul, switching on his bedside lamp.

"Shut it off! Quick!" shouted Rachel, diving for the lamp.

"If you keep insisting on waking me up, I might as well get something out of it," said Paul with another switch of the lamp. "I'm going to read," he pouted.

Rachel promptly shut it off again. "Don't read. Come to the window. It's far more interesting."

"UH OH. MAYBE WE SHOULD CONTINUE THIS INSIDE," SAID Katie in reference to Rich's efforts to remove her splinter.

"You said it hurts to walk.'"

"It does; it seems to shift each time I move my leg," said Katie. "Will you carry me?"

Rich looked Katie up and down trying to figure out the kindest way to tell his wife that he had a better chance of growing back his receding hairline than lifting her. "I've got a flashlight. I think I can get it out right here and now. Just stay still."

"Hurry up. My back is hurting and my bottom's cold. Besides, I think the neighbors can see us."

"You and your paranoia with the neighbors."

It was no wonder Katie was in such a state. Bent over and naked, she waited patiently while Rich used tweezers to remove the offending wood bit.

"Ouch!" she cried.

"Got it!" Rich said victoriously.

"WHY WOULD HE DO THAT?" ASKED PAUL. "PRETTY KINKY, IF you ask me."

"What? What's he doing? You're hogging the window."

Paul and Rachel were now taking turns spying on the Pettigrews.

"Isn't it obvious?" asked Paul. "The way he's bent his head over her..."

"It's not apparent to me."

"He's...he...ehhh, never mind. It's just not something proper people talk about."

"Of course not!" agreed Rachel. "But...maybe you should tell me, you know, just so I'm aware of the dangers out there for little Emily's sake."

"Well, let's just say that he's a bottom man. Probably voted for Obama, too. You were right, honey. I think we should call the homeowners' security patrol."

"THEY'RE WATCHING US," KATIE INSISTED.

"Don't be silly. Who would be up at this hour? We're in suburbia, for God's sake."

"This is so not suburbia," Katie bristled. "We escaped suburbia and all the everyday people that went with it. We're in the Hills...the Hollywood Hills."

"It's still late, Katie."

"Hills people are night people. Besides, we're up and so are they," Katie motioned to the Cox's house. "I saw their lights go on and off."

"Right. On...and *off*. They went to sleep."

"No, they didn't do their routine. Bubble bath for Rachel, followed by a face spritzing, moisturizing, and teeth flossing. Then it's pillow fluffing detail for Paul, followed by an examination of the hospital corners for any necessary re-tucking and then back to the bathroom for ear wax removal duty."

"Uhgg! How do you know these things?"

"Women talk," Katie said simply. "And, I get a good view of

their bedroom from that little window next to our bathtub. Anyway, if they were asleep, why would they keep turning the lights on again?"

"Maybe their obsessive compulsive?"

"More likely they're just nosey."

"Hey, come here," Rich said as he reached for Katie, who had now put her robe back on to avoid anymore stray splinters.

"Rich! What's got into you?" she squealed with delight.

"Must be all this fresh air," he said and pulled Katie onto their bench.

ALTHOUGH RICH HAD TURNED OFF THE FLASHLIGHT, HE AND Katie were still attracting attention. Their kisses became more heated and instead of quietly planting under the moon, Rich's gangly, long legs knocked over the gardening tools that were propped against the bench as he stretched out beside Katie.

"Shh!" giggled Katie, who at this point was more pleased at the fact that Rich was showing her attention than worried about the noise.

"Follow my lead," whispered Rich. "Damn, noisy rabbits," he said loudly and then winked and nudged Katie.

"Someone really should do something about those pesky rodents," said Katie, who ever since high school thespians had a tendency to overact. "There'll be rabbit stew if we catch one."

From her bedroom, Rachel couldn't be quiet a moment longer. Reaching for the telephone she dialed. "Hello, security? Yes, I'd like a patrol car sent to East Haven Drive, right away. The problem? My neighbors are hunting rabbits in the neighborhood, and doing just God-awful things."

THE PETTIGREWS HAD DROPPED THE RABBIT ACT AND WERE

now thoroughly wrapped up in each other again. Rich had joined Katie in her state of undress and was in danger of getting splinters lodged in equally embarrassing areas, but was too absorbed in their current antics to mind. So absorbed, in fact, that they didn't notice the sound of a car easing up their drive.

The men were typical of the type hired by security companies--rejected police academy candidates with beefy builds and muscles aching for action. The ones patrolling the Pettigrew neighborhood had hoped for some excitement as they were bored with their usual work time routine, which consisted of a fifteen minute patrol through the neighborhood followed by thirty minutes in the office. Late nights in a security office had to be the most boring of places and jobs. The men alternated watching late night talk shows with the excitement of bathroom breaks, and then back to the car. The schedule didn't leave them enough time to properly watch the television because their visits to the office seemed to coincide with the network commercial times. It was enough to make a security guard trigger happy.

"Joe, let's check this out and hurry back," the taller of the two guards, named Pete, said to his partner. "Figures that Ariana Grande is on Jimmy Fallon the one night we get a call."

"Lucky guy. You think he'll see any action with her after the show?"

"You're a dog," said Pete as he stepped out of the car and walked across one of the Pettigrew's newly planted flower beds. "He's old enough to be her father. You're a degenerate for thinking such a thought--a disgrace to the uniform you're wearing."

Joe reached for his stun gun and made his way to the backyard while still arguing. "Puh-leaze! I know you'd do her."

"Would not."

"Then you're a homo."

"Crude pig."

"Who you calling a pig?" countered Pete, who was now

pointing his own stun gun, standard issue from 'We're Ready Patrol Co.,' directly at Joe.

Rich and Katie heard the commotion and tip-toed to peer over the fence that separated their front and back gardens.

"Those ruffians," hissed Rich.

"Look at them," concurred Katie. "They've trampled our petunias."

"And they've got guns. Stand back. I'll sneak around to the front and go for help," ordered Rich.

"What do you think they want?" asked Katie while pulling her robe tightly around her.

"You never know with these types. Could be a simple burglary, or..." his voice trailed off.

"Or what?"

"Corporate espionage. They could be sent from the water district to spy on us. Or maybe they've heard about the treasure and are here to steal that."

'What could the water district want with our Indian artifacts?"

"Blackmail. We share in the profits and they keep our water stealing a secret."

"If they know about our water stealing, wouldn't they just put a stop to it?"

"No, they don't care. It's only water. What they want is the big bucks. Now I know we're onto something. I bet those two are government spies," he jerked his head toward the guards.

Suddenly, the guards' attention was drawn to the whispered voices of Rich and Katie. They edged forward; the Pettigrews moved backward; and then, they met, back to back, bottom to bottom. Rich jumped around and Pete, willing his trigger finger to steady, took aim.

"Stop!" shouted Rich.

"The gun!" screamed Katie.

"Against the wall, you two," said Joe.

"Do as he says or I'll shoot," added Pete.

"You'll never get anything out of me," said Rich. "Stay back, Katie."

"You'll have to torture us," added Katie, who was feeling particularly proud of the gallant way in which Rich was handling the situation.

"That's enough, Katie, that's just what these types may have in mind," Rich said, keeping his voice low.

"Hey, stop the whispering and start explaining," said Joe.

"I don't have to explain anything. This is private property and you're trespassing," said Rich. "Do you have a warrant to be here?"

"There's been a request to investigate," replied Pete.

"See Katie? A request. Probably made by one of my firm's competitors, such cronies!"

"Wasn't the complaint made by someone named Cox?" he asked Joe.

Joe quickly checked his log book. "Yep, says here Rachel and Paul Cox of East Haven Drive."

"Rachel and Paul? What would they want with my treasure?" asked Rich.

Pete winked at Joe. "Treasure. Pet name for her, no doubt." He looked at Katie's sizable girth and shook his head. "Go figure," he said to Joe and then addressed Rich. "Listen buddy, just keep it down and do your business indoors. No need to give the neighbors a show. We'll put in that you agreed to a C and D on the I.E."

"Huh?" asked Katie.

"Cease and Desist on the Indecent Exposure charge," Pete explained.

Katie absently started pulling her robe even tighter. "You mean you aren't corporate spies?"

"We work for you," Joe explained. "Well, all of you," he said sweeping his hands towards the neighborhood. "We're your security company."

"At your service," Pete said as he and Joe strode back to their patrol car.

"THAT DOES IT!" SAID RICH FURIOUSLY.

"Come back to bed."

"How can you even think about it after we were humiliated in our own yard?" asked Rich.

"Because we weren't just humiliated. We were interrupted," she said with a renewed attempt at seduction.

"You know, we deserve something good to happen," Rich said.

"That's right, sugar," Katie responded, throwing her arms around his neck.

"I'm going to start pumping the water into our yard first thing tomorrow. That'll show all of them, the city and the homeowners association."

"What about your campaign? What about me?!"

"Katie, we pay those men. We actually pay their salaries through this lousy association. Eighty-eight dollars a month goes to the association, and for what? For the bonus of having secured gates that keep 'undesirables' out. And you know what? I'm thinking that they're thinking we're the undesirables."

"No!" shouted Katie, covering her ears at the horrible sound of his words.

"That's right, Katie. We were practically accosted by those security morons right in our own yard...during, well you know what."

"Exactly," said Katie with a nod, determined not to let Rich forget. "You know, I think Rachel and Paul might still be up."

"Oh?"

"Yeah. Let's give 'em an earful. Show them what good it did to send ol' Pete and Joe round."

"You're the best, Katie."

Chapter 13

It was definitely feeling like a Monday for Katie. The let down from the weekend had struck with a vengeance in the form of 25 unruly six-year-olds. Mrs. Habbernasher called in sick, which meant that Katie was asked to take over her Kindergarten room while the substitute teacher was given the easier task of supervising Katie's pre-schoolers, who were accompanied by a parent as it was actually a mommy and me program in which the mother was the student, learning parenting skills. Katie found that she was much better equipped to tell grown women how to discipline and clean up after their children than to actually do it herself when faced with a classroom of children alone.

The challenges began from the moment Katie entered and a wise-cracking boy pointed to Katie's stomach and accused her of eating Mrs. H. Then, the stress became incrementally greater with each passing hour. Unlike Katie's usual class where the children readily fell asleep at the drop of a hat, the older children argued about taking a fifteen minute nap, a lousy quarter of an hour that Katie had waited anxiously for so that she could go to the teacher's lounge for a much needed caffeine boost.

Katie would finally get one group quiet and ready for a nap when the other side of the room thought breaking into the finger paint was a good idea. The trouble started when Joey Del Rios thought Stephanie Sweeney would look better with a beard. Finally, when Katie had the rogue finger painters under control and prepped for a nap, the first crew would awake. It was a vicious cycle that continued until Katie finally decided that sleep was not in their immediate future and a cup of coffee was surely not in hers. Snack time brought another set of problems. Most of the children wanted to sample others' treats, but were not inclined to share their own snack. This naturally brought about tears, hair pulling and tattle tailing. After a blonde little girl in a designer dress received a helping of chocolate pudding dumped over her head, she ran to the classroom mirror, saw that her hair now resembled Ozzie Osborne's, a terrible look in anyone's book, and wouldn't stop screaming. She had climbed on top of a desk to make her screaming all the more dramatic when the principal walked in to inform Katie that the vice principal would take over and Katie's presence was requested immediately in the office. Although Katie was happy to escape the terrors of the six-year-olds, the alternative of sitting with Mr. Dashell didn't please her.

She followed him to his office and when asked to sit in front of his massive, oak desk, was catapulted back in time. She tried to convince herself that she was his peer and was probably being asked to consult about a new program for the elementary students. The story didn't fly even with her and when she saw the look of disapproval on Mr. Dashell's face, she knew why the older students snickered, 'Dashell's an Asshole!' She was singing a chorus of the rousing tune in her own head when his words brought her back to reality.

"I said, Mrs. Pettigrew, did you hear me? Were you listening?"

Katie felt like a naughty child. "Uh, no sir, I'm sorry. I must have had my mind on something else."

"Well, would you care to share it with the rest of us?"

Rest of us? For the first time Katie noticed the others. When did the board of governors arrive? Three of the five members of the committee were seated behind her, keeping her from making an escape.

"I'll repeat myself then,"Dashell announced. "There have been very serious charges brought against you, Mrs. Pettigrew. Charges involving livestock."

Katie's mind raced to a recent private moment when Rich made an off-color joke about sex on farms. She immediately began to imagine the light sockets being bugged and promised herself to check them the moment she arrived home. "Livestock?" she uttered barely above a whisper.

"Yes. It seems that a rabbit has disappeared from your classroom. A pet rabbit, no less, that belonged to a very prominent member of our community. According to Amanda Exeter, her daughter is heart-broken. Would you care to explain how this could happen?"

Katie's brain was a whirl. A number of possible explanations came to mind, but none would be pleasing to the board. She considered them all:

1. Perhaps the rabbit was as extraordinary as the Exeter family believed and had managed to pick the lock. Cheeky rodent.
2. There could be a rabbit kidnapper on the loose, hoping to milk the Exeters of some spare change. Dirty opportunist.
3. There was always the possibility that Katie had simply left the rabbit's cage open. Stupid. Stupid.

"Mrs. Pettigrew? Are you with us?" Mr. Dashell asked. "As I was saying, there are some very serious charges against you."

"Yes, I understand that they are concerned about their rabbit, but Mr. Dashell, I have no idea how it got out of its cage.

I can assure you that I'll search the classroom from top to bottom. I'll even look under Pete Dupree's desk." She whispered knowingly, "Nose-picker. Under the desk is not a pretty sight."

"That's all very well, Mrs. Pettigrew; however, the Exeters do not believe the rabbit will turn up in the classroom."

"How can they be so sure?"

"Because they believe that you and your husband may have taken the rabbit."

"But, why would we? Rich doesn't even particularly like rabbits."

The moment she expressed that truth, Katie knew she was digging a deeper hole for herself.

"So we've heard. Therein lies our problem," Dashell said more to the Board than to Katie. "The Exeters tell us that a neighbor heard you and your husband discussing burying animal remains...rabbit remains to be specific. They believe it was part of some ritual since the act..."

A nearby Board member suddenly cleared his throat and Dashell continued, "I'm sorry...the *alleged act*...supposedly took place at night." Dashell then paused and looked straight at Katie. "Mrs. Pettigrew, I must ask, did you and your husband partake in any activities deemed inappropriate for public viewing from a woman who is a mentor to children?"

Katie stared on with a horrified expression, but Mr. Dashell didn't stop there.

"And if so, did you and your husband speak ill of rabbits while in your backyard after hours partaking in this act?"

Katie saw the sets of eyes staring back at her. She noticed their disapproving nods. What could she say other than, "Do I have to answer that without my attorney present?"

"KATIE, WHAT ABOUT THE CAMPAIGN? I'LL BE RUINED IF you're convicted of burying animal remains. How sick!"

"It's worse than that," Katie admitted. "They think it was some sort of creepy ritual where we had sex and *then* buried the animals."

Rich buried his head in his hands.

"Rich? Rich, sweetie? You know I didn't bury anything. I hate dirt!"

"How are you going to convince this community of that? The Exeters have power, money, and a name for themselves."

"Don't I know it..." Katie muttered. "But, we're going to have all that when you win this election. Now think positively!"

"What are you going to do?"

"Me? You're in this too," Katie chided.

"I didn't steal a bunny!" Rich exclaimed.

"Neither did I! Have you completely lost your mind?"

"Relax, Katie. I'm just practicing for when I get into office. I'm trying to distance myself from guilt."

"I'm not guilty!"

"That's what they all say," Rich mocked. "Ahh honey, I know you didn't do anything. You don't have it in you to decapitate, mutilate, or even propagate a rabbit."

Suddenly, a lightbulb went off in Katie's mind. "Why do you have that look in your eyes?" Rich enquired.

"You said propagate. That's it. If we're going to be the first family of Hollywood, we have to be more of a family. We're going to have a baby! Oh, Rich, you should've told me sooner!"

KATIE WAS DRESSED TO IMPRESS. OR, AT LEAST KATIE believed it to be so. Wearing a pale pink suit with black trim, a pill box hat in the same shade of pink with spots of light yellow, and high-heeled pumps of pink with a swirl of lime green around each pointed toe, Katie looked like a bowl of spumoni gone awry. To top off the look, she donned dark, cat-shaped sunglasses and believed she pulled off the look described in her favorite blog, "The Chic Fashionista," as worn by Audrey Hepburn, Jennifer Lopez and even Dita Von Teese.

She attempted to be seductive, leaning her back against the wall of the doorway that led to the living room, waiting for Rich to glance up from his newspaper. He rustled, caught a quick glimpse and then quickly buried his nose again and sneezed for good measure in hopes that Katie would think his glance in her direction was merely an attempt to catch some runaway post-nasal drippage and not an appraisal of her fashion sense.

"What do you think?"

"Nothing really interesting today," he said believing that the best approach was an honest one.

"Not the news, silly. Me!" Katie announced and struck another pose.

"Oh, you," replied Rich, knowing that the subtleties of his comments would be lost on Katie. "Where are you going?"

"I'm invited to the Gardening Club's tea party," she said proudly. "Janet got me the invite. It should be good networking for your campaign. I'm playing the part of a Coucilman's wife. How do I look?"

She looked so happy about the party that Rich smiled in spite of himself. "You look radiant, dear. Like the cherry on top of the sundae." And he meant it.

THE PARTY WAS IN FULL SWING BY THE TIME KATIE ARRIVED. Janet and Rachel had converged on the dessert table, sampling petit fours and scones before giving the tea sandwiches a second glance. Ireland was loading her plate with vegetable crudité, not a carbohydrate dared approach. Amanda was doing her best to ignore the Lessers and cozy up to the In crowd. Stacey surreptitiously emptied a vile of something into her teacup and then smiled at Katie and toasted her approach.

"It's a bore here," she whispered. "But I've got my ways of

livening things up," she said patting her handbag. "Wanna put a kick in your teacup?"

"Nah, it's okay," Katie responded. "I quite like tea. As long as it has enough milk, honey, and lemon in it," she said and took a loud slurp.

"Really?" said Amanda, who happened to be eavesdropping nearby. "Is that how it's drunk?"

"Who are you calling drunk?" asked Stacey, sounding as if she already had enough of her own brew.

"Please, Stacey. Will you try not to make a scene," Amanda hissed. "Just once."

Janet walked up in time to stop further outbursts. "Ladies, so glad you could make it. Amanda, I think Rachel was looking for you in the next room."

Amanda turned on her heel, giving Stacey one last disparaging look before she left.

"Did you see that?" Stacey asked.

"Yeah, at least she looked at you," Katie noted. "She just ignored me. And I've known her forever."

"Never mind her," Janet said, patting Katie's arm. "You should know Katie, you look wonderful. Why don't we chat in the living room?" And, knowing that Stacey would relish the chance to pour herself one more cup, Janet escorted Katie away. "Stacey, help yourself to more tea. I must steal Katie for a moment."

"How are you, dear?" Janet asked.

"That Amanda is making my life a living hell," Katie admitted. "Her daughter's bunny is missing and she's accused me and Rich of...of, oh Janet, it's just too awful for words." Katie believed that if she were to be accused of such indiscretions, she might as well take her humility to new heights. She pulled out a matching pink handkerchief from her little, lime green handbag and gently blew her nose into it, dabbed at her eyes, and then wiped the smallest amount of lipstick from her teeth, all in the span of a minute. Janet stared aghast.

"Katie, you really must get a grip. Falling to pieces isn't going to help matters. I'm sure all this talk is just that. You know the way people like to gossip. They'll talk about the latest scandal until the next one pops up and then the first is just a memory. Tomorrow Amanda will be telling everyone that Stacey was so sloshed she couldn't stand."

"You really think so?" Katie asked hopefully.

"Of course. This outing will do you good. By the look of you, I'd say you don't get out much," Janet added and gave Katie's arm a little squeeze. "Now go on and mingle," she said and shoved Katie toward Rachel and Ireland's clique.

"You look fabulous, Rachel. Really fab," said Ireland.

"I owe it all to Dr. Pagatacos," Rachel answered proudly.

"Oh, I've heard so much about him," Ireland exclaimed. "Everyone who is anyone goes to him. How did you get in?"

"I met his wife at a charity fundraiser. Before you knew it, we were chatting about Lypo, Botox, neck lifts, tummy tucks, you know...the usual."

"One of my clients' husbands went to him for a neck lift, chin lift, and rhinoplasty all in the same procedure," Ireland said.

"That's the way to do it," Rachel added knowingly. "If you're going to go under the knife and be out of commission for a week, you might as well tag on another two weeks to really get the works done. But don't let Janet hear us...her husband's plastic surgery business has been a bit slow ever since he had that eyebrow debacle."

"Oh I heard...," Ireland said excitedly. "That poor woman. Her right eyebrow ended up two inches above the left one. She always looked like she was asking a question and then, she couldn't take it anymore...moved to Indiana."

"I thought it was Kentucky?"

Katie took the opportunity to jump in. "Oh, I've been dying for a little Botox. I hear they're doing it in your butt now too, just to get a little lift there."

"Pardon?" asked Rachel.

Remembering her high society manners, Katie rephrased. "I mean buttocks." Still, her words were met with questioning glances. "Botox, short for buttocks, right?" she said in a panic.

"Oh Katie, you are such a whip!" Rachel squealed.

Katie smiled fiercely. "I've meant to get a video so I can do it at home. Rich says that I can kick-box my Botox back into shape in no time. All the celebrity wives are doing it," she added for emphasis.

Ireland was also roaring by now. "Katie, stop. My stomach is hurting; I'm practically ROFL!"

"Rawful?" It was Katie's turn to be confused.

"Rolling on floor laughing," Ireland explained, adjusting the low-plunging neckline of her top that threatened to become more revealing with each one of her exhalations.

"I've heard about it, naturally. But I never knew anyone who actually did it," Katie confessed.

"Honey," Rachel said gently. "Everyone in Hollywood does it. You just don't know they do it because they go to Beverly Hills doctors who know what they're doing."

Ireland concurred. "Yeah, if you go to a Valley doctor you're likely to end up looking like a cyclops."

At that moment, Janet passed by and added her two cents. "Or you could go to David and be assured of perfect results."

"Of course," Ireland agreed sweetly.

"My thoughts exactly," Rachel kissed up.

"Does everyone around her do lypo?" Katie asked naively.

"Well, after having kids, I'd like to," Rachel responded. "A friend had it done and she now has a fifteen-year-old stomach."

"How disgusting! Did she sue?" Katie asked.

"Are you kidding? Wouldn't you want a fifteen-year-old stomach?" Rachel asked in amazement.

"I don't know...," Katie pondered the concept. "It just sounds so alien."

"Katie, they make your stomach as tight and firm and

wonderfully sexy as a teenager. You know, the way nature intended us to look," Rachel explained.

"It's really the only saving grace of my not having children," Ireland chimed in while ever so subtly stretching her spine, allowing a bit of bare midriff to become exposed as her top glided upwards.

Feeling left out of the conversation, Katie meandered to another group of women, but found their dialogue to be just as confusing. "No, it wasn't colic, it started as soon as breakfast was over," said a woman holding a mammoth-sized baby. Katie poked her head into the circle and smiled.

"What a beautiful little boy," she said.

"Thank you, but it's a girl," the woman answered back. "See?" she said pointing to a stick-on bow that had been attached to the baby's otherwise bald head.

"Oh, of course, now I see the resemblance to you," Katie said trying to recover.

The woman ignored Katie and continued speaking to her friend. "Anyway, as I told my husband, colic doesn't start until at least 4 p.m. She does not have colic," she said in a tone that was more fearful than decisive.

"Of course not," the other woman agreed.

"Maybe she's just fussy," Katie offered.

The women stared at Katie as if she had just suggested the child be sent to a nearby zoo to be raised by hyenas.

"Penelope is never fussy. Are you sweetie?" she said to the baby.

"I've heard that a warm bath does wonders. I know it does for me," Katie tried again.

"Well, you can't do that everyday. Penelope's delicate skin will dry out."

"Do you have children?" the second woman asked.

"Well, no. But I...," Katie responded.

"Well, you really don't know anything then, do you?"

"No, I guess I don't," said Katie glumly, before decided to

test out her new revelation. Without realizing it, Rich had stumbled upon the answer. Now, Katie was sure of it. "But, my husband and I are trying," Katie said mustering up a new story. Trying to remember all of the new catch phrases and with it philosophies, she added, "We're thinking of having a midwife birth for us. It's a less sterile environment."

"Ewww," the woman gasped.

"I mean that as in cold, not as in unclean," Katie clarified. "Midwives spend more quality time with the mother to be and a happy mother means a happy, well-adjusted baby. No fussiness," she said pointedly.

Once on a roll, Katie couldn't stop her enthusiasm. "Naturally, I plan to breast-feed all my babies until they're at least a year and can be converted to cow's milk, of which I'll only buy organic," she said proudly. "Unless, of course, little Sarah or Phoebe, those are absolutely my favorite names, proves to be lactose intolerant."

The women stared at Katie half expecting her to take a bow. "Congratulations," Penelope's mom said simply.

"Good luck," the other added.

"I'll let you know when we're successful!" Katie beamed and left the party with a new lease on life.

Chapter 14

K atie returned home to find Rich rearranging potted plants in the garden in an attempt to hide the buried hoses, which resurfaced each week, ironically after their own sprinklers' watering caused the dirt to rearrange itself. As of yet, the hoses had not yielded more than minor droplets of water from the city's supply. Katie was sure that the minuscule amount was caused by condensation, not a force of physics that brought the creek's supply conveniently into their own backyard. Katie was never in favor of stealing city water; nonetheless, Rich's failed attempts now caused her to worry.

The father of her future child should be successful, a man who could set his mind to stealing water and succeed. If Rich couldn't even steal water properly, there was no telling what other shortcomings would emerge. Katie sat at the patio table and looked up from her coffee to spy Rich attempting to maneuver the bulge of his stomach under his waistband and wondered if he had other secrets.

"Rich, have you ever gotten a woman pregnant?"

"No. Why do you ask? Has someone come out of the wood-work declaring me the father of her child?" he asked with concern. "It's not true, Katie. Damn election is going out of control," he said kicking at the earth. "They'll stop at nothing to derail me," he said staring at his protruding hose.

"Relax. It's not that. I was just wondering."

"Why would you wonder such a thing?"

"Well, we've been together seven years and in all that time...," she let her voice trail off.

"What? Because we've never had an accident, you think I can't drive the ambulance?"

"Well...can you?"

"That question is totally without merit."

"Sorry."

Rich looked at Katie and knew it was a time for action, not words. "I'll show you, Katie Pettigrew," he said picking her up, or rather, attempting to pick her up, but settling on leading her into the house.

SEX WASN'T WHAT IT USED TO BE, NOT THAT KATIE WAS complaining. In the old days of their courtship, she and Rich languished in bed. Each romp in the sack was akin to a lazy Sunday morning. There was never anything more pressing than spending time together. But now that Katie had babies on the brain, sex had taken on a more perfunctory role.

"Where are you going?" Rich asked.

"I've got a surprise for you," Katie answered back, having already bounded from their bed and made it halfway to the bathroom.

"Can't I have it with you by my side?"

"Soon," Katie promised, "just as soon as I pick her...or maybe him...up."

"What?!"

"Nothing...you'll see."

Katie left Rich and made a beeline for "The Pampered

Pouch," a chic maternity store best known as the place where all the pregnant celebrities shop. The most amazing feature of the store was that it didn't look like a store at all, but more like an intimate sitting room. Furthermore, this room wasn't just thrown together with mail order furniture and sterile walls like the kind in doctors' offices. An antique french desk made of mahogany stood adjacent to the entryway door with a leather bound book welcoming

guests to sign in. Katie did as instructed and then allowed herself to be escorted to the *lounge*, an area with two ample wingback chairs, large enough so that even the largest of pregnant women would feel like Alice in Wonderland after significant shrinkage. Katie sank into the forest green velvet, gratefully accepted the cup of steaming herbal tea offered to her and anxiously awaited her private consultation.

"May I offer you an almond biscotti? They go wonderfully with our tea", a woman who had introduced herself as Elizabeth asked. She also explained that her job was to make pregnant women feel like the beautiful goddesses they've become. Katie had doubts about whether she would ever feel like a goddess, pregnant or not, but eagerly accepted the offering. She scanned the rest of the room and noticed a row of framed magazine covers. Each one featured very pregnant celebrities including Demi Moore, Brooke Shields, Monica Bellucci, Britney Spears and many others.

Elizabeth followed Katie's gaze. "They're all truly inspiring, aren't they?"

"Oh yes!" Katie concurred.

"By the way, we carry all of the maternity fashions that Jessica Simpson wore, if you're interested in plus sizes."

"Isn't all maternity wear *plus* sized?"

The woman smiled a kind, but also disparaging grin. "Oh no. Monica Bellucci's clothes were part of our petite preggy line, although sadly she chose not to wear any of them on that particular day," her eyes went to the naked photo. "A shame, truly. Forced us to withdraw our advertising from the magazine. Damn photographers," Elizabeth said with sudden vehemence. "Anyway, for those of us who don't possess Monica's sense of freedom," Elizabeth said as she glanced toward Katie, "we offer couture maternity fashion in various sizes. Tell me, Katie, are you couture material?"

Katie searched her mind for the right answer. "I've been told my skin is like satin."

"I see you have a sense of humor. I like that, but allow me to be blunt. Our clientele is sophisticated," she said looking down her nose at Katie. "We don't want our fashions worn on just anybody. It would simply give us a household name, which again, we don't want. We choose to be exclusive because our women demand it. You won't find anything with a bib or a bow. Those are for babies, not the fertile women that grace our doors. Are you in agreement?"

"Most definitely," said Katie, quite enamored.

Elizabeth led Katie with teacup in hand deeper into the shop and Katie discovered how true her wise words were. A tent-shaped dress with polka dots or other non-flattering patterns didn't dare hang next to the upscale fashions displayed. Instead, sleek pantsuits in black, flowing dresses with side slits, and even halter tops were miraculously transformed to fit the pregnant figure and look good, even sexy.

"Just feel this fabric," Elizabeth offered. "It flows over your body and just shouts, I'm pregnant and proud. There's no need to hide such a glorious occurrence."

Katie tried in vain to balance her teacup and biscotti while struggling to rid her fingers of crumbs to stroke the dress presented to her. The teacup began to wobble and while Katie managed to save it, the tea, itself, landed on the wood floors with a splash.

"Oh my, I'm so sorry," Katie gasped. "I'm just so clumsy lately."

"It's your condition. By the way, how far along are you? I'd say about three months, just starting to show," noted Elizabeth while eyeing Katie's stomach.

"Actually, I'm not pregnant...yet." It was Elizabeth's turn to be embarrassed. Katie decided to fuel the sympathy into overdrive. "I so want a child."

"You poor thing. Have you tried IVF?"

Katie was tired of never knowing the latest buzz. She thought of the potential organizations to help childless, sad women like herself, and took a desperate stab at figuring out the acronym. "International Vagina Fraction?"

Upon seeing Elizabeth's confused stare she knew she had it wrong, all wrong. Perhaps it was some sort of disease. "Internal Vulva Fever?"

Elizabeth looked repulsed. "IVF...In Vitro Fertilization!"

"Oh!" Katie exclaimed. "That's not necessary. My husband is very virile."

"I see. Then perhaps the problem lies with you."

"No, I got pregnant at sixteen. First time out in fact. It scared the heck out of me. After that, I was changed."

Katie grabbed a tissue from her purse as Elizabeth offered her a chair and a comforting arm around her back.

"My mom was so angry. She created a reminder phrase about safe sex that I could use with guys I dated. She must have had a new phrase every time I left the house."

Elizabeth looked shocked. "Every time?"

Katie nodded, rolled her eyes and started reciting. "It will be sweeter if you wrap your peter. Don't be silly, protect your willy. If you think she's spunky, cover your monkey. Don't be a prick, cover your..."

"I think I get the picture," Elizabeth insisted before Katie could finish her last thought. "Any way, but you and your husband are ready?"

"Well...I am. I guess I just wanted to see what it would be like. I'm sorry if I've wasted your time. I'm new in the area and the women I've met are just...well, let's just say that I don't really feel like I can be myself around them."

Elizabeth looked pensive and then beamed in Katie's direction. "I know a way that this visit can be successful for both of us. Follow me," she said mysteriously. She led Katie into yet another room located behind the chic boutique section. Inside Katie saw that walls had certificates indicating that Elizabeth was a pregnancy prosthetic expert. A sterile looking table sat in the midst of the room, next to it was a sink and a counter covered with jars of cotton, sponges, equipment and potions. Lined up next to the assortment of colored potions were a display of round molds of varying sizes designed to emulate a pregnant stomach.

"Looking at you, I'd say model BF267 would suit you. You can change behind there," she said indicating a Chinese silk screen. "Just expose your stomach. Everything else can stay on unless you're concerned about the plaster mixture getting on your clothes, but I assure you that I'm a professional."

When Katie appeared next, Elizabeth led her to the table, positioned a luxurious feather pillow under her head and a silk, lavender scented bean bag over her eyes. "Comfy?"

"Very."

"Good. This model fits you precisely and it's quite affordable at $500."

"Oh," said Katie, worrying about how to break the news to Rich. "Is that all? Maybe I should try some others? Maybe one that isn't so...," Katie wanted to say expensive, but settled on "realistic."

"Nonsense. This one suits you." Elizabeth continued her fitting without further interruption from Katie. "We'll just make a mold of your stomach and add the plaster mix to fill it out. How far along would you like to be? Second or third trimester?"

"Oh, I'd say second. Don't want to shock the neighbors too much."

Within minutes, Elizabeth had swabbed off Katie's stomach

with antiseptic, smoothed over a green gooey mixture, and produced a hair dryer to help it harden faster. "Just another couple of minutes, Katie. How are you doing?"

"Well, it feels a little tight."

"Pregnancy has its discomforts, you know."

"Yes, but will it always be like this?"

"No, the tightness will subside when I peel off the mold, but you will have to get used to the extra weight of your new figure."

"I'm ready."

KATIE WANTED TO RUN THROUGH THE STREETS OF HER neighborhood showing off her prosthetic tummy, but didn't dare in her new "condition." Instead, she purchased one of the more revealing outfits available at The Pampered Pouch and decided to wear it home. She was proudly strolling to the mailbox, one hand tucked protectively under her tummy, when Ireland approached.

"Katie, I had no idea. Look at you. When did this happen? How could I not have known?"

"Well, I didn't want to say anything at first."

"I understand. My sister kept it a secret too until she made it through the first trimester."

"Exactly. I'm in my second, so I'm told."

"What do you mean? Don't you know when you're due?"

"I'm not exactly pregnant. I'm just trying it on for size. It's not my real tummy," she whispered.

"You're kidding. It looks so realistic. Can I pat it?"

"Of course," said Katie proudly.

Ireland was in the process of stroking Katie's stomach when Rich drove up. The shock was overwhelming. Katie in a tight outfit. Ireland caressing her. It was all too much for him.

Everyone seemed to be getting attention from Ireland except for him. Now his wife was even making it with her.

"What's all this?" he said in a jealous tone.

"She's beautiful. I just couldn't resist."

"We just wanted to try it out," Katie added.

"That's your explanation? Sheer physical attraction? Shame on you. You should have more restraint. Honestly, if the two of you think this type of experimentation is the new cool, l have news for you."

Rich just couldn't bare that his ideal woman, both of them, were caressing each other. He took a closer look at his wife's stomach, trying to remember when it had grown and why husbands were always the last to know.

"You're pregnant? We just spoke of this? How could this be?" he said pointing to her tummy. "How could I have missed it? It wasn't there this morning!"

"Nice, huh?" Katie said standing up straight and showing off her stomach from different angles.

"I'll let you two love birds have some time alone," said Ireland, as she headed toward her drive.

"Sounds like a good plan. Let's go upstairs, Rich. I'll let you take off my pouch."

"Take off your pouch?"

"It's just a trial tummy to see if I like the feel of pregnancy, the look of it. You know, I've heard that many women's sex drives increase in their second trimester and guess what, that's just where I'm supposed to be. Let's go inside."

"No, this is all happening too fast."

"Rich, you'll have nine months to get used to it, once it happens for real. Now let's go. I think I'm ovulating."

"But we barely discussed you getting pregnant and now look at you."

"I told you. I'm just trying this one on for size."

"But what about romance?"

"It will have to wait. Right now is the time."

"Well you'll have to wait because this time is not right for me."

"You're being way too sensitive. There's a gardening meeting again next month and I want to pregnant for it. Maybe I'll even get a nasty bout of morning sickness and can get some sympathy."

"You certainly won't get any from me. Sympathy or otherwise," he said pointedly.

"Well, what will I talk about at the meeting?"

Rich was growing more exasperated. "Gardening?!"

"Oh Rich, you really don't have any clue about women."

Chapter 15

I f someone had told Katie that a successful party is just as
stressful as a poorly receive one, she would never have
believed them. Before holding the tea party to announce Rich's
candidacy, she worried that something...anything would go
wrong. But with the party having been deemed a success, now
Katie faced the age old dilemma of keeping up appearances.
The neighborhood women were clamoring for another opportunity where they could gossip under the guise of discussing the
more noble topic of community improvement. Katie faced the
seemingly impossible task of enacting a repeat performance,
one which she had been rehearsing for since moving behind
the gates.

If Katie's world was a stage, then she and Rich had practiced their lines and her new pouch provided the best possible
costume design, but to her discerning eye, the set had much to
be desired. Katie admitted that housecleaning was never a huge
priority, although certainly a necessity considering that a bevy of
snobbish belles would soon barrel through her doors. With the
welcome addition of her pouch, she now had an excuse to limit

more mundane domestic endeavors such as dusting and vacu-
uming, if only until she found someone else to do it for her.

However, deciding to hire help was one thing, finding the
right help, according to the women around her, was another
issue altogether. They had warned Katie about the limitations
of help. Part-time, full-time, live-in, nanny only. These were
terms that all came with their own definitions and each woman
had her own opinions of which was most beneficial. After taking
it all in, Katie started the task of interviewing. Thus far, the
people Katie had spoken to all seemed to clean in a "limited"
capacity. Some would do floors and carpets, but wouldn't dust
or do windows, others offered to do laundry but rolled their eyes
at the suggestion of cleaning toilets. One woman even insisted
that an assistant cleaner be hired if she were to accept the job.

"I don't see why we need cleaners when we have you," Rich
pointed out.

"Because everyone else around her has one. I just want to fit
in. Besides, I am not a cleaner."

Rich looked at the mess that was now his living space.
"That's become obvious."

"Don't start. What would the other women think? Can you
imagine Rachel pushing a vacuum cleaner around if she were
pregnant?"

"First off, let me ask you what our bank will think when we
can't pay our mortgage because our living expenses are
too high?"

To Rich's annoyed expression, Katie simply sent one of
deliberate patience right back. "You didn't answer my
question."

"Katie, I can't imagine any of these women pushing
vacuums around whether they're pregnant or not."

Believing Rich's answer lent credibility to her own argument, Katie merely replied, "See?"

"However," Rich continued, "we do not have to do what
everyone else does. Didn't your mother ever teach you that? And

for that matter, you're a teacher. I know teachers are the ones always saying, 'Just because Billy is throwing sand, doesn't mean you have to.' Right?"

"Mother did say things like that, and I chose to ignore her."

"I give up," Rich answered. "You figure out how we're going to pay for cleaners. Maybe you can do some extra teaching."

"For nursery school students?"

"Maybe you could tutor their older siblings? Something!"

"I'll figure it out," she said with a wave of her hand and returned to the phone book to search for more cleaning crews, a job that made Katie as tired as if she had actually done the work herself. She was about to give up when a bright pink car with green lettering reading, "Courageous Cleaners...No Job Too Messy" pulled into Rachel's driveway. Although Katie didn't relish the idea of admitting that her home had become somewhat of a pig's sty, if Rachel could risk the embarrassment of having such a motto parked in front of her home, than Katie could as well. With one hand cradled under her prosthetic tummy, she ventured out to head off the cleaners before they got to Rachel's door.

"Excuse me? Hold on a moment, would ya?"

The young woman carrying a vacuum, mop, and assorted cleaning products gave Katie an annoyed stare for stopping her in the midst of hauling such a heavy load. She struggled to keep a hold of the supplies while Katie took her time crossing the lawn, making a big show of her delicate condition. In the end, the woman gave up and dropped everything, waiting impatiently.

"Thank you," said Katie. "It's hard for me to get around quickly these days," she said motioning to her stomach. The woman merely stared. "It's also hard for me to do heavy cleaning," Katie continued, but still the woman made no comment. "Oh! You probably don't speak English!" Katie said delighted. "Parlez-vous Francais?" Katie inquired. "It would be just fab to have a French maid," she said more to herself, and then when she got no response. "On second thought, a French maid would probably not be good for a marriage, too much folklore about their overactive sex drive, you know," Katie realized and gave a sudden nudge to the young woman's ribs. "You never know how much of those rumors are based in truth. Espanol?" she tried, but to no avail. "You can't be German...nobody around here has a German maid."

Katie hung her head, trying desperately to figure out a mutually understood language.

"Ma'am, I understand you perfectly. What I don't understand is what you need," the woman said in perfect English.

Katie beamed. "I'll cut right to the chase. I've got a big party at my house next Tuesday and I need help. I really shouldn't be inhaling cleaning products in my sensitive condition. Besides, the place is a mess and I don't know where to start."

"Sounds like an offer of a lifetime," the woman said sarcastically.

"I'll pay you time and a half," Katie suggested.

"Again, sounds tempting, but Tuesdays, as you can see, is the day I work for Miss Rachel."

"Just this once?"

"Double pay?"

"Fine, but I want windows, toilets, the works."

They shook hands, exchanged numbers, and Katie waddled her way back to her house.

KATIE GAVE THE LIVING ROOM A QUICK ONCE OVER BEFORE opening the door to the first of her guests.

"Katie the place looks wonderful, so put together and tidy. You really shouldn't have gone to so much trouble," said Rachel who stood at the door with a woman Katie had never met, a woman who was decidedly more pregnant than Katie's pouch made her appear to be. "Katie, this is an old friend of mine, Julie. The others have all met her before."

"I hope you don't mind that I'm tagging along. I just love this neighborhood and any excuse to visit. And look, now I've got two reasons," she said patting her stomach. "Your wonderful tea and my pending arrival. We're thinking of moving here because we're going to need more room soon. You know how it is...although my husband and I are looking at one of the larger models," she said surveying the surroundings.

Katie was getting used to the way Briarwood women spoke and she was ready. She knew that like on the battlefield the first attack would come fast, and the retaliation needed to be just as swift. She immediately shot back. "We decided to downsize with this purchase. The last place was too big for just the two of us. The little one," she said patting her stomach, "was a total surprise...a blessing from above."

Julie was adequately put in her place. "It's lovely," she said, her voice carrying through the entryway.

"Is that Julie?" Stacey exclaimed as she came bounding to the open door. She whipped past Katie accidentally bumping her, obviously unconcerned for her unborn and non-existent child to make a beeline for the unexpected guest. "Come in here and let me take a look at you."

Julie proudly pirouetted for Stacey and Janet, who had also convened in the doorway. The party may have been at Katie's, but the belle of the ball was Julie. Katie worked to contain her disappointment. "Ladies, can you step inside?"

"Yes, come on you two, there's plenty of time to catch up. We've got all afternoon," Rachel pointed out to Katie's dismay. For the first time, she wished she had never offered to host the party. This friend of Rachel's was also a friend to everyone else, making Katie feel like an unwanted guest in her own home. Stacey and Janet buzzed around her like bees to a hive, a very plump hive at that.

"So Julie, how far along are you?" asked Katie at an attempt to fit into the conversation.

"Seven months," she said proudly.

"Nearly ready to pop," Katie retorted.

"But you'd never know it looking at you," Rachel said with the loyalty of a sheep dog. "If I could look as good as you pregnant I'd force myself to have sex," she laughed manically. "Paul would be thrilled."

"Thanks, but it's all in the clothes."

"I've been to the Pampered Pouch," Katie joined in. "The absolutely best stuff, don't you think, Julie?"

"Definitely," she agreed and Katie beamed, happy to be in the know.

"So, Julie," Katie continued, "would you like a canape? They are loaded with calories I'm afraid, but don't let that stop you. Had I known you were coming..." her voice trailed off.

"Don't be silly," Julie said and grabbed not one, but three of the appetizers. "I don't believe in depriving myself when I'm pregnant. I mean, we have to put up with so much poking and prodding, why not indulge in the little things?"

"Like pregnant sex," said Rachel from behind Katie's shoulder. Pouch or no pouch, pregnant sex was an alien subject to Katie.

Julie chimed in, "Best I've ever had."

"What do you think, Katie?" asked Rachel. Katie looked at her and to her horror, noticed a satisfied glint in Rachel's eye. She had been set up.

Katie stammered nervously, twisted a ringlet of her hair, and avoided eye contact with the entire group. "I could go on forever, but I've got to get the next batch of canapes out of the oven," she said and escaped before further scrutiny could be brought on herself. Once in the kitchen, Katie caught Rich nibbling on her appetizers, but for the first time, she wasn't angry.

"I only had one, I swear."

"Never mind that. Something weird is going on with Rachel."

"What do you mean?"

"Don't know. She just seems pissed off about something," said Katie. "She actually backed me into a corner about my pregnancy."

"That sounds like a good thing. Honestly, how long are you going to keep this up," he said motioning to Katie's pouch.

"Until I get a real pouch."

"You were doing fine in that area before you made this purchase," he said patting her tummy.

"You're just what I need for my ego."

"Don't mention it. Can I have another one?"

"Don't you dare," she said and removed the tray.

Katie was just coming out of the kitchen when she heard Rachel's voice, "She actually hired Rosa right out from under me."

"Rachel, it is a free country. Rosa can work for whomever she chooses," Janet chided.

"On my day?" Rachel asked incredulously.

"Oh," responded Janet.

Stacey concurred, "She didn't. How could she?"

Katie decided it was time to brave the worst. If she had committed some kind of suburban faux pas she wanted to hear about it to her face. "How could I what?"

The three women just turned and stared. "Come on, you know what you did," Rachel scolded.

"No, I don't," Katie responded.

The two went back and forth with accusations flying. "Tuesdays are my day," said Rachel.

"I didn't know you had a monopoly on the day," Katie answered sarcastically.

"Do you always steal other people's employees?"

"Employee?" laughed Katie. "I bet you pay her under the

table. Probably don't even claim her on your taxes. Does the I.R.S. know about your Tuesday arrangement?"

Rachel sent a level glare Katie's way. "Just what are you saying?"

"Nothing," Katie said innocently, "except I had no idea it was such a big deal to you." Out of the corner of her eye, Katie caught a glimpse of Harry Greene's flashy red Porsche. Rachel was still ranting, but suddenly Stacey came to Katie's rescue.

"That reptile!" she exclaimed.

"I wouldn't go that far," mumbled Rachel under her breath, shooting Stacey with a horrified look.

"No, not Katie, Harry!"

"Thanks Stacey," Katie added as the group moved closer to the window. Harry was carrying a small paper sack, which he handed to Dean. Ireland came outside next, wearing her usually skimpy garb. Dean gave her a pat on the bottom and apparently sent her back inside for something he had forgotten.

"If he gets their listing I'll just die," Stacey said.

"I didn't know they were selling," said Janet.

"It doesn't look like he's listing their house," Julie pointed out. Ireland had returned with a wad of bills, which she handed to Dean. He counted out a hefty stack and gave it to Harry.

"Since when do real estate agents take money up front?" Rachel asked.

"When they're doing drugs on the side," Katie answered. The other women stared at her in disbelief.

"How do you know it's a drug deal?" Rachel asked with renewed interest in Katie. It was the first time her voice had warmed since she had arrived.

"I used to teach at middle school," Katie said by way of an explanation. "Once you've spent time with middle-school-ers...well, let's just say it hardens you. I much prefer the nursery age. Less corruption. Just the occasional rogue potty-goer, you know...a seat wetter."

Once Harry accepted the cash, Ireland dipped her finger into the sack and placed it inside her cheek.

"Coke," said Katie knowingly and then proceeded to perform a play by play analysis of the deal. "Ireland has just tested the merchandise. She's now telling Dean that it's primo stuff and can they wind this thing up so they can get high and have fantastic, non-pregnant sex." The other women laughed and Katie was once again in the swing of the conversation.

"Oh my God. Dean just looked over here," Janet said, ducking behind the curtains. The other women fell to the ground military style. Katie stayed in place and simply waved. Harry, Dean, and Ireland waved in return. Ireland held up the bag and motioned for Katie to join them. Katie politely shook her head, but mouthed a thank you. At least Ireland and Dean were friendly, she thought as she gathered up another platter of canapes and told the women it was okay to return to their places.

Chapter 16

K atie soon discovered that Rachel wasn't the type of person to stay angry. All it took was for Katie to seek out her advice and Rachel turned sugary sweet. She had debated about a more traditional piece offering such as baking cookies, but decided that Rachel, in her quest for perfection that extended from body to home, would not appreciate the extra calories. Instead, Katie feigned decorating ignorance, which in reality was not much of a stretch.

Her inspiration came from a home decorating magazine article she spied at the grocery check out line. "Does your home have the right white?" the headline questioned. Katie, who was getting a taste for the bold colors Stacey had suggested during her makeover, couldn't imagine anything more boring than a home decorated solely in white, but knew she was onto a hot topic. From the grocery store she went straight to a local paint store for her ammunition. Ignoring the display of whites, she moved to an assortment of reds that ranged from the bold "Rhapsody" to a shade just a few hues deeper than a magenta known as "Love Me Tender." Then, armed with enough decorating magazines to make herself look sadly pathetic, she showed up at Rachel's door.

Before knocking, she took a liberal amount of saliva and carefully smeared her lower lashes to give the appearance of fresh tears. A quick snort of saline spray supplied the necessary nasal drip. Rachel answered to find a bewildered and babbling Katie.

"You've got to help me," Katie started as soon as the door opened. "It's just horrible."

"Katie, slow down. What's wrong?"

"It's all over the walls," she continued. "Red! The magazines said it would bring 'old world charm to a modern house' but it just looks like..."

"Close the door, Rachel," a voice from behind interrupted. "She's probably spilled the blood of another one of her student's helpless pets."

"Amanda, shush!" Rachel ordered.

"Katie, tell me what's wrong," she said applying an arm to her shoulder. "Just ignore Amanda. She doesn't know how traumatizing a decorating faux pas can be."

"What?!" Amanda shrieked.

"Because you are so talented," Rachel placated. "But some of us," she said pointedly motioning to Katie, "aren't blessed with an innate design sense."

Katie hadn't expected to run into Amanda and immediately turned up her performance a few notches. "Rachel, only you would understand, that's why I came over immediately. I wouldn't expect Amanda to...to...," and then Katie sobbed even harder. "How she could bring up such a hurtful experience at a time like this? She brings up blood when I have a color patchwork quilt smeared over my walls? Well, it's indecent."

"Oh please," Amanda said from the background. "You'd have to be a decorating ditz to paint a post 19th century Mediterranean style home anything but soft hues of earth tones."

"Well that's just cruel," Katie sniffed.

"Amanda, I have to side with Katie. Not everyone has our interior instincts. Come on, Katie, I'm sure it's not that bad. I'll come back and take a look with you. Amanda, give me a minute."

Rachel walked Katie across the street to her own house only to have Rachel instantly repelled at what greeted her. "My God," Rachel exclaimed. "You were right."

Katie started an impromptu round of tears. "Can you help me? Can you forgive me for taking your cleaning crew? I don't know how to fix this," she said with a wave of her hand.

"Of course you don't, dear. You obviously have no idea," Rachel said and although the statement was belittling, Katie knew that she had restored her relationship, which was her ultimate goal. "It's going to take longer than I expected. Let me just text Amanda and tell her I won't be able to go shopping after all. She'll understand when I tell her what a dump your place is."

Katie felt oddly triumphant. With one performance she managed to win over Rachel and take Amanda's place within her afternoon plans.

"Katie, it's no surprise that this happened," Rachel said pointing to the walls. "You shouldn't try this alone. Luckily, I can help."

"Thank goodness," Katie gushed. "I don't know what I would do without you."

"It's nothing, really."

"It's just that you're so kind, not at all like Amanda."

"You should give her a chance."

"Not on your life. She tried to get me fired over a rabbit of all things."

"Apparently her daughter was heart broken."

"Well that may be, but it doesn't mean I had anything to do with it."

"Well," said Rachel uncomfortably.

"You don't think that I..." Katie let her voice trail off. She noticed that Rachel was staring between her and the red stained walls. She had to admit that her attempt to appear as a decorating misfit gave off the impression that she was a descendent of Charles Manson.

"Maybe you should just take a leave of absence," Rachel suggested.

"Why would I?"

"It would give you time to really learn about home decorating. You could take some courses, get more involved in the Gardening Club, maybe even patch things up with Amanda. I want to help you, Katie. But, there's only so much I can do with so little to work with."

"What do you mean?"

"Katie, honey, just look at this place. If I'm to turn this house into a showplace I'm going to need some help and Amanda is an expert in this area. I'm afraid that it's pretty overwhelming. If there's anyone who can help Rich's campaign, it's Amanda. You want her in your corner."

Katie stopped to assess the situation. It was bad enough that she had to suck up to Rachel, but to do the same to Amanda was just unbearable. "But isn't it just a matter of repainting?"

"Oh Katie, that's what I mean. You're really so naive when it comes to this," she said with a wave of her hand over the room. "We need to do a complete overhaul. If you were to shop retail it could cost a fortune."

"A fortune?" Katie gulped thinking about Rich and his reminders about budgets and living conservatively in the weeks leading up to his election.

Rachel continued, "I think the best place to start is by you quitting your job."

"What?! Why would I do that?"

"You're going to need to study up on decorating. First, you're on to a good start with these," she said flipping through a couple of Katie's interior magazines. "I think the monochromatic look would suit your new lifestyle as a councilman's wife. Politics can be so stressful that it's nice to come home to simplicity."

"Fine. White it is. That's easy."

"Oh no, not so fast. Winter white? Swiss coffee? French vanilla? There are many shades to choose from, as you can see by your, uh, experiment," she said pointing to the red walls. "Then, you'll have to learn about pillows to offset your white."

"I'll just go down and buy a couple at that cute shop down the street," Katie suggested.

"Katie, dear," Rachel said shaking her head and clucking her tongue. "Custom. You must go custom when it comes to pillows. It's very important."

"Why?" Katie said, reaching for a hanky to mop at the beads of sweat developing on her forehead.

"Well there's the matter of the trim. Twisted rope? French bouillon fringe? This brings me back to my original point that you have no time for work. You need to learn all this and more."

"There's more?"

"Yes. For instance, I notice that you are still fluffing your pillows, which is so 1990s. You're a good 25 years behind. The karate chop is in," she said with a whack to the nearest pillow. The blow might as well have been to Katie for she felt ill and clutched her stomach.

"See, Katie? Just another reason to quit. A woman in your condition should not be on her feet. Let me help you to the couch," she said and led Katie to the sofa.

By the time Rachel left, Katie was sure that her friendship had been revived, but she worried about what would become of her relationship with Rich as a result. Rachel's plan was for Katie to swap a job that paid a modest salary for the lifestyle of a stay-at-home mom who spends a small fortune on decorating. Even Katie's poor math skills could figure that this idea didn't calculate.

Trying to imagine the conversations before her had Katie's head reeling. She would have to tell her principal why she would be quitting and the subsequent explanation to Rich. For the first time in her life, words escaped Katie's mind. She decided that the only way to get through the days ahead was to consult with a professional, so she contacted Janet.

"Let me assure you, Katie...you've come to the right place, but in your words, tell me why you need a psychiatrist?" Janet asked.

"Because if I don't handle this correctly, I'll lose everything. My marriage, my sanity, everything! I don't have the money to quit," she admitted, knowing that what she told a physician would remain confidential. "Besides, Rich is likely to lose the election from the stress of our pending non-existent arrival, not to mention the strain of raising a non-child on a single income."

"I see. Katie, you sound a bit over-cooked."

"Is that the professional term?"

"No, but I think it's a fair description. You've been over-analyzing the situation too much, kind of like a watched pot."

"So you'll help?"

"I'll help you develop an exit strategy that's a win-win for both parties," Janet agreed.

"Excellent...really great," beamed Katie. "That's just the type of mumbo jumbo bullshit that's likely to get me a big buy out on my contract."

"I'm not a lawyer. I can't guarantee you any settlement, especially if you're not even pregnant. But maybe we can address the insanity issue."

"I'm insane?"Katie said hopefully.

"We'll see what we can come up with," Janet said gently.

RICH WAS JUST GETTING USED TO THE IDEA OF KATIE'S TRIAL pregnancy when her news about being insane hit him.

"And you think this will help me win the election?" he screamed.

"Not the insanity part," she admitted. "But the stay-at-home mom image is very popular with families today. As for the other..." Katie tapped her finger on her chin, "maybe we can appeal to the bi-polar, ADD, post-traumatic stress disorder set?"

"I don't think so," Rich replied curtly. "Besides, how do you plan to suddenly overcome your insanity once the school district pays you off?"

"Miraculously. I'll find a higher source," Katie said lifting her eyes skyward. "That will get you the evangelical crowd in your corner. I'm sure He...," she paused for dramatic effect, "would send me a sign of why I should leave my job. If I receive a sizable payoff due to stressful working conditions that affects the well-being of our unborn child, then that's just icing as well as a way to relieve me of my stress," Katie explained.

"It's that simple? Who cooked up this scheme?"

"Janet helped."

"Can't she lose her license for this?" Rich wondered aloud.

"Fortunately, she really believes I need help. I'm going to go to her once a week for counseling," Katie smiled cheerfully.

"Of course you are. And how much will that cost?"

"Just $125 an hour, but our insurance will pay."

"What insurance?! You just said you were quitting your job! And Fugenics hires me as an independent chemical researcher. Remember? I rely on your insurance and now we both need it."

"Relax. Once you get into office we'll have insurance provided by the city."

"How could I forget?" Rich asked and started to rub his temples in a futile effort to subside an oncoming migraine.

"Rich, when you win the bid for city council we'll be able to decorate with the right white, I'll no longer be insane, and we might even be able to get pregnant for real. Isn't it great?" she said giving him a bear hug.

"Great," he yelped under her grip.

Chapter 17

K atie woke up and dressed with purpose. She couldn't wait to get to work and realized that months had passed since she felt this way. It could only mean one thing...it was time to quit.

"No point in staying if I'm not enjoying myself," she said aloud as she pulled on her pantyhose and then cursed as she ran them in her hurry to get ready. "Oh, forget it," she mumbled to herself while tossing them across the room. "Who do I need to impress?" The knowledge that she was void of a job as well as constricting nylon gave Katie a sense of new found freedom. On a whim, she decided to toss her bra as well. "Forget this stuffy business attire," she said searching her closet. Her eyes finally rested on the last outfit she had purchased with Stacey, but never had the nerve to wear. A midriff top and low-riser jeans beckoned although she admitted it looked better on the mannequin. She reached for the outfit without a care in the world. It no longer mattered that her tummy protruded below the confines of the top and over the waistband. She relished the sight of her large breasts and decided she would dare others to stare. In her pretend pregnancy, the female form was something to be cherished. By the time she stepped outside the house, she had created a fashion minimalist statement and was mentally ready to bare all to her principal.

She drove straight to the school, omitting her usual stop at one of the umpteen Starbucks that spouted from every corner within a one mile radius of everywhere. When she pulled into the school parking lot, she noticed with annoyance that someone had taken her assigned parking spot. She circled the lot and decided on the vice principal's spot. "I'll only be a minute," she reasoned. In her haste to leave, she had slipped on tennis shoes without socks and now her feet stuck to the bottoms of her sneakers, causing a strange squeaking noise and an increase of perspiration, which would only worsen if she increased her walking distance. She cut off a minivan headed for the handi-capped spot and pulled into her desired spot. The minivan's horn blared, Katie smiled and extended her finger to the driver, and then locked her car and proceeded to the administration office.

"He's in a meeting," the principal's secretary announced before Katie could enter the closed door.

"Will he be long?"

"Shouldn't be. Why don't you have a seat? You've got a few minutes before class." The secretary then noticed Katie's uncon-ventional outfit. "You are going to class, aren't you?"

Before Katie could answer, the door to the principal's office opened and the woman who had been driving the minivan walked out. "Thank you Principal Riley for your time."

"Always a pleasure. We'll be in touch," he replied before turning to Katie. "Mrs. Pettigrew, what a surprise at five minutes before the hour," he said glancing at his watch.

"That's actually why I'm here," said Katie, following him back into the office. "I'm afraid I can't return to class. The strain of it is too much for me in my delicate condition."

"Condition?" he said looking at her.

"I'm with child," she said proudly patting her tummy.

"Oh. I had no idea. How far along are you?"

"Well, actually my husband and I are just in the planning stages, but my doctor... my psychiatrist, actually...believes that any extra stress may make it difficult for me to conceive."

"I see," he said coldly.

"Yes, I've found the children to be unruly and the parents to be unappreciative. Teachers are taken for granted," Katie added.

"So you're quitting," he said.

"Quitting is such a harsh term. I was hoping more for disability."

"But you're not disabled," the principal pointed out.

"Soon," Katie beamed, again patting her stomach. "By the way, can pregnant women use the handicapped spot? I wanted to park there, but someone else nabbed it. I had to use the vice principal's spot. He's not going to mind, is he?"

"Perhaps you should be going," the principal said with increased annoyance. "I think a leave of your duties is the right thing after all."

"Oh, one more thing," said Katie happily, believing that she had successfully implemented Janet's exit strategy. "I hope there's no hard feelings. You know that I'll send my own child here."

"That remains to be seen."

"I'm definitely going to have a child," Katie answered quickly.

"That remains to be seen as well, but I was referring to our long waiting list. Employees get priority, but as you are no longer an employee...," his voice trailed. "Then, of course, there's the business of undergoing the interview process with our board of governors before admittance is granted."

"Well, maybe you could give me someone else's spot, someone less deserving. For instance, someone like that woman who was just in here."

"And why would you believe that she is less deserving?"

"Fraud," Katie said simply.

"As in pretending to be pregnant when one is not?"

"Exactly," said Katie, not realizing that the dig was directed at herself. "I can see we're on the same page. That woman is not disabled. If she were, how would she have gotten in here to see you before me? I cut her off and took the vice principal's spot, which is much closer to your office than the handicapped spot. Obviously, she's not hobbling her way around."

"No, she's not," the principal said, his anger rising. "Her daughter is disabled and was in the car with her. She had planned to meet me, but decided to stay in the car and read instead."

"A handicapped daughter?" Katie said feeling embarrassed. "I guess that counts."

"Is there anything else, Mrs. Pettigrew?"

"I guess not. Can't wait to meet the board of governors. They're gonna love my Rich. He's running for city council, you know." The principal was slowly closing the door as Katie continued to talk, "Oh, and I intend to be very involved in the PTA," she said in one last ditch effort to ensure her future child's spot as the door to the principal's office closed once and for all.

———

"YOU QUIT?" RICH EXCLAIMED.

"I told you I was going to," Katie responded.

"Yes, but so soon?"

"No time like the present. Speaking of time. We don't have much to waste. We need to get pregnant so that we can get our child on the waiting list for the school."

"What waiting list?"

"It's huge, unless of course, you work there."

"But you did work there, Katie."

"Yes, but I don't want our child to think they only got in because I was a teacher. She'll be treated like a second class student, the others thinking she doesn't have the social merit to get in."

"So, let me get this straight. Had you kept your job our child could be admitted, but now that you quit, we have to get on a waiting list?"

"Yes, but I think the whole teaching angle is overrated for a number of reasons."

"Go on."

"Well, there's also this interview with the board of governors, all those fancy shmancy people. If they think we need my job then they'll reject us anyway. They want the upper crust to be admitted. People like Amanda."

"You don't like Amanda."

"I don't like Amanda, but I wouldn't mind being like Amanda. Here look at this." Katie pulled out a large manilla envelope and dumped the contents onto the table. It looked like a fanatic's dossier. Inside were hundreds of magazine clippings that included people who made the best dressed lists, society columns, who wore it better columns, reviews of chic restaurants and who was in attendance and each one of the articles had something in common -- Amanda Exeter.

"What is all of this?"

"I've been following Amanda for years...decades actually. Ever since we were in grade school. She was even on the best dressed list back then, along with the girl most likely lists."

Rich gave Katie a puzzled look. "What's 'most likely'?"

"Most likely to succeed, most likely to be a debutante, most likely to marry Jeff Gold -- he was the class hottie," Katie explained.

There were even notes attached to the articles that detailed recipes that Amanda had supposed sampled during her many nights out on the town. Katie never intended to duplicate any of the recipes for nouveau cuisine, but she wanted to be in the know in case she ever had the chance to frequent one of the restaurants Amanda had visited and was lucky enough to be seen in similarly sophisticated attire. Katie dreamed of the day she could order fois gras, crostini, gravlax, and other dishes that she normally would need an interpreter or at least a dictionary to understand. The envelope also contained folded inserts from magazines that if opened revealed the latest perfumes and colognes that Amanda had been quoted over the years as saying were her favorites.

Katie carefully peeled back the paper from one of the tear-offs and rubbed the page against her wrist. "Smell this," she said holding out her arm to Rich. "Nice, huh?"

"A bit gluey, if you ask me."

"Well, it's from the September issue...2010," she admitted. "It probably isn't meant to last more than a few months in the magazine, but fresh from the bottle it's truly luxurious. At least that's what Amanda said in this article," she said while sadly scanning one of the pages. "That Amanda," she said shaking her head, "she's got one thing...style. I just want an eensy bit, just a millisecond to walk in her shoes. It's just impossible to keep up with her."

"Be patient, Katie," Rich said taking her in his arms. "You said it yourself. Once I become a councilman you'll have all the prestige that goes with it." Katie was a handful, in more ways than one, but Rich loved her and in spite of all her foibles, what he wanted most was for her to be happy because he knew that she felt the same about him. As if echoing those very thoughts, Katie spoke up.

"The right job, the right school, it all goes together." Katie had discovered that having a house behind the gates of Briarwood was no longer enough. She had discovered that keeping up with the Jones' was intoxicating. The closer she got to achieving status, the farther she fell from it. It wasn't enough to imitate the women she admired, she wanted them to admire her as well. "It's a very good school. You're sure to meet loads of influential people at the PTA, the types who could help your campaign. Besides, wouldn't you want our child to go there?"

Rich thought about it a moment. "I suppose if I had a child, I would want him to go there."

"Good, then it's decided. Let's pick out something nice to wear to the interview. We can play dress up," she said leading him into the bedroom. "You always like that game," she said with a wink and a nudge.

Chapter 18

The Hollywood Chamber of Commerce boasted that the city's temperatures were at least ten degrees cooler than the staggering heat of the San Fernando Valley, where mountain ranges kept the smog and congestion imprisoned. Still, this news did nothing to appease Katie's overactive sweat glands. The thermometer read 98 degrees, driving most of the city's inhabitants to the beach or members of Briarwood to the exclusive community's pool.

"Community pools are so pedestrian," Katie complained to Rich.

"The pool was one of the reasons you wanted the house," he reminded her.

"I'm just practicing, Silly. I love the pool."

"Practicing for what?"

"It's something that Amanda would say and when in Briarwood... you say things like that, or that we only bought the house in the Lowlands for resale purposes."

"Is that what our house is called?" Rich asked sadly.

"Oh sorry, I never meant to tell you, but yeah. Amanda's house has its own pool and is in the Highlands, the uber-snobby-cool part of Briarwood. We're in the part where the houses are more of a stone's throw from each other."

"So, people like Amanda don't use the community pool, even to spend time with friends?"

"People like Amanda would never actually swim with people she doesn't know."

"You do it at the beach."

"That's different. The ocean is bigger, less chance of getting e-coli from some snot-nosed kid's weak bladder problems," she yelled from the bathroom. "Speaking of children, have you seen my pouch?"

"No, thank God. How long are you going to keep that up, anyway? Can't we just wait until you have a pouch...err, a bigger pouch," he noted to himself.

"Not until we conceive and I am properly rotund," Katie announced coming out of the bathroom wearing her bikini, pulling up the front panel to cover her protruding stomach. "Ah, there it is," she said spying it under the bed.

"The picture of motherhood," Rich said watching her slip a cover-up over herself to hide the pouch. "Why do you bother covering up?"

"One can't go out in my condition without some semblance of modesty," she said properly. "Besides, I'm going to sunbathe with Ireland and I can't bear the idea of being next to her perfection."

"You'd look a lot better without that thing," Rich insisted.

"Are you saying you're not attracted to me? Do you have something against pregnant women?"

"Of course not!"

"Of course not, what? You're attracted to me like this or pregnant women?"

"What's the right answer?" Rich said hoping for diplomacy. "I'm attracted to you and I have no intention of seeking out pregnant women for any type of indiscretion."

"I see," she said unconvinced. "But if I were truly pregnant and my shape started to take shape, then what?"

"You already have shape and I love it."

"You think I'm fat!"

Rich was trapped. It was the fat talk. He thought he had perfected the art of avoiding it, but somehow it managed to sneak up on him again.

"Katie, you are not fat. Cuddly, perhaps. Besides, I like a woman I can hold onto," he said, his eyes drifting across the street to where Ireland was rubbing suntan lotion on herself. She smoothed her hands over her arms, down her toned stomach, her fingers reaching just under the lines of her bathing suit to ensure that no rays dared leave their mark.

"Gee thanks. I'm going to Ireland's. Remember her?" she said waving a hand in front of Rich to gain his attention. "Poor girl. All skin and bones. It's surprising she found a guy like Dean to love her."

RICH WATCHED KATIE HIKE UP HER POUCH AND WALK ACROSS the street. The moment she arrived, Ireland was off her chaise lounge, fawning over Katie. She even patted her tummy again! Rich still couldn't believe it. He had a paunch, which he believed to be more natural than Katie's pouch, and yet Ireland never seemed to give him a second glance.

"Must be something wrong with her," he mumbled, desperate to reassure himself that he still had it, whatever *it* might be. Or, at least desperate to know once and for all that Katie wouldn't have an easier time winning over a girl than he. After pacing in front of the window for three-quarters of an hour, a pitcher of iced tea left on the counter served as the offering he needed to intrude on Katie's afternoon. Rich gave himself one last look in the hall mirror, sucked in his gut and smoothed his hair. "Ahh, what the hell," he said exhaling, his stomach returning to its normal, flaccid state.

Katie was snoring contentedly in the warm sunshine when Rich arrived, his newly applied after-shave causing Ireland to look up and sniff the wind. "Shh," Rich whispered. "No need to wake her. I just thought you two might like this," he said indicating the iced tea.

"Well, aren't you just the prize?" Ireland beamed.

"Should we go inside and get some glasses?" Rich said more eagerly than he had practiced.

"What about Katie?"

"She was up late last night. Let her rest."

"Sure, why not."

And Rich followed the longest legs he had ever dreamed to be in close proximity to into their own home. He would have followed her anywhere, of course while reminding himself that he was married and hoping for a momentary memory lapse. Wishing for a chance to just touch one of those perfectly toned and tanned legs, he followed closer, hoping to accidentally stumble into her, just for one excuse.

"This is going to feel great," she said interrupting his thoughts and turning suddenly.

All thoughts and no courage, Rich stumbled to a halt. "Huh?"

Ireland giggled, "The iced tea, remember?" she said and held up two glasses. "Honey, come here," she called.

He was making progress. Already she was using pet names. "Sweetie?" she called again.

Rich wasn't the touchy feely type, but for a girl like Ireland, what the hell. "Sugar?" he called out tentatively.

"Of course, here you are," she said handing the sugar bowl to Rich. "Oh there you are, Honey. I've been calling you."

Rich looked over his shoulder to see that Dean was also home and then to his dismay, he watched Ireland cross the room on those perfect legs, lean one seductively over Dean's and coo into his ear, "I was very hot, but Rich brought over some iced tea. Wanna have some?"

"Wouldn't miss it," he said nuzzling her neck and leading her back outside and away from Rich's fantasy. "Hey Rich, what's up?" he said slapping Rich on the back, causing him to sputter the sip he had just taken. "You coming?" he said holding the door.

"Right behind you," Rich said, trying to hide his disappointment.

Rich noticed with annoyance that Ireland could not seem to talk to Dean without touching him. "You're home early," she said reaching to brush his hair off his forehead. Rich swung his head around, hoping to create a windswept look to his modest locks. But only Dean seemed to notice.

"Got a neck problem there, Rich?"

"No," he said sullenly.

"Come on. Let me take a look," he said and turned Rich around so that he was facing the back of him. Dean immediately placed a beefy hand behind Rich's neck. He could practically take his entire head in one hand.

"Really, it's not necessary," Rich objected as Dean began to massage the back of his head and neck. To Rich's dismay, the only one in the group who seemed remotely interested in him was Dean. He stiffened with every passing movement of Dean's hand, trying to figure out a polite way of moving away. It was a delicate situation that offered no solution. He couldn't offend Dean or he would inadvertently anger Ireland. He tried to imagine Dean's rough hands as Ireland's delicate ones, her fingers bathed in a luxurious oil that smoothed away all of his tensions. But it was no use imagining the impossible and the roar of a sports car punctuated the sentiment.

The car carried Harry Greene, and although Rich believed that like Stacey, Harry was only out for a quick buck, Rich had his reputation to think of. Ensuring that he didn't get the wrong idea, he made a quick jog over to the car to offer a friendly welcome and distance himself from Dean's most public advances.

"Did I catch you in the middle of something, ol' boy?" Harry asked nodding toward Dean. "Wouldn't want to interrupt a quiet moment," he said with an elbow to Rich's ribs.

"Nothing going on here,"Rich said a bit too quickly.

"Nothing? How can you say that with these two beautiful creatures lying about?"

Rich had always hated over the top gallantry, particularly because Katie was always pointing out how he should be 'more of a gentleman.' The idea of Katie being taken in by Harry's slick as oil demeanor sickened him. Still, it was a more appealing option than having oil slicked on him by Dean.

"Ireland, my dear, you do have a way of stopping traffic," Harry said moving away from his Mercedes. Rich and Dean turned to watch Harry kiss Ireland's hand, who then inadvertently wiped the back side of it on her beach towel. Katie, who had woken to all the commotion and was not used to such attention, smiled when Harry turned toward her. "Katie, you look positively glowing. There is nothing more beautiful than a woman with child," Harry said admiringly. "I saw you and had to stop to tell you so."

Rich couldn't help but think that even without Ireland's scant bikini, the sight of Katie lounging on the front lawn in her maternity bathing suit filled to the brim with her Pampered Pouch test tummy would attract attention.

"Rich? What are you doing here?"

"Just thought you might like some tea."

"What a considerate lad," Harry said with raised eyebrows indicating to Rich that he didn't buy the line for one minute. "If I had a wife like you, Katie, I'd do the eight days a week."

"Oh you're just saying that," Katie said.

"Absolutely not," Harry argued. "Rich, isn't she a picture? Quite a sight, I must say."

"I couldn't agree more," Rich said and then watched in horror as Harry grabbed the sun tan lotion.

"Here, Katie let me help you. It's important to keep well lubricated during pregnancy. Wouldn't want to give the little fella, or gal, sun exposure. May I?" he said indicating the lotion.

"Oh, alright by me," Katie said and turned over onto her side, careful not to squish her pouch.

"You know, he's right, Katie," Ireland chimed in. "You could get a nasty bout of stretch marks with pregnancy if you don't moisturize."

"She's not even pregnant," Rich protested. "It's just a damn pouch!"

Embarrassment crept up Katie's cheeks. She flushed red and reached for a towel to cover herself up.

"Don't!" Harry protested. "You're beautiful," he said and then suddenly reached for Katie and planted a kiss on her hand, allowing his lips to hover in place for a moment before creeping up her arm.

Katie was too stunned to react, which made Rich's reaction even more extreme. "Pervert!" he yelled and threw the first punch. Harry went down, landing on top of Katie. Ireland screamed. Dean took the opportunity to grab Rich, but he mistook his embrace for that of Harry and threw another punch, which landed squarely on Katie's jaw. For the briefest of moments Katie saw the three of them standing over her, but then she fainted. "Let go of me," Rich insisted. "Katie? Katie? Get off her," he said pulling Harry up by his collar.

"If I were you I'd keep your voice down," Harry said straightening his shirt.

"If I were you I'd butt out."

"It's really no wonder she's suffering from natal depression," Ireland whispered to Dean.

"Natal depression?" Rich said in disbelief. "I told you all. She's not even pregnant."

Suddenly Katie came to. "He's never accepted the child," she cried.

"There, there," Harry said patting her pouch. "Let me help you home. We'll take a little walk across the street to clear your head."

"Rich, I think you should let her cool off," Ireland suggested. "Why don't you come in and have a drink with us?" Dean took him by the elbow, indicating he should listen or fall prey to another impromptu wrestling match.

"Well, I'll be..." mumbled Rich while allowing himself to be led into the home by Ireland and Dean.

HARRY DIDN'T BELIEVE IN WASTING TIME. HE INSISTED THAT Katie lie down and then offered to make her a sandwich to regain her strength.

"I'm fine, really," Katie said.

"Have a bite to eat. You'll feel better."

"Well, I ate just a half hour ago. I really should watch my weight."

"Nonsense, you're eating for two."

"Well Harry, technically Rich is right. I'm just in the trying out phase."

"Then you should try out a nice ham and cheese."

"You're really too kind."

"Nonsense. Now go lie down while I whip up something fantastic."

With Katie safely tucked inside her bed, Harry raided the house, and not just the refrigerator. He searched under the stairs. He looked behind cupboards. Finally, he decided the best place to hide his stash would be inside Katie's new decorator throw pillows. After planting two kilos of cocaine within the plush confines of the Pettigrew's upholstery, he returned to the kitchen and made not one, but two sandwiches.

Having polished off his sandwich, he reached for his cell phone. "Mission accomplished," he said into the mouthpiece. "The dust is stashed. No, they don't suspect a thing. The guy's an idiot and his wife isn't much better. It was a cake walk. Listen, I'll catch you later."

Chapter 19

After wrestling with the sheets for more than an hour, Katie finally fell into an aggravated sleep only to wake throughout the night. By morning, she felt no more rested having spent the better part of the evening contemplating what outfit would impress the school admission committee. As she stared at her closet she was no closer to making a decision, although Rich had efficiently dressed in his usual uniform of grey slacks, white shirt, and grey cardigan.

"Can't you find something more with it...trendy...interesting? Please, anything, but grey," Katie pleaded.

"This is business-like and professional. I thought you would approve."

"Yes," she said hesitantly, "but it's also so boring. We only have one chance with the committee," she reminded.

Katie was determined to make an impression, more importantly, a statement. "Rich this is important. It's all about little Cheyenne's future."

"Cheyenne?"

"The university acceptance rate among Native Americans is higher than any other demographic. Why not give our child a fighting chance at a prosperous future? Besides, I can't stand it when couples start talking about so and so if it's a boy, or this and that if it's a girl. Cheyenne is a completely bi-sexual name."

"I believe you mean asexual, but either way I am not naming my child Cheyenne."

Katie contemplated Rich, who for the first time seemed to accept her non-existent pregnancy. "Oh Rich," she beamed, "whatever you say," she said and planted a huge kiss on his lips. "You're so opinionated. I love it!"

"You love it?" he said, pulling her in closer. With Rich, reverse psychology always worked, even when it was non-intentional.

"Definitely. You're so powerful," she said, nibbling his ear.

Now wanting to please Katie, he said, "I hear that green is a power color. Perhaps it would make more of a statement than this old grey thing."

"The color of money," she beamed.

"THIS IS IT," KATIE SAID TAKING A BREATH. "IT'S GOING TO go our way; I just know it."

"I hope you're right. It would be a shame to be dressed like a leprechaun for nothing," Rich said giving her hand an affectionate squeeze.

The entire way to the meeting Katie practiced her lines, described how she and Rich had moved to Briarwood to seek a better and safer life for their future family. She imagined telling the school board of her esteemed teaching background, how the children loved her and she them. And then she would deliver the real clincher...as if they were her own. She imagined being asked to head up the P.T.A. and leaving with each board member's name and address so that an invite to her baby shower could be sent when the time was right. She and Rich were definitely Bishop Oaks School material and she was going to prove it.

When she and Rich entered the conference room, the air conditioning was turned on too high, mirroring the icy reception that followed. Katie shivered involuntarily when a familiar voice requested she take a seat.

"Oh my god," she whispered to Rich. "It's Amanda."

"Amanda who?" he asked too loudly.

"Hello, Mr. Pettigrew," Amanda interjected, "I'm Amanda Exeter, chairperson for our Admissions Committee. I haven't had the pleasure of meeting you around Briarwood as I have Katie, probably because our homes are nowhere near each other, but we'll talk now as I'll be conducting this afternoon's interview. Please...if you would like to take your seats."

She pointed to two chairs arranged in front of a long table in which five other women and one man sat. "Have a seat," Amanda repeated, this time more like an order than a request.

Katie and Rich shifted uneasily, sitting in front of the firing squad of their unborn child, waiting, endlessly it seemed, as the committee shuffled and read from files, which appeared to be threatening dossiers on the Pettigrew lifestyle.

"We'll just proceed if you're both ready," Amanda said. "Each of us will be asking a series of questions. If for any reason you do not feel comfortable in answering anything just inform us, but I will mention that your reticence will be duly noted in our files."

"We have nothing to hide," Katie declared.

"Uh, yes," Rich chimed in. "Fire away."

"Very well. I'll start," Amanda said with a mischievous glint in her eye. "Katie, under what circumstances did you leave your employment here at Bishop Oaks School?"

"Well, I wanted to start a family."

"Yes, but I'm curious why you left before becoming pregnant. You realize that our employees are given special consideration when it comes to reserving a place for their children."

"I've also heard that the committee prefers that Bishop Oaks parents have at least one stay at home partner so children receive optimum attention," Katie said in her practiced manner.

"So you quit to devote yourself to becoming a full-time mother?" another woman asked.

"And to prove that we didn't need Katie's income," Rich offered.

"To prove?" Amanda interjected. "You mean you do need Katie's income?"

"No, that's not what he meant," Katie added. "Tell them what you meant," she said to Rich and then whispered, "Tell them what we practiced."

"Oh I mean, we didn't think this was the best place for Katie to spend her time."

"Is there something wrong with Bishop Oaks in your mind?" the man on the committee asked.

"Um no," Katie stammered. "That's not what we mean either. Can we just move on?"

"Certainly," Amanda agreed. "Katie, it notes in your file that there was a complaint logged against you during your tenure, although in your application you write that you had an exemplary record of employment. Can you explain?"

"You placed that complaint," Katie said with hostility.

"Honey," Rich offered to help, trying to uncover the mess he created from the previous question. "Don't you mean that Amanda merely opened up suspicion?"

"No!"

"Well actually, that's correct, Rich," Amanda replied. Rich beamed like a child who had just recited the multiplication tables.

"I was not found guilty of any misconduct relating to your rodent," Katie said angrily.

"Rabbit," Amanda corrected.

"Technically, Katie gets that point," Rich offered. "Rabbits are from the genius of rodent."

"Ah, the scientist in you speaks out," Amanda noted. "Rich, we understand that you have been trying some experiments in your own home. Do you believe these practices will be safe for young children to be exposed to?"

"Of course. Just simple shit solutions."

"I beg your pardon," the older woman on the end seat stated.

Katie elbowed Rich in the ribs. "I mean manure," Rich explained. "I'm creating my own synthetic manure."

"Why would you do that?" Amanda asked.

"Why not? It's profitable."

"Do you often do things for money regardless of the consequences?" she asked.

"Absolutely not. Money is never a factor," Rich said.

"I see, but Bishop Oaks can be quite expensive. We want to make sure that admission won't become a financial burden to our parents."

"Oh in that case, money is very important," Rich replied.

"You seem to be wavering, Mr. Pettigrew. Which is it?"

"Let me explain," Katie offered, seeing the chance to deliver her most practiced aspect of her speech. "We are upstanding members of the local community who look forward to contributing to the future success of Bishop Oaks School through the attendance of our unborn child and the contribution we will make as parents."

She and Rich beamed back at the committee.

"Thank you both," Amanda said. "I believe this concludes our examination."

Katie and Rich got up to leave, but were stopped by one last question from Amanda.

"I nearly forgot. We'll be conducting an on-site visit of your home. Is next Tuesday convenient? I hope so," she said before the Pettigrews could respond. "That will be all," she said and closed her file in a final dismissal of Rich and Katie.

As Rich and Katie walked out of the room they both agreed that the interview went quite well.

————————

KATIE WAS ENJOYING THE LUXURY OF A MID-AFTERNOON NAP when the sound of machinery coming from her own backyard woke her. "Over here, boys," rang Amanda's voice over the sound of a bulldozer.

"What's going on?" Katie yelled from the upstairs window.

"Just taking soil samples," Amanda explained.

"Soil samples? Whatever for?"

"DNA testing. The committee has reason to believe that my daughter's bunny is buried in your yard."

"The committee or you?" Katie accused. "When are you going to stop this witch hunt?"

"When the bunny is found, dead or alive! Dig away, boys!"

"You can't rip up our entire yard!"

"Of course not, Katie. Just this small portion right here where I notice there are fresh mounds of dirt as if someone else has been busy digging."

Katie watched in horror, praying that Rich's hoses would not be found. "Ms. Exeter, we found something," one of the men shouted. "Should we bag it?"

"Yes, by all means. Don't contaminate it."

"Contaminate what?" Katie asked.

"As I suspected, we've found animal remains in your yard," Amanda said triumphantly, holding what she believed to be a rabbit bone.

"That's Rich's dinner from last week."

"You see," she said to the rest of the board, "I told you they were just low life cannibals."

"I meant that you're not holding a rabbit leg, just a chicken leg."

"Either way, I'd say your guilty of something. If it's not my daughter's bunny then you're still guilty of burying garbage. Not exactly the behavior we look for in our congressmen."

"Nonsense. Rich is conducting a green campaign. Burying garbage is just what his constituency expects. We're creating our own compost."

"I'm still going to insist on a complete autopsy to be performed on this," Amanda said indicating the bone, which was now being placed into a hermetically sealed bag.

"She's taking our bones. Aren't you going to do something?" Rich asked Katie in a panic.

"That's the least of our problems. We've got to find that damned rabbit."

IT DIDN'T TAKE LONG FOR KATIE TO HOP ON THE TRAIL OF the Exeter's lost rabbit. Both she and Rich had tracked mud across their new carpeting upon returning from the school meeting. "Just look at this!" Katie exclaimed. "It even looks like rabbit droppings and I've got the Gardening Club coming next week."

"If they're all about gardening they should be used to a little mud. Anyway, how do you know you didn't bring it in?"

"Because I wouldn't," she said simply. "And, what is that smell?"

Rich leaned down to sniff the carpet. "It's not mud, that's for sure."

"What is it?" Katie asked leaning down on her hands and knees.

While Katie was sniffing the carpeting, Rich stood up, walked behind her and checked out her shoes. "Told you!" he said triumphantly. "You have dirt on your shoes as well."

"Impossible. That school is kept so pristine. There's nothing for me to step in."

"Let's see," Rich said as he leaned down to take a sniff. The

MIA FOX

view of Rich leaning over Katie's backside was all Dean and Ireland could see as they arrived at the Pettigrew's front doorstep and peered through the window.

"Maybe we should come back another time," Ireland suggested.

"Maybe this is just the right time," Dean argued. "I knew that Rich was a kinky monkey, but I didn't know just how far gone he was."

"Let's leave them alone to their romance," Ireland said, tugging on Dean's arm. "They've obviously forgotten we were coming by. We'll give them a call later."

KATIE AND RICH WAITED UNTIL AFTER DARK TO RETURN TO the school. They reasoned that the droppings they stepped in might belong to Amanda's rabbit and therefore it was worth checking out. Katie had prepared their covert operation bag containing a video recorder, carrots as bait, and the rabbit's cage, which Amanda had left in Katie's classroom, an empty reminder of the rabbit's disappearance. "I don't see why we have to break into your old school," Rich huffed as he jarred a window open. "Don't you still have your employee key?"

"They made me return it when I quit. Anyway, we have to do this or we'll never be able to step foot here again."

"That's likely to happen anyway if we're caught."

Rich was propping Katie into the window when the night janitor's whistle reached their ears. "Quick pull me back," Katie whispered.

Rich tugged at Katie's legs to no avail. "Why'd you wear leather? It's sticking to the window sill."

"Just keep pulling. I think he's coming this way."

"Undo your pants," Rich ordered.

"This is not the time!"

"Just do it!"

Katie undid the button and zipper on her pants. "Hold on tight," Rich instructed as he pulled her pants by the ankles until they slid off. He dropped them in the bushes next to him and then went back to the task at hand, pulling Katie, who this time eased through the window just as the janitor entered the room.

"Get the video camera," Katie instructed. "He's holding something. Looks like a rabbit!"

It didn't take long for the couple who was passing by to shoot a video from their phone. They were walking home from the observatory where they captured a rare asteroid shower on video. Considering that on the way home they stumbled upon a bottomless Katie with Rich at her heels on video, it was their lucky night. They went directly to the police station and by the time the emergency patrol was called on the scene, Katie and Rich had managed to enter school grounds, giving the officers reason to book them for breaking and entering.

"But officers, we had good reason to break into the school," Katie implored.

"You can tell us at the station," the taller of the two responded.

"It'll be too late. The evidence may be gone," Rich added.

"What evidence," the other officer asked.

"Stolen property," Katie said. "Livestock to be specific. I figure the janitor must be involved."

"Jim, take these two into the car. I'll check it out."

It only took fifteen minutes for the officer to return. "Looks like your story checks out."

"It does?" Katie and Rich said with shocked relief.

"Yep, that janitor's closet is a mini pet store, kind of creepy. Aquarium, mouse cage, turtle bowl, and your rabbit."

"Did you hear that?" Katie smiled at Rich. "Let's go home,

honey. I can't wait to plan a party to rub the news in Amanda's face."

"Not so fast," the officer said. "You were still caught on school grounds without cause."

"Do you know who you're talking to?" Katie demanded. "We're not just two burglars, you know."

"That's right. We had plenty of cause!" Rich exclaimed. "I'm running for city council. I can't let my constituency down. I've made a pledge to eradicate this town of crime."

"Oh Rich, I'm so proud of you," Katie added. "Officers, we hope we'll have your vote in September. Being tough on crime is a big part of our campaign. Maybe you'd like to endorse Rich?"

Katie quickly removed the lens cap from her video camera and began aiming the device at the two police officers.

"Hey, what are you doing," the one named Jim demanded.

Katie started to bark orders like the most seasoned of Hollywood directors. "For the commercials, silly. Rich, stand between them. Jim, put your arm around Rich. Nothing too friendly, if you know what I mean." She waited impatiently, tapping her foot, while the police officers shuffled around Rich.

"Jim, maybe we can call this one even," the other officer said. "I'm not very photogenic."

"I know what you mean, Al. Hey lady, can you turn that thing off? We'll come back tomorrow and book the janitor on the stolen property charge..."

"You mean kidnaping, officer," Katie corrected. "That terrible Amanda Exeter charged me with kidnaping."

"Well, not officially, Katie," Rich said gently.

"It was just so awful," Katie continued. "And then when you two showed up, well, I nearly passed out in my delicate condition," Katie said patting her tummy, which was plump, but certainly not pregnant considering she left her pouch at home.

"Er, Honey, your pouch was left behind, remember? The mission? No baby on board for this one," Rich reminded.

The officers looked from Katie to Rich with growing concern. "Are you two alright?" Officer Jim asked.

"Maybe we need to do a breathalyzer, Jim?" the one named Al asked.

"No, no need for that," Rich jumped in sensing that their freedom was becoming short-lived. Katie, let's go home and let these nice officers get on with their work."

Chapter 20

In Katie's new world of social climbing, nothing could be better than a built-in excuse to entertain, even if it were a narrow escape from police arrest and proving Amanda wrong. To really make a big deal of it all, Katie drove past her neighborhood market and continued along the main road an extra fifteen minutes to the newer, better, more expensive gourmet market, the store where locals dressed up to shop rather than tie their hair up in a pony tail and don a pair of sweat pants. For the occasion, Katie was wearing her casual chic look: black stretch pants, black sweater, cat-shaped sunglasses, and booties.

Even the parking lot seemed outfitted in high fashion black. Concrete pavers had just placed a fresh layer of tar, making the lot gleam a smooth onyx. The car tires moved easily over the fresh pavement that was now void of pot holes. Katie felt free as she veered the car in and out of the orange cones that marked the wet from the dry pavement. She maneuvered the vehicle like a Formula One driver, weaving carefully, gaining speed, but suddenly losing control as a pair of mallard ducks waddled into her lane. The car screeched to a halt, leaving significant tire tracks in the fresh tar before coming to a rest. Katie looked around nervously for any other patrons, but saw nobody in the lot. As she got out of the car, she noticed that not only were there deep indentations in the lot, a great deal of tar remained on her tires and had been kicked up to the lower fenders of the car.

"Damn ducks!" Katie shouted at the passing mallards. The ducks, being used to humans as they had made the fountain in the market's covered patio area their own wading bath, took Katie's address as invitation for food. They waddled closer, waiting. "Go away! Shoo!" Katie shouted, waving her arms. The ducks squawked back; Katie shouted once more, "Stupid foul," and stormed into the market, unaware that Rachel had pulled into a nearby spot and witnessed the exchange.

Katie was now hoping to get in and out of the market as soon as possible to avoid the tar drying on her car and anyone from the market noticing the damage she had done. She went straight to the Service Deli and still brooding about the mallards, decided that a duck theme would be appropriate. She picked up duck paté and water biscuits for an appetizer, a chinese duck salad for an entree, and a mandarin orange frozen mousse for dessert. "Will this be all?" the employee, whose name tag read, 'Gayle, may I serve you?' asked.

"Yep, that's it," Katie answered back.

"Have you tried our fresh baguettes? Just out of the oven," Gayle enquired.

"Sure, that sounds good," Katie answered, while looking to the parking lot to make sure no notice had come of her car.

"And some fresh, creamery butter?"

"No, just the bread."

"Baguette," Gayle corrected.

"Whatever," Katie answered.

"It makes a difference, you know."

"Sure."

"You don't sound convinced," Gayle said sweetly. "Would you like to sample one?"

"Listen, I'm really in a hurry, and I bought the damn thing, anyway," Katie snapped.

"We don't want you to buy it if you're not totally happy. Don't take my word for it, try some," she said taking a knife to Katie's baguette.

"Wait, I wanted to buy that," Katie protested.

"No, I insist that you taste it."

"It's not necessary. I just want to buy it."

"How do you know?"

"I just do. Now give it to me," Katie ordered, reaching over the counter to grab the baguette.

"Do I have to call security?"

From Katie's point of view, the girl's sudden change in demeanor was a welcome reprieve from her may-I-help-you banter. "Listen," Katie pleaded, "I've had a really difficult day. I just need to get home."

"Of course," the girl softened. "I'll just ring you up. I'm sorry. I just thought you might be disappointed in the baguette if you were expecting bread. It's much harder you know. Well, not hard, as in stale, just not as mushy as bread, not that our bread is soggy, more like soft..."

"Stop! I don't care. I don't!"

The girl stared for a moment, a rabbit trapped in headlights, and then burst into tears. An older woman suddenly approached from the room beyond the service deli. "Gayle?" she said placing a motherly arm around her shoulders, "What's happened?"

"This woman just started shouting at me for no reason," she sobbed. "I was just trying to be helpful. Really, I was," she said, this time turning toward Katie.

"Gayle is our Associate of the Month," the woman informed Katie. "We've never had a complaint," she said, her voice trailing off.

"I'm not complaining about your employee. Now if you'll just hand me my groceries."

MIA FOX

"Gayle is an Associate," the woman said crisply, still holding Katie's groceries.

"And?" Katie asked, arms outstretched to the bag.

"You said employee. She is an Associate."

"Alright. Associate, employee, whatever."

"It makes a difference. It's like asking for bread and getting a baguette."

"That's just what I was telling her," Gayle chirped.

"Now then, we'll help you to your car," the older woman announced. "All part of our service."

"No!" Katie shouted, remembering the tar. "I just want to take my baguette, my duck stuff, the dessert, and leave. I want to be alone."

"I *vant* to be alone," the older woman said in a heavy accent. "I just love Greta Garbo. Very good!"

"I mean it," Katie said grabbing for the groceries.

"Nonsense, it's our service motto...always be of service to our guests. Notice I didn't say *customers*," the older woman said and grabbed for the groceries.

Katie reached out again, only to be intercepted by Gayle. "No guest should lift a finger when in the presence of a Belton Farms Associate."

Katie was not about to let these two follow her out to the lot. "Let's get one thing straight. I am a customer. You are employees. That makes me always right."

The two women looked at each and then back at Katie, who was clutching her baguette. "Will that be all?" they asked in unison.

"Yes! That is all!" Katie shouted, turned on her heel and then bumped right into Rachel.

"Katie, is everything all right? You seem a little agitated."

"That?" she said motioning to Gayle and her supervisor, "just role-playing the part of a difficult customer."

The two Belton Farms employees looked unconvinced. Katie pointed the baguette in their direction as if carrying an armed shotgun. "Gayle, you did wonderfully! I'll let the secret shoppers association know that Belton Farms is doing A-Okay. Truly superb service," Katie beamed.

"Don't mention it," a scared Gayle replied.

"This is my very good friend and neighbor, Rachel," Katie introduced. "She feels the same way I do about this wonderful establishment. I'll leave you two now," Katie said and walked off, noticing with relief that Gayle looked too horrified to say anything other than her polished line to Rachel. As Katie made her way to the supermarket front doors she could hear Rachel's first request: "No, I don't want egg salad; I want eggless egg salad. What do you mean you've never heard of it? It's tofu made to appear like egg..." Katie smiled, understanding the exchange as if she had finally learned a foreign language. She knew she had finally mastered the art of shopping in upper class suburbia.

KATIE HAD COME TO REALIZE THAT THE NEIGHBORHOOD women all had one thing in common. Well, actually they all had money in common, but in addition to that, they all seemed terribly busy although half of them didn't work. But oddly, they were just too busy to work. There were school functions, Gardening Club meetings, shopping appointments, beauty appointments and those were subdivided into appointments for hair, nails, facials, Botox, waxing...it was all enough to leave one feeling utterly exhausted. And nothing made Katie feel more overwhelmed than to be underwhelmed. She needed more to fill her time now that she wasn't working. To sit around simply wouldn't do for she knew that important people always had some place to be. But with virtually no hobbies, this would prove challenging. Fortunately, Katie was always up for a challenge.

She started off her week and morning with a cappuccino at the local coffee bar with the newspaper in hand to *peruse* (never read). Afterward, she would go for a quick massage, which had to be a proper one at the local health club, certainly not one of those foreign $25 service ones that were cropping up all over town. After lunch, the afternoon was filled with organizing her organizer for she was certain that many important events involving Rich's election and the Gardening Club would arise.

In fact, she had already planned the menu for the Gardening Club meeting that would take place at her house, and found herself surprisingly calm at the prospect of having the women back for another visit.

Things were looking up as she had finally been able to hire Lola, one of Rachel's maids, thanks to Janet. Janet had casually placed Lola's number in Katie's cell phone as she still harbored a deep resentment that Rachel had lured Lola away from her last year with the promise of every Friday off from work. Janet felt what comes around, goes around, and when Katie mentioned feeling overwhelmed, Lola was not only a solution, but also a form of quiet revenge.

She told Katie that 'help around the house' would simplify her life. Katie wasn't sure about that because ever since having Lola around, even for the one hour in which she was stealing her from Rachel's employment, it added extra stress to Katie's life because she had to hide her from Rich, who didn't believe they had the money or need for extra help.

Katie found that she had to put in even more work now. She had to tidy the place before Lola got there because she was told that Rachel was a neat freak and Lola liked it that way. Then, after Lola left, Katie would run around and surreptitiously leave a few shoes and garments of clothing hanging around the sofa or Rich would notice the difference in the environment. It was pure exhaustion, but worth it if it meant keeping up appearances.

On the day of the Gardening Club meeting, Katie didn't dare do anything to rearrange Lola's cleaning efforts. In fact, she took pride in giving the living room the white glove test even though nobody had been in there since Lola scurried back to Rachel's place. Rich had tried to take his morning coffee and newspaper into the room, but Katie was quick to reprimand, insisting it was the formal room reserved for company only. Satisfied that not even any dust had the nerve to settle itself in the space, she moved into the kitchen to lay out the party food on polished, silver trays. She had only been gone half an hour when she returned with the first of the trays and discovered Rich asleep on the living room sofa.

"Wake up! What are you doing in here?" Katie screeched. "The Club members will be here any minute."

"Huh? I must have dozed off."

"In here? Why?"

"You said we were going to have a party in here. It's the only chance I get to sit on this sofa."

"Then by all means, sit, but don't sleep. I need you to do that butt thing. Here," she said handing him a throw pillow. "Indent it."

"Just do the karate chop. I can't just do it on command," Rich objected. "It takes time."

"I told you, the karate chop is out. Your butt print is in. Now come on, they'll be here any minute. Just do it."

"Not if you're going to talk like that. It puts me out of the mood."

"That's ridiculous. Men are always in the mood. It's what they do. They mess things up."

"Well, maybe I'm not like other men," Rich said feeling miffed.

"Of course you are," she said softening, knowing that she would have to sweet talk Rich into giving her pillows the interior decorator's equivalent of a good rogering. "Here," she patted the first pillow. "Tempting, isn't it?"

"Yeah, I suppose," he said hesitantly.

"Try it out," she suggested.

Rich sat down and then stood up, only to reveal a slight

indentation, not the bold canyon that had made such an impression on Rachel once before.

"No, that's not it. Try again," Katie said.

"I can't just perform like a trained seal," Rich objected.

"Rich, you can do it," Katie encouraged. "Just try not to think about it so much. Just let your body enjoy the moment. Be a slob; live it up!" Before she could give any more motivational messages, the bell sounded. "I've got to get that," she said motioning to the door. Just do your thing and be done with it."

Rich tried to get the right butt impression, but couldn't duplicate his previous work. He closed his eyes and tried to visualize himself feeling completely at ease as he started to bounce his bottom up and down on the pillow just as Katie returned with Janet and Ireland.

Horrified at the sight, Katie recovered quickly. "Oh he's so young at heart. Isn't it refreshing?"

In the meantime, Rich had placed his hands over his ears in order to help him concentrate and was oblivious to the audience he now attracted.

Before Katie could move to stop him, Janet spoke up. "I've seen this before. Your husband is digressing into early childhood. It might be stress related, perhaps from his campaign work?"

"I'm sure that's not it," Katie said.

"No, I'd say not," Ireland added, noting that Rich now was maneuvering his bottom in frantic circles over the pillow.

"Oh no. It's not that either," Katie spoke up.

Ireland merely smiled; Janet looked concerned.

"Rich!" Katie shouted. Rich jumped to attention, leaving the perfect butt impression. "It worked!" he beamed, leaving a different type of impression with Janet and Ireland.

Chapter 21

"Why do we have to go to this touchy feely thing?" Rich complained.

"For lots of reasons," Katie answered, staring at the bleak and empty road ahead of them. They had been driving for an hour, heading south on the way to Palm Dessert, as the car thermometer seemed to increase with every mile driven.

"Name just two."

"It's good for your campaign and I promised Janet."

"I can't see how going on a marriage retreat could be good for my image."

"Think of it as a networking weekend. Absolutely everyone is in therapy."

"I don't want to be in therapy. I relish being normal."

"Rich, you are not normal, and that's a good thing. Normalcy is overrated. It's downright boring."

"Are we there yet? Check the map."

"Nearly. I've just got enough time to do my hair," Katie said plugging her curling iron into the cigarette lighter.

"Is that safe?"

"Of course. I do it all the time."

"I've never seen you do it."

"You don't drive with me."

"You mean to say that you do your hair while driving? It's bad enough that women try to put lipstick on while driving."

"Rich, I can do an entire exercise regime while behind the wheel. Butt squeezes, tummy tucks, pushing on the steering wheel for my pecs," she said proudly sticking her chest out.

"It's working," Rich admired.

"That's my guy," she said happily. "No more complaining. This will be fun, you'll see. Oh and Ireland and Dean are going to be at the retreat too."

"She is? I mean, they are? Maybe it won't be so bad."

The outside temperature read 115 degrees when Rich and Katie pulled into the circular driveway of Janet and David's vacation home. It was typical of the second homes owned by couples in the area in the fact that it was as large as their primary residence. The sprawling Mediterranean house was painted pink like a desert sunset and in spite of the heat, the massive lawn surrounding the drive remained a deep green. Palm trees dotted the property line as if to block the view of neighbors that in reality were too far away to sneak the most indiscreet peek.

"This is their weekend getaway place?" Rich asked in disbelief.

"Stacey says they got it for a cool mil."

"What's so cool about spending a million dollars in a place that ten months out of the year is hotter than Hates?"

"It's impressive Rich and you know it," Katie argued.

"I suppose if you like flaunting."

"Who doesn't?"

Within minutes of their arrival, a man of about 20, dressed in white shorts and shirt, which made his bronze complexion all the more noticeable, appeared from the house, ready to heave the Pettigrew's bags from the trunk. He was followed by another tanned and gorgeous youth who proceeded to take the car to its remote parking spot. The Pettigrews had only been outside for a mere five minutes waiting for this action to take place, but still, Rich had broken out in a sweat and Katie's hair seemed to frizz before the eyes.

"This darn humidity is making me ugly," complained Katie.

"You're fine, but I look like I just stepped from the shower," Rich said fanning his arms out, exposing the spreading yellow stains from his armpits. He turned to yet another white-clad wonder, this one a girl with a blonde braid extending down to her waist, a waist small enough for a man to encircle with his fingers, and a face too beautiful to be marred by a rogue droplet of sweat.

"Care for a spritz?" she asked sweetly, indicating a tank strapped to her shoulder that had a receptacle with a shower head on one end and a hose with a pump on the other.

Rich eyed her uneasily. "I'd rather have a spritzer. Got anything stronger than water?"

"I'm sorry, Sir, I'm just the spritz girl. Perhaps inside," she said and held the massive oak door open for Rich and Katie.

The interior of the home was another scene from a decorator's magazine. Everything was white, so clean and pure that Katie and Rich felt indecently dirty just standing in the entry.

Rich mopped his forehead with the back of his arm. "I wish I would just stop dripping. It's this damn polyester top you made me wear."

"It's known as 'resort attire' and I thought it would be perfect."

"Perfect for what? Sponging the sink?"

"Just change. But be quick."

Rich didn't wait to be shown to a guest room, which from the look of the house might be quite a hike. He stripped off his shirt in the entry while Katie rummaged through her carry-on bag for a replacement.

"Hurry up. I'm practically naked."

"Hardly," a familiar voice sounded.

Rich and Katie looked up to see Ireland coming down the grand spiral staircase that led to the front door in her usual attire of a bikini and matching sarong. Her hair was wet and upswept. She carried a small towel that she used to catch any runaway water drops.

"Here," she said throwing Rich the towel. "Looks like you need it more."

"What I need is a shower," he answered.

"We just arrived. Had to wait outside while they sorted out the car," Katie answered as an explanation.

"Well, I think you two look wonderful as always."

"Where is everyone?" Katie asked.

Ireland pointed toward the next room. "The first of what is promised to be many exciting seminars is going on in there," she said with a roll of her eyes. "Personally, I've had all the personal growth I can take for a lifetime and I've only been here since last night. Harry has the right idea. He's by the pool sunning and arguing with Stacey about Palm Springs real estate value. Dean and I have been swimming, as you can see by my wet welcome and we're getting water logged. It's the only way to stay out of their battles. I swear, those two should be married the way they argue and carry on. Come outside and rescue us from more of their bickering."

"Maybe we should check in with Janet and David?" Katie asked. "Especially if we're supposed to be in there," she said angling her head toward the closed door of the room that was in fact a home theater.

"If you want my opinion," Ireland continued, dripping ever so slightly onto the tiled floor, "the architect intended that room to be a theater and any other use is blasphemy. Let's go play," she said tugging on Rich's arm. "Oh, Rich. You've been working out. Maybe we should get high? That way, we won't notice the unbearable heat."

Katie quickly slid her arm protectively around Rich. "We don't want to be rude, honey."

"Of course not," he said smiling at Ireland. "Lead the way to the pool!"

"No, Rich," Katie said as if to a disobedient and unruly sheep dog. "I meant, we don't want to be rude to our hosts."

"Oh," he said crestfallen. "I suppose she's right."

Having finally located a shirt in her overnight bag, Katie plunged the neck opening over Rich. "Couldn't you have found one of mine?" he complained.

"Yours are in the other suitcase, which is still in the car."

"I think it suits you," Ireland cooed. "Pink spandex is your look," she said giggling. "Kind of kinky, too."

"I think we better get going," Katie insisted. "Rich, let's find our room before heading over to the theater...honey cakes," she added for good measure.

"I'm telling you, she was already high...or maybe drunk," Katie said once they were alone.

"She was just happy to see us."

"No, she seemed happy to see you," Katie said glumly. "She was fawning all over you."

"Really?"

"Don't sound so pleased with yourself. It was just the alcohol taking away her inhibitions."

"I've never known Ireland to have any inhibitions even when she's sober," Rich remarked. "Anyway," he said taking a hold of Katie's hand, "I'm here in this hotter than Hades head shrinking weekend with you."

"You could have a worse place to spend the weekend. Will you just look at this place?"

Katie and Rich had been assigned to the Blue Room, according to their invitation. And, like it's name implied, it was decorated in cool blue tones that combined with the overall white theme to make one forget about the incredible heat. The bathroom featured a large, circular tub with jacuzzi jets. A shower designed for two had a bench seat that faced three separate shower heads, one at head level, a second at the waist, and a third at a strategically placed and decidedly more private level. The connecting bedroom had a double, four-poster bed piled high with pillows and sheer silk drapes clinging to the frame, creating a cocoon-like environment.

"What's with the mosquito netting?" Rich asked. "And, how are the two of us going to fit in that bed?"

"It's romantic, which is the whole point of this weekend."

"It is? You told me the point of the weekend was to keep campaigning."

"Of course. That's what we're here for, but we can't let Janet and David know that. We have to assimilate."

"Assimilate? Like joining our neighbors at the pool?" he asked hopefully.

"Alright, but no hanky panky."

"Katie. You know me better than that," Rich chided.

EVEN IF RICH HAD EVERY INTENTION OF KEEPING HIS HANDS to himself, Janet and David's itinerary put an end to that. Katie and Rich had just lathered themselves up with suntan lotion, laid claim to two lounge chairs by a table, and were in the process of ordering two tall iced teas when the rest of the weekend guests descended on the pool area.

Janet called out to Katie and Rich, "Hi, you two." She turned to Ireland and Dean next. "You've been MIA for the last three sessions, but we've got you now," she smiled mischievously.

"That's right," David chimed in. "We decided to bring the party to you," he said holding up a basket of apples.

"Oh no," Rich said panicking.

"What is it?" Katie whispered.

"I'll bet they're going to play that stupid teenage game."

"Which one?"

Harry suddenly appeared from behind Katie, and took hold of her shoulders. "The fun one."

"Excuse me? But you've got your hands on my wife," said Rich, suddenly chivalrous.

"Sorry ol' boy. No offense meant," said Harry, but added quickly to Katie, "I'll see you later."

"What did he mean by that?"

"Nothing, Rich. I'm sure he's just being friendly. Let's grab an apple. We don't want to be stick in the muds."

What ensued was a grotesque game of flesh and fruit.

"I thought we weren't supposed to use our hands? And what's up with these blindfolds?" asked Katie in a worried tone as a pair of hands shoved an apple between her ample breasts.

"You can pass with the hands, you just can't receive with them," explained David from a loudspeaker.

"But, are we really supposed to touch each other?" she asked with growing concern as the hands squeezed her breasts together to hold the fruit in place.

"Free love, Katie. It's all part of our get-to-know-you session. Now hurry and pass that fruit," David called out.

"Katie, don't you go and get to know anyone too well," Rich shouted from his line as a pair of hands came from behind him to nestle just below his crotch. "Ireland?" he asked hopefully.

"You wish, mate," Harry responded, in more ways than one.

Miserably, Rich accepted Harry's apple between his legs and then hobbled to the next person in line, twisting his ankle and falling to the ground. The accident put an end to the ill-fated game as Rich angrily removed his blindfold, disqualifying his team.

"Spoil sport," Harry tisked.

"Pervert," Rich replied as he hobbled off to his room with Katie's aid.

"I'VE HAD ENOUGH," SAID RICH AS HE ICED HIS ANKLE.

"It'll get better. You need to walk on it."

"Not my ankle. This weekend. I've had enough," he repeated.

"Let's focus on your campaign," Katie suggested.

"I thought we were and then that stupid game started up."

"Well, it looks like we have free time from 3 p.m. until dinner," said Katie reading from the schedule that was left in their room.

"Oh goodie. And if we're good can we have milk and cookies?" Rich asked sarcastically.

"It's not that bad. Let's go back to the pool. The water will probably make you feel better."

THE PARTY WAS STILL IN FULL FORCE WHEN RICH AND KATIE returned. Ireland's bikini top was lounging by the side of the pool; Dean was absent-mindedly rubbing oil on her back, while Janet was putting him in touch with his inner child through chakra therapy.

"Just repeat your affirmations, Dean," Janet instructed. "I deserve love," she said pressing on his forehead, the site of his first chakra.

"I deserve love," he repeated.

"Dean, honey, can you stop?" Ireland requested. "You're not rubbing the oil into my back in a counter-clockwise rotation. David said that my skin's elasticity will become just ruined if I go against the grain."

"Shall we continue?" insisted Janet. "Dean, you really need to focus on your affirmations, not other distractions," she said pointedly at Ireland, who walked off in a huff. "Now then, let's continue. I deserve respect."

"Of course you do, Janet. I'm sorry."

In spite of her training to remain calm, Janet was becoming undone. "No Dean, repeat the affirmation."

"Oh, of course. I deserve respect," he said in a monotone.

At the other end of the pool area, David was just beginning his talk on the latest plastic surgery trends. "Will you look at that?" Rich said in disgust. "He just used this weekend as an excuse to promote his practice"

"Well what's wrong with that?" asked Katie. "You knew that it was a weekend retreat for Janet's practice."

"Yeah, that's bad enough, but to get hit on by both of them?"

"Janet and David believe in supporting their partners to the fullest extent possible."

"You sound just like them. I think we better get home before you become a complete convert."

"It makes sense," Katie argued. "Why bother working on your mind if you let your body go south?"

"South?" asked Rich.

"As in downward spiral. Listen, I think I'll just take a quick listen," she motioned to David and his growing crowd of enthusiasts.

"What about my campaign?"

"You go on ahead. Oh, Ireland's over there," Katie said pointing to the deep end of the pool. "Go on," she nudged.

"I'm a terrible swimmer," Rich said.

"You're not that bad. I can't believe you're even arguing. It's Ireland for God's sake."

"You don't mind?"

"I said you could talk to her. What's not to mind about that?"

"Of course," Rich nodded.

Rich looked down the other end of the pool at the topless woman doing laps and decided that he wasn't one to argue with his wife, certainly not at a couple's retreat. And so, he dived into the pool in pursuit of Ireland.

"I'M TALKING PARTIES, LADIES," DAVID SAID WITH enthusiasm. "I mean, what could be more fun?"

"You mean you do it in our house?" asked Katie in amazement.

"By all means. The more the merrier," David replied. "In fact, for the group Botox rate, I insist on at least four women."

"The parties are truly marvelous," piped in Janet. "You get your injection and then a massage, manicure and pedicure. You just keep rotating from chair to chair, and nobody is ever left out."

"Musical plastic surgery," mused Katie out loud.

"It's the latest craze," David rebounded.

"Yes, but do you really think surgery should be a craze," Katie questioned.

"Oh Katie, you should try it," Janet insisted. "That little frown between your brows will be gone in an hour. I'm talking poof! All gone! In just one hour!"

Katie took the mirror that Janet had handed her and examined her face. She tried to raise her eyebrows to eliminate the pesky frown that she had previously not noticed, but now seemed to be not so much a frown, but a mass of lines that were cast so downward they were practically suicidal.

"How much does it cost?" asked Katie.

"Katie, really, you can't put a price tag on beauty," said Rachel.

"So true," added Janet. "You know Angelina Jolie's lips?

Well, David's office did them and now everyone is coming in asking for Angie's lips."

"I never really noticed them," said Katie thoughtfully.

"Exactly," said David proudly. "Subtle, but effective."

"Come on, Katie, it'll be fun," Rachel coaxed. "Amanda had a Botox bash last summer and it was the talk for absolutely ever."

"Well, if Amanda had one...sure, sign me up," Katie beamed at David.

"You won't be disappointed. The results from my most recent party are phenomenal. Just take a look at Ireland," David leaned in, whispering.

"Ireland's had Botox?" Katie asked in shocked delight.

"Nobody's perfect, my dear. I just make them look that way."

"What else has she had done?"

"Take a look over there," David instructed, nodding across the patio to where Ireland was rubbing suntan lotion on her bronze skin. "See those?" he said with a raise of his eyebrows.

"Fake?"

"Completely false. Was a small b-cup before she met me."

"What about that perfect nose? That's got to be a phony too," Katie said hopefully.

"Sorry, love. The nose is hers. Now, Katie, about your ears," he said escorting her to a lounge chair.

"Come on, Rich. It'll be fun," Ireland insisted.

"I'm just not the party type," Rich said squeamishly.

"This is good shit," Dean insisted.

"I'm sure it is, but my campaign," Rich argued weakly.

"Well if that's what's holding you back, we'll never tell," Ireland said.

"I didn't mean that. I'm really not into it and the campaign is just one more reason not to start now."

"Actually, it sounds like the campaign is just the reason to start," Dean said. "I remember when I was under stress with my business," he said, letting his voice trail off.

"What business?" asked Rich.

"Don't have it anymore. The pot made me realize that I'm not cut out for such hard work. You should try it. Being an over-achiever is not worth it."

"Well, maybe some other time," Rich said. "I think Katie is probably wondering what I've gotten up to."

"Nothing yet!" Ireland squealed, giving his arm a tug. "But we can change that."

"Err...we better not." Beads of sweat were starting to form on Rich's forehead and he doubted the humid weather had anything to do with it.

"Oh Rich, you are a sweet one. Here take this," she said handing him a potted plant. "Consider it the house warming gift we never gave you."

"Really? No hard feelings...that I don't want to...well, you know. I mean, you don't have to do this."

"It's nothing, really."

"Katie will love it. She's always going off on how the house needs more greenery," he said happily.

KATIE WAS COMPLETELY ENRAPTURED LISTENING TO DAVID discuss how a few nips and tucks could make her look just like Ireland. Ireland was stoned and therefore, oblivious to the disap-proving eyes of the other women. And the husbands were either talking business or giving others the business. Everyone was occupied; nobody noticed Harry and the accident that was about to befall him. Nobody, that is, except Rich.

Rich watched Harry's antics on the diving board and was

privately surprised that his gymnastics did nothing to gain the others' attention. Nobody even noticed when Harry misjudged his double somersault and whacked his head on top of the diving board on his way down to the pool. Rich paced back and forth on the pool deck, carefully watching the crowd while weighing the benefit of diving in after Harry immediately or waiting for him to float unconscious to the surface.

The decision came easy for Rich as Harry's immobile body soon sprouted a sufficient amount of blood to cause Janet to shriek about the efficiency of their pool man.

"David, did you add the right amount of chlorine this morning? The pool is turning colors. I specifically remember Bob telling us to add the entire bottle that he left behind yesterday. Did you do it? Because if you did as he instructed and it still looks like this," she said pointing a disapproving finger, "we'll just have to give him notice. This is absolutely unacceptable."

"Do whatever you need to do," David called absently without bothering to look. His mind was on the money he was going to make once he persuaded Katie and the other women to hold a plastic party, as he liked to call the gatherings.

Rich looked at his watch, calculated the time in which Harry had been unconscious, and wondered how long before Janet realized that he wasn't simply floating in her pool. He decided the time had come, and threw off his shirt dramatically and then, spreading his arms in order to make the loudest splash he could muster, proceeded to save Harry.

The water fountained over onto David, who cursed loudly as his before and after photos of recent clients proceeded to get soaked. The others standing with David looked over to the pool and grew silent as the drama unfolded. Rich had turned Harry onto his back and was dog paddling over to the shallow end. The crowd ran to meet him. "Stand back," Rich shouted. "I need space. I'm trained in C.P.R."

"You are?" Katie asked, a bit too loudly.

"Maybe we should call the paramedics?" Janet suggested.

But Rich didn't waste time. Mouth-to-mouth ensued and soon Harry was sputtering pool water. "Let's put him over there," David said, pointing to a chaise lounge under a tree.

"Get some ice, will you?" Rich ordered Janet. "And a waiver of liability from my office while you're at it."

Together, David and Rich heaved Harry onto the lounge and simultaneously grabbed for the ice pack. "I've got it," Rich said.

"No, I better take over. I am a doctor, you know," David said.

"Well, I'm the one who saved him," Rich sounded, much like a child.

"Rich, you're a hero," Katie shouted, realizing the need for damage control, and then, turned to Ireland for support. "Did you see? Isn't he wonderful?!"

In a voice that was as stoned as it was admiring, Ireland replied, "That was beautiful, man. Just amazing. A real turn-on," Ireland added, and then moved closer to Rich.

Katie immediately intercepted Ireland's approaching body. "That's enough."

Suddenly, a moan erupted from Harry, stealing the scene from Rich's heroism. "What is it now?" Rich inquired with annoyance.

"Headache," was all he said.

"I know just the thing for it," Ireland offered.

"Yeah," Harry agreed. "Just a lift."

"We'll take it from here," Katie insisted, and then to Rich, "Don't let him go off with Ireland. We need to milk this for all it's worth."

"Come on, Harry," Rich said taking him by the arm.

"You got a lift?" Harry asked.

Not catching his meaning, Rich innocently replied, "Of course. The car's this way."

THE DRIVE BACK TO BRIARWOOD WAS UNEVENTFUL FOR RICH and Katie. With little traffic, they were able to get home in just under an hour-and-a-half. The only annoyance for them was Harry, who became angrier with every mile driven.

"Listen, just give me the damn cigarette lighter," Harry grumbled.

"No smoking in the car," Rich said.

"You shouldn't be smoking at all considering what you've just been through," Katie added.

"Yeah, what were you thinking? Jumping around like that," Rich agreed.

"I was high," Harry said as way of an answer.

"It was quite impressive," said a naive Katie. "Do you have formal training in high diving?"

"You're kidding," Harry laughed. "Didn't know you needed training for that. Now what about my lift?"

"Oh it's no trouble," Rich said.

"Happy to do it. Just let your clients know about Rich," Katie added.

"Ahh, so that's the rub," Harry said, a light going on. "You want my clients to know about you. That's cool. Didn't know that you were trying to get into the business."

"Of course I am," Rich exclaimed. "Why do you think I'm going to all this trouble with the campaign if I didn't really want it?"

"Makes sense. I like your liberal policy. So can I ask you two for one more favor?"

"Anything," Katie said with a smile.

"Can I hold out at your place for awhile? The fuzz is on my tail and after this ordeal I don't have the energy to deal."

"The fuzz?" Katie asked questioningly at Rich, who shrugged his shoulders.

"Probably means headache or something. You know how these limeys talk."

"Harry, anything you need," Katie said, as they pulled into the driveway.

"Thanks, mate," Harry replied. "Real kind of you both. You won't even know it's here."

"You mean you're here."

"Just ignore him, Rich. The poor man...can't even speak straight. We better get him to bed right away."

HARRY WAS THE FIRST HOUSE GUEST THE PETTIGREWS HAD entertained in their new home. Katie wanted everything to be perfect so while Harry was showering, she went into the garden to pick roses for the guest bedroom. Rich pitched in by finding a pot for the houseplant given to him by Ireland. "This looks nice," he said, placing it in the corner of the room. "Just like she said. A little greenery cheers up a room."

Harry emerged from the bathroom in time to admire the thriving cannabis. "I couldn't agree more," he chuckled, and plucked a leaf. "Should we try it out?"

"What are you doing?" Rich shouted. "It's just been transplanted. It's very fragile."

"You had me fooled, that's for sure," Harry commented. "Never knew you were such an aficionado."

"Well, horticulture is a hobby of mine. Plants need time to get used to their environment before you cut them. Shouldn't touch this one for at least a month. It'll really be something then."

"A month?"

"The difference will be noticeable," Rich said.

Harry laughed loudly. "Rich, my man, never had you pegged," he said and headed back into the bathroom.

KATIE DECIDED THAT HAVING HARRY STAY WITH THEM WAS another opportunity for self-improvement, if only for an evening. Learning a second language was something she always wanted to do and since she failed miserably at Spanish while in high school, she decided to try her skills at the queen's English.

"How's your fuzz?" she asked Harry.

"Beg your pardon?"

"Your headache," she said pointing to her own head.

"Ahh, I thought you meant, never mind," he said shaking his head, laughing to himself. "Fine, just fine. I did get rid of my stash, by the way."

"Stash. Funny, so many words for headache."

"I never thought of it that way. Always look forward to it, myself."

"What an excellent attitude toward life," Katie mused. "I knew a woman with cancer who said virtually the same thing. She said that the pain made her still realize that she has a life to live. Such an inspiration."

"Yeah, well, thanks for putting it up. It won't be here long," Harry assured.

ONCE HARRY LEFT, A DAY LATER, RICH AND KATIE GOT BACK to business.

"Rich, I've been thinking that you need to change your campaign to appeal to different audiences. Maybe you should learn to rap, while you're at it."

"Why would I want to rap?"

"Get the black vote," she said simply.

"But we live in the middle of white suburbia," Rich argued. "This is the most Wonder bread community I've ever seen."

"What about the English vote? Maybe you should do commercials in English."

"My commercials are in English. You mean Spanish?"

"No English, like the kind Harry speaks."

"You want me to do a Madonna? Put on an accent?"

"Madonna doesn't know English," Katie said knowingly. "Just because you can put on an accent doesn't mean you know the nuances of the language. For instance, did you know that the English refer to themselves as 'it'?"

"It?"

"Yes. Harry kept thanking me for putting 'it' up. He never said thanks for putting me up."

"You must have misunderstood. He's a strange guy. Kept wanting to pluck Ireland's houseplant."

"Really? Why would he do that?"

"Don't ask me."

"You see?" Katie said. "We really don't know anything about the English customs."

Rich thought for a moment. "You could be right. I wouldn't want to say something that could be misconstrued. There are thousands of English living in this area."

"And they're such a generous, helpful people," Katie added. "Do you know that Harry insisted on repaying us for the ride."

"He did? You didn't accept, I hope."

"Of course not. He kept saying that he didn't know what he'd do without a lift, but I told him it was our pleasure. He even called me angel."

"That cad."

"Don't be jealous. It was just the concussion talking. Said he was going to leave his angel dust here until the fuzz settled. Crazy stuff like that."

"Sounds like you have a new fan."

Katie took the plant given to Rich by Ireland in her hands. "He's harmless," she said, but couldn't help feeling a bit pleased.

Chapter 22

Rich's bid for city council rested on the public's acceptance of his 'green' campaign and Rich intended to not only preach green, but to also live it. He believed his compost mix had now been perfected. It combined multiple types of manure with chicken bones and any leftovers that he could sneak from the refrigerator. To his amusement, the plants seemed to thrive on the concoctions that Katie made while he was unable to stomach them. Returning to habits from boyhood, he would surreptitiously spit any vile meat that Katie put in front of him into his napkin and then take the offensive material to the garden late at night where he added it to his manure and created more of the same.

The potted plant that Ireland had so kindly given him had nearly outgrown its original confinement so Rich decided to make one more addition to his garden. Within weeks of being transplanted and enjoying Rich's compost, the plant had grown from a mere houseplant to a veritable sapling. Rich then split it apart from itself, planting smaller versions along the entire border of his garden, creating the private retreat he had always dreamed of.

"What have you been feeding that thing?" Katie wondered aloud one day.

"It's my own special mix," Rich beamed.

"Amazing," she agreed. "If the bid for city council doesn't work you can always go into the compost business."

"I intend to anyway. With results like this," he said displaying the forest before their eyes, "the possibilities are endless."

"Maybe you should start marketing it right away. Your success in the business front could branch off to improved voter turnout. People are more likely to drive to the polls if they think they're backing a winner."

"You think?"

"Definitely," Katie said. "But there isn't much time."

"For what?"

"Oh Rich, you have so much to learn about politics. We need to keep entertaining, networking, *schmoozing*."

"Schmoozing! That's all we've been doing. Every time I turn around there's a new group in here, Katie. I just want to sit in our garden alone. The way it used to be."

"Nonsense," she argued. "We've got plenty of time for being alone. Now there's work to do," she said, pounding her fist atop of a nearby throw pillow for emphasis. A cloud of dust billowed from the pillow. "Honestly. I don't know why Rachel was so upset about my stealing Lola. I could do better myself," she said fanning the air.

"I thought you said you didn't have time to clean."

"Well I don't," Katie said recovering quickly. "I have to keep up appearances, you know. Manicure on Monday. Facial every other Tuesday. Pilates class on Wednesday. Gardening Club on Thursday. And in between all of that, I'm thinking about campaign strategies for you."

"What do I do?" Rich asked with concern.

"You work for that funny little company and create all those cute little experiments," Katie said as if she were talking to an indulgent child. "Without your science brain this wonderful compost would never have been created and the world would never know what to do with all of this shit."

"Is that our new campaign motto?" Rich asked worriedly.

"It's in the works, but something like that. Now then," she said getting up. "You go experiment. I'm going to get the house ready and meet with the caterers."

"What caterers?"

"Didn't I tell you?" Katie asked innocently. "I've put Rachel's caterers on a retainer so that they are at our beck and call. She suggested it. Apparently, Nicki Minaj and George Clooney do the same thing. You want to be like Nicki and George, don't you?"

"I'm not sure. Well...maybe George; Nicki...I'm not so sure."

"Nonsense! Of course you do," Katie said patting his hand. "With the caterers on our personal payroll, we can throw a party at the drop of a hat, which is what we need to do now. We haven't had one for at least a week."

Katie left to plan the next campaign party before Rich could argue, or more importantly, before he could ask how much his new catering staff cost. This party, she decided, would also include a fundraiser. She knew that all politicians needed to raise funds, although she was never clear on what they spent the money on. Flyers and invitations were one thing, but she believed that her own wardrobe was far more important. And why shouldn't the tax payers pay for her to look beautiful? If there was one thing that Katie found offensive was Mr. Blackwell's hit list of poorly dressed women. If she could save herself from appearing on it once Rich was elected into office and others from the unbearable pain of seeing it, then she was surely doing her service to society.

She glanced at the hall mirror, saluted herself, and set off to clean the house in a way that Lola had never tackled. She was a cleaning missile, seeking dirt in the most remote places, and hopefully burning calories in the process so that the new wardrobe would be even more deserving.

"What's the hurry?" Rich asked while observing Katie moving frenetically throughout the living room.

"Killing two birds," Katie replied. "The place needs cleaning; I need to lose weight."

"Yes, but what's the hurry?" he asked again.

"I just have so much energy. It must be that protein drink I've been having each morning. Besides, there's so much to do, so many muscles to build, so much damn dust," she said swatting another pillow and sneezing with each billowing cloud that emerged. The more she swatted, the faster she moved and the more determined she became. It wasn't until she vacuumed the staircase for the third time, polished the wood floor, and cleaned the grout with a discarded toothbrush that Katie passed out on the kitchen floor.

"Katie!" Rich screamed when he came into the kitchen. For the first moment in the last three hours, there was no sound of polishing, aerosol cans, or other cleaning clues. "Katie, wake up!"

He threw water on her face to no avail. Lifted her arms above her head. Bent down to listen to her heart, which thankfully was still beating. He was about to call an ambulance when Katie finally stirred.

"What happened?"

"You passed out. I was just about to call the ambulance."

The news was the best medicine. Katie jumped up and cried, "Don't you dare. Just look at the way I'm dressed!"

"You need a doctor."

"I'm not going anywhere. There's too much to do."

"Normal, healthy people do not just pass out."

"Call Janet. She'll tell you that I'm normal. She's my analyst."

"Since when? We go to one awful retreat and now she's your analyst. You don't need an analyst."

"Ah ha! So I am normal?"

Feeling had, Rich admitted, "Alright, you're normal, but certainly not the picture of health. Just look at yourself."

She moved to the hall mirror once again and instead of the vibrant woman that had earlier saluted, a tired and pale face with dark circles under her eyes stared back. "Perhaps I do need some help. Call David. He's a doctor."

"A plastic surgeon."

"Well, he had to pass all the exams before he became a plastic surgeon. He'll do."

"If that's the best I can get you to do, I won't argue. Let's go."

"Fine, but let me put on my other jeans. These are my fat jeans," she said by way of explanation and marched herself upstairs.

"You shouldn't be so concerned about the way you appear."

"Rich, that's sweet, but this is Briarwood. Women just don't go around without makeup and manicures, dressed and coifed. It's expected if you're going to live here."

Rich watched Katie go down the hall to retrieve a new set of jeans and wondered where the old Katie had gone.

DAVID BOYER'S OFFICE, LIKE THOSE OF MANY SUCCESSFUL, Beverly Hills' physicians, was decorated with as much care, style, and money as some homes. In actuality, his office decor probably cost as much as some annual college tuitions.

Tiffany lamps displayed a soft light, a necessary effect for middle aged patients who preferred to be seen as air-brushed beauties that was simply impossible to achieve in harsh, bright light. Adding to their comfort level, the guests as his patients were called, could sit under the gentle glow at a mahogany Louis XIV desk with inlaid wood designs. Others preferred to peruse magazines and read how Jennifer Anniston maintains her youthful appearance while seated in wing-back chairs covered in crushed, velvet upholstery and adorned with decorative throw pillows. Each chair was carefully positioned precisely at a forty-five degree angle within each corner of the waiting room, a placement which David's feng shui advisor insisted was necessary for the positive flow of his office.

Apparently, the feng shui advice was indeed working for the flow that moved throughout his office was to the tune of over 500 new clients per year, each willing to spend upwards of $5,000 on treatments ranging from tummy tucks to eyelid lifts. Of course, there were plenty of breast augmentation surgeries still being performed, but David found that the patients desiring this procedure were the under thirty crowd and he preferred to target a more mature client. When it came to his practice, David found that maturity did not breed the confidence that women tend to believe they possess once they hit forty. On the contrary, the over forty-year-old woman generally became a basket case of insecurity, much to his delight. He couldn't recount the number of times women had come to him fearing about being 'replaced by a younger model' or 'gravity taking its toll.'

Breasts were for beginners, he joked. The successful plastic surgeon focused on Band-Aid procedures, those that gave a quick fix, but didn't solve a thing. From his point of view, the aging dilemma was a wonderful problem. It was one that could not be beat, which guaranteed David his own feng shui flow, that of money straight from his clients' purses and into his pockets.

When Katie came in she was in the state of mind like so many of David's first-timers. She was suffering from an acute desire to regain her youth and had exhausted herself in the process. "My God, what's happened to you?" David exclaimed.

"It's nothing, really," Katie said modestly. "Rich insisted I see a doctor when I passed out this morning. I'm sure that I've just been working a bit too hard and not sleeping enough. That's all."

"Nonsense. Just look at your eyes!" David knew it was key to establish fear in his clients. Not a fear of him, but a fear of the aging process, an invisible opponent of which only he was the savior.

"What's wrong with them?"

David ignored the question, preferring to steamroll Katie's insecurities. "And, your entire skin tone," he said inspecting her face with a magnifying glass. "Just look at these pores. Tsk, tsk."

"My pores?"

"Positively gray. Here, take a look." He shone the spotlight, as he liked to refer to it, the harshest most unkind overhead light imaginable, directly onto Katie's cheeks and nose before handing over a mirror, a triple-grade magnifying monster.

"Oh my God!" Katie exclaimed, much the way David had when he first laid eyes on her. "Just look at me."

"Now, now. We can fix it."

"A prescription? Sleeping pills? Rich says I need more sleep."

"Now, I don't mean to belittle your husband, but he's not a doctor, is he?"

"No, no he isn't," Katie admitted as she now took note of the elegant decor around her, realizing that once again her desires were not in sync with her wallet.

"Well then, let me decide what you need. Just sit back down," he said pointing to his examining chair. He leaned in closer, prodded her face with different metal scopes, and came to a conclusion. "Katie, your elasticity is positively shot."

"My what?"

"In laymen's terms, your skin is saggy," he said bluntly. "That's what's giving you this gray, tired look. Your pores are too big, your cheekbones are not prominent enough to compensate for the poor structure of your chin, and your eyes are too sunk into your head."

"It sounds like I need an entire new face," she said with despair. "I could never, uh, go you know. Under the knife."

"Of course, not. And I wouldn't recommend it for you. Way too drastic. That approach is only for women who can't emit your type of inner radiance and beauty. Mere models. The empty headed shells of female society."

"Oh, them," said Katie, nodding in acknowledgment.

"For you, a more subtle approach is preferred."

David proceeded to describe a treatment plan that he had designed that provided his bread and butter. He long ago realized that it was easier to find ten women to happily submit to a $500 treatment each month, than to find one client willing to undergo a $5,000 procedure once a year. Forget the young bimbos wanting big boobs. He wanted the has-beens, those who were already in the habit of taking time for beauty treatments each month. His ideal client was the once beautiful who hoped to become that way again, but he'd make an exception for Katie.

"I'm not sure," Katie said in reference to David's proposal.

"Think of it the way you would a manicure, pedicure, or facial. Even a car payment. It's a necessary expense."

"But it seems more extreme, so self-indulgent."

"No. It's just beauty maintenance. Tell me, would you hesitate to pay the watering bill? The gas bill? Of course not!" he answered before Katie could point out the obvious flaw in his reasoning. "Tell me, Katie," he said taking her hand in his own. "Why should you deny yourself a few Botox and collagen injections?"

"Well, when you put it that way," she said with pause. "But, what about the expense?"

"Minimal," he said with a wave of his hand.

"And the discomfort?"

"Not more than a little pinch. I can even use a local anesthesia, if you like."

"And you say I'll look ten years younger?"

He smiled and tipped the exam chair backwards.

"Tomorrow you'll look in the mirror and see a vibrant new you looking back."

KATIE HAD INTENDED TO TAKE A TAXI HOME RATHER THAN ASK Rich to pick her up from David's office. She had also intended to take a quick detour and pick up something fabulous to wear, something young and hip to match her new and improved younger face. She intended to buy a new lipstick to show off her collagen enhanced, pouty and fuller lips as well as a new eye shadow to draw people's attention upwards to her wrinkle free, albeit a bit frozen looking forehead. Instead, she was being spoon fed ice chips and promised that the ambulance would be here soon.

"What happened?" Rich asked in a panic.

"Just a slight adverse reaction to the procedure," David answered calmly.

"Slight reaction? Just look at her!" Rich raised his voice. "She's...she's...well just look!" He pointed at Katie's face, which was swollen, blotchy, red, and most upsetting, without any movement or expression except one wayward eyebrow that made her look maniacally surprised. "Can she hear us?" he suddenly asked worried.

"Mr. Pettigrew, I'm sure your wife will be fine. We're just sending her to Oaks General as a precaution," the nurse said. "You can even ride with her."

The ambulance arrived and two men entered David's office, stretcher in hand. They leaned over Katie and started to confirm statistics.

"B.P. dropping. Better get some oxygen," one said to the other, who hooked up a gas mask.

"What's wrong?" Rich asked, rushing forward.

"Sir, we'll just need you to step back."

"I'm her husband," he said, and then remembering Katie's

instructions about taking his campaign to the streets, added, "Candidate Rich Pettigrew for City Council!"

Katie opened her eyes. "That's my boy," she said weakly. "Remember to campaign hard. Add medical malpractice to your list of topics," she said finally as they carted her off on the stretcher.

David watched after her sheepishly. "That bit about malpractice was a joke, right? This sort of thing happens all the time. I mean, it doesn't happen all the time. Oh, I mean it's a normal adverse reaction. Happens to some of the people, but usually just the highly unusual. She isn't like any woman I've ever examined," he said finally.

Rich wiped a tear from his eye and watched the ambulance pull away. "You can say that again."

Chapter 23

The hospital doctors confirmed David's statement that Katie's reaction was unusual. While they couldn't or wouldn't make a statement against David's practice, they did say that Katie was probably not the best candidate for Botox simply because of her poor circulation caused by age, excess weight, and just plain bad genes. Rich decided not to burden Katie with this news for fear it would exasperate Katie's new facial flaws with more frown lines. Instead, he told Katie that the doctors felt her reaction was caused by extreme stress and over-exertion.

Katie had recently read that Mariah Carey had passed out during a concert for similar reasons and Rich knew that she would be pleased to be afflicted with an ailment worthy of celebrity status.

"You know, Britney Spears has said she will take six months off for just this reason," Katie spoke in a barely audible voice.

"Yes, I know," Rich humored her. "Miley Cyrus had the same problem."

"That's right," Katie said, sounding pleased. "Just think, Mariah, Britney, Miley, and now me! However, I don't know what they have to be stressed out about. They don't have a husband running for council. They don't have to make their house a showplace for the local busy-bodies."

"Honey. Try to remain calm. The doctors want you to stay under observation for a couple of days."

"Is my condition serious?"

"No, you don't have to worry."

"Oh," Katie said, sounding disappointed. "What about the Botox? When can I re-do my forehead?"

"You can't. It's what got you in here."

"No, the stress got me in here and if I remove frown lines I won't be stressed. I'll be happy, carefree, young again!"

"It's just not a good idea, honey."

"How about another round of collagen instead?" Katie asked hopefully.

Rich took a look at her puffed up lips, now in a downward turn, much like a plump caterpillar. "I hate to see you like that," he said, referring as much to the caterpillar that was now Katie's mouth as the sad expression on her face.

"Collagen is my friend," she said simply.

"Katie, I love you just the way you are."

"Oh Rich."

Katie's tone was a mixture of love and amazement, unsure if she could muster up the courage to love herself in the same way that Rich did.

LIKE A GOOD NEIGHBOR, IRELAND INVITED RICH FOR DINNER during Katie's absence, and like a typical man, Rich both daydreamed and fretted about the possibilities. He came home from work, showered, changed his clothes three times and finally decided on his white tennis shorts with red polo shirt and navy blue socks, a bold look if he had ever seen one. With confidence, he selected a bottle of wine from his cupboard, the kind with a cork, and strode across the street.

He found a note on the door inviting him to come in. He loved Katie, but for a brief moment he allowed himself the fantasy: this was his house and Ireland, his wife, was waiting for him.

"Rich? Is that you? I'm in the kitchen. Come on in."

He found Ireland standing on a chair, giving her more height needed to stir a large pot that was more like a cauldron. He looked up and then turned quickly realizing that the open window and the breeze billowed her skirt up, giving him a view. "Smells great," he said awkwardly. "I'm really looking forward to dinner."

"This? It's just a new wax formula I'm toying with. I mix different types of wax with perfumed oils and plant extracts. You can't eat it, silly."

"What do you do with it?"

"You're going to find out. I thought you could be my guinea pig for the evening. I've been doing this all day so I just ordered a pizza for dinner. I hope that's okay."

"Sure," he said feeling a mix of emotions. Katie would never invite someone around and then order takeaway. His perfect image of Ireland was fading. "So, do you need any help?"

"Yeah, go in there and take off your socks," she said pointing to the living room.

"My socks?"

"You can take off your shirt, too, if you like."

"What do you have in mind?" Rich asked, trying his best not to sound nervous and instead appear suave.

"It may not be dinner, but I've got a complete menu planned for you. First we'll start with reflexology for relaxation, then move on to chakra therapy to balance you, and finally, some affirmations to cleanse you and leave you feeling recharged."

Not knowing what was involved in any of this, but believing that his feet were a very private part of his body, Rich nervously looked around the room.

"Uh, when's Dean coming home?""

"Who knows?" Ireland answered easily.

"Well, wouldn't you rather practice on him?""

"On Dean?" Ireland laughed. "God no, he's completely blocked. His negative energy will sap all of the positive flow from my body and steal it directly into his. It's a terribly greedy process that always leaves me with a migraine."

"Oh dear," said Rich, suddenly feeling the onslaught of performance anxiety. "But, won't he mind if you're, you know, doing whatever it is you said you would be doing, to me?"

"Don't be silly. Dean would be positively thrilled to know that you were open to it. He's always going on about how we should have you over for this and that."

"He is?" said Rich, now feeling even more uncomfortable.

"Now Rich, off with those socks," she said jumping off her perch and leaning down before Rich. Ireland didn't wait for Rich to make his move. She had a grip on his ankles, pulled down the socks, pushed Rich to the floor, and removed the offensive cotton before Rich could protest, even mildly. Ireland grabbed a pot of her goo and started to work it into Rich's leg. Although she told him to lie down and let the flow of energy enter him, he just couldn't keep his mind from wandering. He thought of Katie in the hospital, Dean who knows where, and Ireland kneeling between his legs with her hands on his thigh. It was all a bit much for him and he squirmed uneasily. "Don't by shy, Rich. I need the practice and you obviously need the release," she said reaching higher onto his thigh.

"The what?" he said alarmed. "You didn't say anything about..."

"What's all this?" Dean said, suddenly appearing at the doorway.

"Nothing!" Rich exclaimed jumping up and dumping hot wax onto the carpet in the process.

"What do you mean nothing? Ireland, if I've told you once,

I've told you a thousand times, you need to be more careful about where you put that wax."

"It was only my leg!" Rich said in a panic.

"I'm referring to this spot over here," Dean said pointing to the hardwood floor entry. "Ireland, honey, be more careful next time. Hey, good seeing you, Rich. I'm just going to grab a quick swim before dinner."

"Sure sweetie," she said and returned to Rich. "Now then, where were we?" she asked.

"What about Dean?"

"I told you. He's not into it, but he'd probably watch if you wanted."

"No! I thought this was supposed to be relaxing."

"Just breathe. Concentrate on your mind's eye."

"My what?"

"That little space in your mind, not to say that your mind is little. Anyway, that spot that just empties itself into blackness. That's right," she said feeling Rich's muscles give into the massage of hot wax for the first time. "Now repeat these affirmations: I am virile. I am free."

"I don't think that's a good idea," Rich protested.

"Don't you want to feel virile and free?"

"I meant the wax. It's starting to pull the hair on my leg. It kinda hurts."

"It'll leave you silkie soft. A waxing is a side benefit."

"I don't think so. Just get it off."

"This is the only way," she said, starting to rub more feverishly, up and down his leg.

Rich looked around, checking to see if Dean had returned or forgotten something. "You sure Dean doesn't mind if you're rubbing another man's uh, appendage?"

"Of course not. Dean isn't the jealous type. Besides, he's always impressed with a man who can take pain."

"Pain? This is great," said Rich, who for the first time was starting to feel his chakras become enlightened, his mind relaxing. Until, Ireland placed a strip of cloth across his thigh and pulled. "Oh my goodness gracious me!"

"That's the cutest swear I ever heard. You are a gentleman Rich Pettigrew. And, you've got the silkiest legs in Briarwood!"

Katie was in good spirits upon leaving the hospital despite her brush with permanent facial freezing. A bouquet of flowers arrived each day of her stay, all from Harry Greene. Naturally, Rich bristled about the attention calling it an obvious display of marketing and a ploy to get in the Pettigrew good graces. "He's just trying to get us to list our house. Tell him we work with Stacey."

"I thought you didn't like Stacey either."

"Real estate is a dirty business. She's the lesser of two evils."

"Oh Rich, you're just jealous."

"I'm not jealous. Just disgusted. Sending flowers to a married woman. It's outrageous!"

"You're right. It's something my husband should have thought of. By the way, what has kept you so busy lately? If it weren't for Harry, I wouldn't have had any attention the last few days. Speaking of which, he said he would stop by this afternoon. Can you run a quick errand after dropping me off? We need some wine."

Rich thought back to the previous night at Dean and Ireland's house and began to wish he hadn't taken over a bottle of wine. He had practically finished off the bottle himself in an attempt to relax and settle into Ireland's chakra therapy. "I hardly think you need to worry yourself with entertaining Harry the moment you get home from the hospital."

"Oh look, he's already here." As they approached their driveway, they could see Harry's red Porsche.

"Showy and pushy," Rich said with disgust. "He's in my space."

"It seems in more ways than one," Katie said with delighted amusement. "You're cute when you're jealous."

"I told you, I'm not jealous!" he said slamming the door. Before he could walk around the car to Katie's side, not that Rich had planned to undertake such gallantry, Harry already had his hand on the passenger door.

"Allow me," Harry said opening the door. "My God, who is this beautiful teenager?"

Rich made gagging noises. "For Pete's sake."

"Shh. Don't be rude," Katie said under her breath before stepping from the car. "He might hear you."

"I should be so lucky."

The threesome made their way into the Pettigrew house only to have Harry immediately excuse himself to the kitchen to prepare a light snack.

"He's becoming a permanent fixture around here," complained Rich.

"Don't complain. He's helping out and pulling his own weight. Besides, I think it's rather nice of him to check up on me."

"I can't even remember why he's here."

"Wasn't he having his place painted?"

"I thought he said it was being fumigated."

"Maybe it's being fumigated before being painted?" Katie suggested.

"The whole thing is suspicious if you ask me. He should be more covert about his intentions."

"Rich, what are you going on about? What intentions?"

"He obviously has a crush on you."

"Don't be ridiculous. Do you really think so?"

"That does it. I'm going to have a word with him." Within moments, Rich returned. "Where have you hidden him?"

"What are you talking about? He went in the kitchen."

"He's disappeared."

"That's impossible. Let's search the house," Katie suggested.

Rich quickly searched the living room, made his way upstairs, and then doubled back down again when he heard a loud shriek from Katie.

"Sorry, Love," Harry said getting up from where he had crouched behind the couch. "Didn't mean to frighten you."

"What's going on?" Rich demanded.

"Dropped a cuff link," Harry replied.

Rich eyed Harry carefully. There was something about him that didn't quite add up. "You're not wearing a french cuff shirt," he said, feeling all the part of a detective.

"Never do," Harry admitted. "I had them in my pocket. They were going to be a gift for you."

"For me?" Rich said shocked.

"Yes. You could do with a little style. I thought they might help you look the part at Amanda's Dreamscape Charity Tea Party."

"The Dreamscape Tea..." asked Katie breathlessly. "Oh, what I wouldn't do for an invite. I simply must be invited."

"Why would you care? Especially after all she's done?" Rich asked.

"Everyone will be there. It's a total insider's party. There's even paparazzi," piped up Harry.

"You see? We should just forgive and forget?" Katie replied.

"An excellent motto," said Harry, who was now rearranging the couch cushions that he had accidentally dropped to the floor. "I could probably swing you two a ticket. After all, you did help to solve the mystery of her lost rodent."

"Rabbit," said Katie. "A sweet creature, never meant to cause harm. I'm sure under other circumstances Amanda and I would become close friends. I mean, we've known each other for years. We're practically sisters."

"Are you sure about this?" Rich asked. "She did try to have us arrested."

"An innocent mistake. Now if you two will excuse me, I've got to figure out what I'm going to wear," Katie said and practically ran up the stairs. She bounded two at a time and then stopped, "Harry, you're wonderful. How can we ever thank you?" and then continued to the second floor.

With Katie safely out of sight, Harry turned to Rich. "So, did you get any action across the street?"

"I beg your pardon?"

"Come on. I saw you sneaking over there while poor Katie was laid up."

"First of all, I did not sneak. I was invited for dinner and Dean was there the entire time."

"That just adds to the guilty pleasure," Harry said smugly.

Rich ignored him. "Second, what is this business about poor Katie. She just needed a little rest. Now she's back. End of story."

"Is it?"

"What are you getting at?"

"Listen Rich," Harry said, leaning in and placing a hand on his shoulder. "Katie is all for Janet and David's free expression mumbo jumbo. The way I see it, she would be in favor of a little split action. You get a go with the two lovebirds across the street and I'll keep an eye on Katie, sort of make sure she doesn't get jealous."

"Awfully kind of you," said Rich sarcastically, "but no thanks."

"Suit yourself, but I can only imagine how upset she's going to be if she doesn't get invited to that tea party," he said and produced an invitation, waving it at Rich.

"Hey," Rich said trying to swipe the invite.

"Not so fast. This one has my name on it, but I can get one for you two...if..."

"If what?"

"If you keep helping me out like you did after Palm Springs. You know, let me leave my 'cuff links' here awhile longer. I just checked my stash and it's fine."

"Listen, Harry, I know you come from the other side of the pond, as they say, but what are you talking about?"

"That's my boy, play dumb. I see that you've been providing similar boarding services for Ireland's *houseplants*."

"Huh? That was just a plant, nothing expensive like cuff links. If you think I'm taking political bribes..." Rich's voice trailed off.

"I see what you're getting at. You're holding out for the big ticket. Well, well, maybe you'll be a better politician than I gave you credit for."

"I don't know what you're talking about."

"I love it!" Harry laughed loudly and handed him an invitation. "Hey, let's make sure to hook up with Dean and Ireland at the tea. We can toast to our new found friendships," he said and elbowed Rich in the ribs.

Chapter 24

It was Katie's first lunch with the girls since she had been home. Determined to make a good impression, Katie made herself a hearty sandwich and polished it off with a glass of chocolate milk. If she planned her digestion accordingly, she wouldn't be hungry when it was time to order and she could actually be happy about selecting a meager salad, the food of choice among the Briarwood women.

"Katie you look ten years younger," Rachel exclaimed as she opened her door to her. Turning to Stacey, she asked, "Isn't it amazing?"

"To die for," Stacy concurred.

"It's nothing, really," Katie said modestly.

"It really changes your whole look," said Rachel thoughtfully. "You know, maybe that's just what we should do."

"What?" asked Katie.

"I know just the place," said Stacey, already on the same wave length as Rachel.

"Fill me in!" Katie insisted.

"Katie, you are going to experience a total image reconstruction," said Rachel.

"You mean a make over?" asked Katie, who sounded a bit offended, believing that Stacey had already made her over and there was nothing more to do.

"No, no," said Stacey. "That implies that there's something in need of, well, making over. This is an image alteration, a reconstruction of your outer persona."

"Oh," said an unconvinced Katie. "What's the difference?"

Rachel took Katie by the hand. "Tons of difference. Endless differences. Too many to even speculate!"

"Let's forget lunch and go to the spa instead," Stacey suggested.

"I don't need to eat," Rachel added, looking to Katie.

For once, Katie was on the same wave length. "I never need food," she beamed.

The women drove Katie to *Celestial*, the newest and most chic day spas and clothing boutiques to open in the area. The boutique was known as much for the price of its inventory as for its upper class clientele. The concept was inviting: first you buy, then the spa makes you look fit to wear the clothes. Katie eyed a myriad of t-shirts displayed on an oversized farmhouse cutting block. Flowing, cotton dresses were hung from the ceiling on a pot rack. A grandfather clock in the corner of the room contained display shelves with crystal jewelry. "How charming," she said looking around the cozy room. "It's like a little cottage."

"They call it shabby chic," Rachel corrected.

"I know the designer," Stacey interjected. "Celeste goes to England each summer to fill a container. Met a gorgeous Oxford man last year," she continued while fingering one of the $50 t-shirts. "It's a shame that there aren't more quality men here."

"What about Harry?" Katie asked. "He's English. Very good looking and you're even in the same business. I think he's rather dreamy."

"Harry?" Stacey said with shocked horror as if Katie had

suggested rubbing beet juice on a stain. "Oh and what business are you referring?"

"Why real estate, of course."

"Hah," Rachel added and took Stacey by the arm.

"Have I said something wrong," Katie asked worriedly, not wanting to once again eliminate herself from Rachel's circle.

"Now Katie," Rachel patronized. "Just stick with us and you'll be alright. But for God's sake, let us dress you, make you over, and get rid of any ideas of the virtues of people you really know nothing about."

"Yes, ma'am," Katie said obediently.

———

By the time Katie returned home, she had a new understanding of her neighbors and what made them different from everyday people. She and Rich had lived in Briarwood for three months, but it was only after today that she felt she had been given a cheat sheet about the rules.

She had learned that you can't buy a Target t-shirt for $6 one day and then buy a Celestial t-shirt for $50 the next. You have to just make a clean break, rid your closet of cheap clothes and dress the part of the upper class if you're truly going to fit in. Rachel and Stacey's motto was 'never look like a lesser.' Katie mused that *lesser* sounded an awful lot like *leper* and it might as well have. It meant you were doomed if you didn't always have your makeup in place, your clothes looking perfect, and an attitude that leaned toward superiority.

"A bad impression is made in just ten seconds," Stacey had said.

Rachel concurred, "You never know who might see you when. Better to always be safe."

Katie intended to follow suit and proudly wore her new $200 outfit out of the store.

"How do I look?" she twirled for Rich in a pair of faded jeans and a t-shirt.

"Fine."

"Fine? Is that all? These are new."

"They look old. Just look at the seat of your pants," Rich pointed to where the fading was more prominent.

"It's supposed to look like that. They take extra time with the fading process to make it look naturally worn. What about the shirt? It's a Steve Star."

"A who?"

"Just the newest and latest. Rachel and Stacey said I looked absolutely fantastic in it."

"Why are they so keen on you all of a sudden? A few weeks ago, Rachel wasn't even on speaking terms with you."

"Oh that," said Katie with a wave of her hand. "Just a little misunderstanding over the help."

"The help? Katie, what's gotten into you?"

"Nothing," Katie bristled. "I just mean that nothing as mundane as all that business would come between true friends," she said breezily. "Rachel now understands that my wanting Lola was a compliment to her good taste."

"Friends. A compliment!" Rich shook his head.

Katie placed her hands on her hips. "What?"

"She's our neighbor, but that doesn't mean she's your friend, nor does it mean you should want her as a friend. That has to be earned. Instead, you treat her like some sort of weird status symbol of suburbia. Someone you aspire to be like."

"Don't be silly."

"Oh yeah, you're right. That would be Amanda."

"Listen, I don't have to aspire to be like Rachel. We live here, don't we? And, we're going to the season's hottest party! Woo hoo!" Katie no sooner started to do a little dance.

"Katie, about that party," said Rich, thinking about Harry's proposition and getting increasingly worried.

"Please," Katie said holding her hand up in the stop position, "I'm doing my happy dance."

"Katie..."

"Actually, for now on I want you to call me Katharine. Rachel and Stacey say it's much more me and very Briarwood."

"I've never called you Katharine," Rich said. "Only your father calls you Katharine, and then only when you're in trouble."

"Don't be silly, Richard."

"I'm warning you, Katie. Start calling me Richmond and it's straight back to calling you what we called you in high school."

"You wouldn't," Katie gasped.

"I always thought that Matey Katie was kinda cute. Had a double meaning, if you know what I mean," Rich said nuzzling her neck.

"Don't you dare...*Richmond*," she said thoughtfully.

"I warned you," he said and without warning, he hauled Katie toward the bedroom.

Chapter 25

The party had all the makings of high society. A doorman, strolling violinists, ice sculptures, the works. "Now I know we've made it," Katie said in awe of her surroundings. "We're at Amanda's charity party and I'm not her charity case!"

"It's something, that's for sure," Rich agreed.

"Why don't we throw parties like this?" asked Katie surveying the scene. "It's so classy."

"Yeah, an open bar, too," Rich added. "Come on, I could use a beer."

"Don't you dare. You can't order a beer."

"Why? I'm thirsty."

"But this is a tea."

"But there's booze too. It's Amanda's way of getting men and their wallets here."

"You can at least order something more appropriate for the occasion."

"Like a martini, shaken not stirred," said Rich delighted. "I've always wanted to do that."

"James Bond you are not. How 'bout something like a wine spritzer?" Katie pleaded.

Rich looked over at the bartender, a big guy with muscles the size of cantaloupes. "Do I have to?"

"It would be very appropriate," she said primly. "Oh look, Janet and David are here," she said, starting to wave frantically. "You go get the drinks. A Dubonnet cocktail for me. I hear it's a favorite of Queen Elizabeth. Very lady like," she added and pranced across the room.

Rich made his way to the bar, pausing to stop at least three circulating waiters to sample their wares. Carrying a plate with samplings of toast points and caviar, crab-stuffed mushrooms, and salmon sashimi along with calamari, he approached the beefy bartender. "I'll have a Dubonnet cocktail and a wine spritzer, please."

"Interesting choices," the bartender said as he started to grab bottles.

"How so?" asked Rich, getting defensive.

"Oh, you just don't see many men ordering that sort of drink."

"Well, it's for my wife."

"Both of them?"

"Can I just have the drinks?" Rich asked impatiently.

"Sure thing, but you should know that I have the utmost respect for you."

"You do?"

"Yeah, I've seen your campaign posters. That's really cool that you're running for council. Most people just stick with their daily grind, never try to make a difference. Me and my buddies were talking one day, saying how you'll go places."

Rich couldn't believe that a guy who looked like a Chippendales' dancer actually looked up to him and discussed him with his buddies. "Aw, it's nothing, really."

"No man, you're the type of guy who isn't afraid to take chances."

But then, as the compliments continued to pour in, Rich

wondered if the fact that he looked like a Chippendales' dancer and admired him was cause for concern.

"Yep, you're a risk taker, I can tell. Just look at that food you've got," he said pointing to Rich's overflowing plate. "Sushi, octopus...you're cool. Me? I've always been a bartender. Never had the guts to take risks. You obviously don't have those fears. Just look at that stuff," he repeated, staring at the food.

Rich wasn't sure if the bartender was truly impressed with his choice of appetizers, revolted by the thought of eating them, or just plain hungry. Either way, he felt obliged to offer him something as it was obvious that Amanda's form of charity did not extend to the hired help. "Er, you wanna try some?" he said holding out his hands.

The bartender looked as if nobody had ever shown him the kindness that Rich had demonstrated. He jumped over the bar, his beefy arms going encircling Rich's mid-section in an enormous hug. Then, he delicately extended his chin, opened his mouth and flicked his tongue in lizard-like fashion toward the appetizer held between Rich's fingers. The entire move happened within a span of nanoseconds leaving Rich open mouthed as well. Before he could recover, the bartender had performed the same trick twice, which gave nearby party guests a prime view of their candidate for council hand-feeding the bartender.

"Delicious," the bartender said, licking his lips, fingers, and then wiping his mouth with the back of his hand. The display positively sickened Rich, who quickly excused himself to find the bathroom and wash his hands.

"Where are you going?" Katie asked heading Rich off before he could pass. "Did you get my drink?"

"I didn't get it. I feel sick."

"You don't look too good," she admitted.

Rich was about to leave again when Ireland and Dean strode over. "Rich, you naughty boy," Ireland teased.

Rich immediately reddened and wondered if she were referring to his recent escapades at their house or the scene with the bartender. Either way, he didn't want word getting out. "Sorry, I'm just headed for the restroom."

"Want company?" she asked boldly.

"He certainly does not!" Katie answered for him.

"Ireland's such a kidder," Dean said quickly. "You're going to have to be more subtle," he said to her in whispered tones, "now that we know for sure. He's totally a swinger! Did you see him and the bartender? I'd say it's time to bring out the big guns."

"We'll catch you later, Rich," and then, as an afterthought she said, "Oh, and you, too, Katie. Lovely outfit," Ireland added and waltzed away with Dean.

"Gotta find the bathroom," Rich muttered. "I really don't feel good. Got this terrible pain and..."

Katie shooed him away with her hand, "Uggh. Just go and do your business. It's not exactly cocktail conversation."

"I don't have to do any *business*. I think I need a doctor. Might be my appendix."

"Now?" Katie complained. "I was just starting to have fun. I don't want to leave. I bought this new dress and everything," she whined. "Maybe David can help you."

"No way. I'm not having that quack examine me. Just look what happened to you. Maybe Janet," he reasoned.

"She's a psychiatrist," Katie said flatly.

"Better her than that plastic phony she's married to. She went to medical school just as much as he did."

"I'm gonna find her," he said, gripping his stomach.

"What should I do?" she asked.

"I don't know. Mingle, look at the sights, find me a bottle of aspirin," he said and left.

Rich was making his way through the crowded room, had Janet in sights and was headed her way when Ireland stopped him in his path. "Rich, wanna come out and play?" Ireland asked coyly.

Momentarily, Rich forgot the pain in his abdomen and could only see the loveliness that was Ireland. He felt an adrenalin rush that made him have no intention of doing anything but listen to the delicate words that would trickle off her tongue.

"You husky beef cake. Take me hard and fast. Dean and I'll show you a good time. We'll..."

Rich listened in shock as Ireland proceeded to whisper a string of expletives describing what she and Dean wanted to do and how the deeds would be done. The pain returned, this time coupled with nausea. Unable to determine whether the bout was brought on by Ireland's pornographic description or a true medical emergency, he politely excused himself to search out Janet.

It seemed to Katie that the charity tea wasn't all it was cracked up to be. Everyone was discussing the usual topics of conversation that she had long grown bored of. One group of women were talking about the foibles of their designers, maids, nannies, or other "people" who were in their employment. She passed by a circle of men discussing their golf averages and the new lounge at the club house. A group of pregnant women debated whose morning sickness was worse and their past labor pains. Having forgone her pouch in favor of a more svelte look in honor of the charity tea, Katie quickly dodged past this last gathering and continued out of the living room, down the hall, and found herself facing the rear staircase of Amanda's massive home.

"It figures. Amanda wouldn't be content with just one staircase," Katie said aloud, and then, looking around and finding herself alone, decided a quick peak of the second story couldn't hurt. "I'll just say the bathrooms downstairs were occupied," she reasoned to herself.

—————

JANET FOUND RICH BEFORE HE FOUND HER QUITE BY accident. On his way to locate her he stopped off in the restroom and due to the extreme pain he experienced, never came out. Janet was on her way in to make a pit stop when the sound of moaning caught her attention.

Having been familiar with the reaction a good party has on Ireland and Dean, Janet believed the frisky couple had commandeered the bathroom for their own private party. "There will be none of that at this party," she said primly, knocking on the door. "This is a respectable event and if you don't stop immediately, I'll call Amanda."

The groaning from within only worsened.

"Do you hear me?" Janet called. "If you don't open this door right this minute, I'll let myself in." The door didn't budge, but the sounds from within grew.

"That's enough," Janet exclaimed, her hand now firmly planted on the handle. "I'm coming in. You better make your-selves decent. There are other people who need the facilities for more appropriate reasons." She swung the door open with mighty force, landing a firm bang onto Rich's head as he was doubled over onto the floor.

"Rich! What are you doing?" she asked, and then with a quick peek inside, added, "so alone."

"Food poisoning," he moaned and then rolled over clutching his stomach.

"Don't be ridiculous," she said staring at Rich. "Amanda always hires the top caterer."

"My stomach," he pleaded. "Need a doctor."

"Alright. If you insist,"she said stepping into the powder room and closing the door behind her. "Where does it hurt?"

"Here," he said pressing a hand to his lower abdomen.

"It's probably those jeans. Putting on a few pounds? A little tight around the mid-section? Just a brisk walk and you should be fine," she said only to have Rich return her thoughts with more groans. "Oh, fine," she said with annoyance. "I'll just unbutton them and prove there's nothing wrong with you." With her hands on his fly, she stopped herself once more, "You're not a pervert, are you?"

"Good gracious," he gasped, "what kind of doctor are you? I think I'm dying!"

"First off, don't be so melodramatic. Second, I'm a psychiatrist and you know it. Haven't had to touch a patient since medical school."

"Please," he moaned. "I need help."

"I'm not debating that!"

KATIE COULDN'T BE MORE PLEASED WITH HERSELF AS SHE twirled in front of the mirror in one of Amanda's evening gowns, her own clothes discarded in a pile next to her. "Ahh, this is the life."

She perused the closet full of dresses with shoes to match each and every one, deciding if she should try on another. "Maybe this will be how I live in my next life, or hopefully when Rich is elected," she said while peeling the first dress off her. Before putting her own clothes back on, she did her best waltz and hummed "I Could Have Danced All Night," her own voice drowning out the soft rumble of the nanny cam as it rotated in her direction.

KATIE CREPT DOWNSTAIRS, CAREFUL TO AVOID BEING SEEN and thus forced to explain why she was in the upstairs wing to begin with. Now that she had changed back to her own clothes, she felt drab, depressed, and overall ready to leave the festive environment. Unfortunately, Rich was not in his usual party hangouts. She checked the bar and the various food stations. Since Ireland was also alone, there was only one other possible place that Rich could be located...the bathroom. "Probably found a good magazine and decided to hang out for the duration," Katie muttered to herself as she rapped on the bathroom door. Only a moan and a subsequent "hush" came from behind the closed door. "Rich? Is that you?" Katie asked, her curiosity growing.

"Thank god it's you," Janet exclaimed, having opened the door a crack. "Quick, get in," she said and tugged Katie's arm while opening the door just long enough to allow her to enter.

"What's going on?" Katie asked staring down at Rich, with his pants unzipped.

"He came wailing to me about needing a doctor," Janet complained. "I think he might actually be sick. He's certainly not trying anything perverted."

"You sound disappointed," Katie accused.

"Nothing of the sort. Just surprised. As a psychiatrist I know his type."

"I'm not a type," Rich protested and then moaned from the added effort of speaking.

"Rich, keep quiet," Janet ordered. "I think he's right. Looks like his appendix," she explained to Katie. "Can you help me get his pants lowered? It's hard with him rolling around on the floor."

"Maybe we should take him to a proper doctor?"

"Proper schmoper. Get going," she ordered, pointing to Rich.

DUE TO RICH'S INCAPACITATED STATE, IT TOOK BOTH KATIE and Janet to help him remove his pants. Their struggles were caused by the dead weight of Rich's legs as the pain in his abdomen was too great for any movement except the occasional gripping of his side. "This brings me back to my interning days," Janet reminisced. "Now, you see this?" she said pointing to Rich's lower stomach.

"What is that?" Katie asked pointing to two large knobs that protruded from Rich.

"Awful isn't it?" Janet announced with delight. "Textbook case. Maybe I should go back into this type of work. Quite lucrative and you don't have to listen to people complain all day."

"Uhhgh," Rich wailed.

"Well, at least they don't complain about their love life," Janet corrected. "Now, as I was saying before being so rudely interrupted," she said with regards to Rich, "this is a busted appendix. Must come out."

"Where?" Katie inquired, leaning over Rich's face.

In turn, Janet stood straddling Rich's body and pointed, "Right there."

It was in that awkward position, with Janet at one end of Rich and Katie at the other, that Ireland and Dean made their discovery.

"Oh my gosh!" Ireland shouted as she opened the door to the bathroom.

"We're not quite finished," Janet said professionally.

"I would never have guessed," Dean uttered.

"It's always the last people you suspect," Ireland agreed.

"Well Rich is normally so healthy," Katie commented, not wanting word of his condition to affect his bid for city council.

"One night on his back is all he needs," Janet added.

"So the three of you thought you would go at it here?" Ireland announced with shock.

"Don't be so surprised. This type of thing can happen at any time," Janet said. "Have you had yours done?"

"Rich, you two-timer! And with your own wife. Honestly, Dean, I've never heard of anything so disgusting," she said and walked out.

"What's her problem?" Katie asked.

"Some people are just squeamish around medical stuff," Janet reasoned and then turned to Rich, "Ready to take a little trip to the hospital?"

He nodded weakly as Janet dialed the ambulance from her cell phone and Katie proceeded to slide his legs back into their trousers.

Chapter 26

A manda pursued volunteer opportunities much in the way a lovestruck teen pines for their first love. It was a burning desire that filled her to the core. Not because she enjoyed performing the seemingly goodwill gestures that she lauded on those who were less fortunate than herself, but because she hoped to one day be awarded the President's Volunteer Service Award, the premier award if there ever was one.

Although Amanda strived to be seen as the epitome of goodwill, Kyle, her elder step-son, whom she rarely spoke of because in her opinion his biological mother was a tramp, did not share this desire. Whereas Amanda's social standing in the community evolved from her work for numerous non-profit organizations and constant volunteer presence on the school board and PTA, her willingness to "give back" failed to rub off on Kyle.

Of course, it was easy for Amanda to be generous with her time. Her husband's salary and multiple investments, not to mention his umpteen rental properties in areas Amanda considered so undesirable they bordered on his being labeled a slumlord, she couldn't deny that it lent her a lifestyle that made it so she would never have to work. Although she and Kyle had never seen eye to eye, there was one trait of Amanda's that Kyle had learned to emulate, and that was her love of money.

It's not that Kyle was a bad seed; he was just a teenager. And, like most teenage boys, he had a fondness for girls and a keen interest in pornography. It was this last point that Kyle believed would also assist him in his quest to mod out the car that his family bought him, but was too 'family' for his taste.

While Katie was sneaking a peek at Amanda's closet during the party, the family nanny cam was taking a glimpse of Katie in all her greatness. What neither Amanda nor Mr. Exeter knew was that Kyle had developed the uncanny ability to alter the program direction of the nanny cam, edit and splice the film, and then return the camera to its original position before either parent noticed anything had gone awry.

Believing that the night of the party would result in some prime footage, Kyle performed his tricks and hit the jackpot when Katie proceeded to undress in front of the camera. As he sat at his computer, he couldn't believe his luck as the images downloaded in front of him.

There were shots of Katie from every angle as she turned and preened in front of Amanda's mirrors believing she was playing make believe rather than a part in a homemade, adult movie. As Katie maneuvered into Amanda's gowns, under garments, and shoes, the camera caught the action. There were shots of Katie bending over as she slipped into silk stockings, shots of her squeezing her own breasts together as she attempted to fit them into the tight bodice of a corset, and more shots of Katie lounging buck naked on Amanda's chaise lounge, holding only a mirror to admire herself in the chic surroundings. Kyle's fine editing skills converted Katie's dress up game into a steamy series of suggestive poses.

With the assistance of digital technology and a high speed connection, the images of Katie were downloaded to Kyle's favorite Internet porn site within minutes. The site not only provided guests with viewing pleasure for a small subscription fee, but also purchased home movies from certain amateur directors. Kyle had proven himself to be of director quality and now relied heavily on the income each month of which half he put away for his car and the other half supported his budding cocaine habit, which Harry Greene was generously helping to cultivate. This recent addition starring Katie Pettigrew was not his best work, but the sheer amount of footage was sure to bring him in a few hundred while WeCYou.com would make ten times that amount from the visitors of the site each day. By the end of the week, Katie's face and then some, would be smiling at strangers throughout the world.

Chapter 27

R ich awoke in the hospital with a pain in his abdomen and a nurse standing over him. "Mr. Pettigrew, there are some people here to see you." The nurse moved aside and in her place Rich thought he saw an angel, a woman so beautiful, dressed in white. It was Ireland. She leaned down and kissed him lightly on the forehead.

"You poor man. Here, we brought you these," she said and placed a bouquet of flowers on the bedside table.

"We?" Rich managed.

"How ya doing buddy?" Dean said, stepping forward so that Rich could see him without straining.

"Oh," Rich said in a disappointed tone. "I thought you were alone." As long as he was heavily medicated, he was going to take full advantage of his fantasies. "You missed me," he said more as a statement than a question.

"Of course, silly. And we wanted to apologize for behaving so rashly at the party," Ireland said sweetly.

"When you're better, man," Dean said.

"We'll have our little private party when you get out of

here," Ireland responded nonchalantly. "Dean and I discussed it, and we don't mind sharing you."

At that moment, Rich noticed the nurse and wondered if she had remained in the room for the entire conversation. He liked the idea of Ireland being attracted to him, was confused over the attention Dean gave to him, but under no circumstances would he want strangers to get the wrong idea about his marriage. It didn't take long to confirm his worst fears. "Mr. Pettigrew," the nurse said briskly, "the police are here. I'll show them in."

"Wait," he begged. "You don't understand. I didn't do anything. These people are just playing a practical joke."

His pleas were met with unsympathetic eyes, followed by the nurse turning away and two large officers returning in her place. Rich was sure that once he recovered he would become the newest toy for the prison population. Labeled a pervert, he was sure to get the most attention, the kind he certainly didn't want. All because of a woman. He was old enough to know better.

"I think we should go," Ireland nudged Dean in the ribs.

"Yeah," he agreed, and then to Rich, "later, man."

When scared, Rich usually took the safe route. In this case, that meant playing dead. With the pain radiating from his side, he decided it wasn't such a stretch so he closed his eyes, tried his best not to breathe, and waited for the police to give up and leave. They didn't.

"Mr. Pettigrew, we have a few questions for you," a hearty voice, that introduced itself as Officer Brolin boomed. "Mr. Pettigrew?"

"Looks like he's asleep," the one known as Officer Hodgson noted in a gentler manner. "Let's come back."

"The nurse said he just had his appendix out. Not like it was brain surgery. He can sleep later. You give it a try."

Officer Hodgson did his best to wake Rich. "Mr. Pettigrew, we found your car."

Rich opened his eyes and stared with obvious confusion,

albeit some relief over not being labeled a pervert. "Your car was missing?" Officer Hodgson prompted.

"Missing?" Rich said blankly.

Officer Hodgson continued, "Seems a local teenager went out for a joy ride. Last name is Exeter, first name Kyle."

"Kyle Exeter," Rich managed with confusion, trying in his mind to piece it together.

Officer Brolin spoke to his partner. "Maybe you were right. The cut in his side seems to have leaked some brain fluid. Maybe we should come back."

"Mr. Pettigrew," Officer Brolin continued, "we're just happy to give you the good news. We'll check with your wife again, maybe return when you're feeling better."

The moment the police were out the door, Rich reached for the phone to dial Katie.

"Katie, the police might come by."

"Why?"

"They said our car was stolen."

"Oh that. Did they find it?"

"It was missing?"

"I couldn't remember where I had parked it," she said simply.

"They said Amanda's son took it out for a joy ride."

"Really?"

"Katie, they think Kyle stole our car. You can't let them think that if you just misplaced it after the party. Did you stay at the party after I was taken to the hospital?"

"Of course not. I wouldn't stay and party knowing that you were about to be operated on. Janet drove me home. She said I shouldn't drive what with the shock of seeing you hauled off in an ambulance. So I let her take me home and then I made a lemon cake."

"You baked?" Rich said with hurt dismay.

"It's not like I planned it," Katie said defensively. "There was a packet of powdered sugar on the counter, so I decided to use it up. You must have left it out. Delicious cake. I couldn't stop eating it. Anyway, by the time I had my fill, I walked back to the Exeter's, but I couldn't locate the car. I figured it had been stolen. If I knew it was Kyle, I would have just talked with Amanda about the matter."

Rich stared at the phone and shook his head. "Katie, something weird is going on. Try to hold down the fort. I'm going to get myself discharged."

"Bye love," she said replacing the phone as she popped another piece of cake in her mouth.

As the police left the hospital, a disturbing the peace report came across their radio frequency. "That's near here. Want to take it?" Brolin asked his partner.

"Sure, I'm up for a party."

The disturbing the peace site took them to the home of the Pettigrews, where Officers Brolin and Hodgson got out of their car and seemed to attract at least as much attention as the loud music. Curtains from the next door neighbor's home suddenly moved. A window across the street opened. Curious eyes strained to see the happenings without being noticed. "Tell me, where does neighborhood watch stop and downright nosiness begin?" joked Hodgson.

"I thought perhaps it was my new cologne causing the stir," quipped Brolin. "Let's go," he said pointing to the door.

After five minutes of ringing and knocking without any answer, the two officers tried their universal key. What they found was more shocking then they could have imagined. Katie Pettigrew dancing with abandon to "You Make Me Feel Like a Natural Woman" in leopard print pants and matching bra. Intently holding a cucumber as a microphone and singing her heart out, she didn't notice the police who were now a fascinated audience.

Brolin leaned toward Hodgson so he could hear. "She looks familiar. Did you see the bulletin this morning? The Internet scam?" he clarified.

"What?" Hodgson shouted, pointing to his ears. "It's too loud."

"The porn scam!" Brolin shouted. "She's our live wire. The latest download."

"That's her?" Brolin turned to scrutinize Katie.

"That's her," Hodgson confirmed.

"She's also got the same last name as the guy we just visited. Sure seems happy about her husband being gone. I think we should have a word with Mrs. Pettigrew. Cut the music."

Hodgson found the socket for the stereo and pulled the plug. Katie spun around with obvious annoyance, believing a power outage had occurred, but quickly realized that something much worse was happening.

"What are you doing here?" she demanded.

"Mrs. Pettigrew?" Brolin asked. "We'd like to have a word with you."

"If this is about the car, it's no big deal. We'll sort it out with the neighbors. They should have a stern word with their son and it'll be over. Thanks for your trouble," she said holding the front door open for the officers.

"Mrs. Pettigrew, there was a disturbing the peace complaint. Would you mind sitting down a moment?" Brolin continued patiently.

"Well, if I must," she said and took a seat on the couch. Yet Katie couldn't sit still. She rotated her ankle, crossed and uncrossed her legs, fluffed the cushions.

"Mrs. Pettigrew, you seem agitated. Have you taken any illegal substances recently?" Hodgson inquired.

"Me? Never touch the stuff. Well, maybe a white wine from time to time, but that's it."

"You won't mind if we have a look around?" Hodgson inquired.

"Suit yourself. Oh, I have a lovely lemon cake. Would you like some?"

"No thank you. We're on duty," Brolin said.

"Not that I have much left. It was so good! But, here...I saved a bit," Katie insisted. "It's so delicious. You can't help yourself."

Then, as if to elaborate the point, Katie grabbed the slice in her open hand and shoved it into her mouth whole. "It's to die for. Best I ever made," she mumbled.

Hodgson and Brolin looked at each other with dubious suspicion. Brolin leaned over the cake platter, gave a sniff, placed a pinky on the powdered sugar topping and took a hesitant lick. He nodded to Hodgson. "Cuff her."

"What? Don't you like it?" Katie asked. "It's always been Rich's favorite."

With that comment, Hodgson added a second order. "When you're done, call the hospital and have that Rich Pettigrew put on 24-hour watch. We'll haul him in when he recovers." He turned to Katie and spoke evenly, "Mrs. Katie Pettigrew, you are being placed under arrest for possession of cocaine and attempted forced distribution of this illegal substance. Furthermore, you are under suspicion of illegal pornography, a crime in this state."

"Coke? I don't do drugs. And as for porn, well, I don't even go to the movies."

Brolin merely continued where Hodgson left off, "You have the right to remain silent. Anything you say can and will be held against you in a court of law."

Katie sat back down and started to cry. Hodgson turned to Brolin. "Maybe we don't have to cuff her? She's in her own house and the neighbors are watching. Let's just take her in a more civilized manner, what do ya say?"

Brolin thought it over. "You can leave her the way she is, I guess." Then, he turned to Katie, "Mrs. Pettigrew, do you plan to cooperate?"

"Yes. Anything to prove my innocence."

"Very well. Stay here while we do our investigation," Brolin conceded.

Katie sat back down on the couch and reached for another slice of lemon cake.

"Hodgson!" Brolin barked. "Get that cake away from her. She's high as a kite and she's continuing to eat her way through the evidence."

"No wonder my diet hasn't been working," Katie sniffed. "It's all that Harry Greene's fault."

"Now who would that be?" Hodgson asked more gently, now that Brolin had left the room.

"Just some real estate agent. He gave me the powdered sugar, at least that's what I thought it was."

"So you had nothing to do with it?"

"Nothing at all," Katie insisted.

Hodgson was starting to feel sorry for Katie when Brolin returned. "You better come see this." He produced a gloved hand that held a small bone. "They're buried everywhere. Looks as if they tried to hide it with cannabis, which are sprouting up everywhere. I'm telling you," Brolin said shaking his head, "there's enough pot to supply all of east Los Angeles. And, enough bones to be a small animal, maybe a rabbit. I think we're onto something big. Coke, pot, porn, and now Satan worship. I'll take her down to headquarters. You stay here and start questioning the neighbors. I'll be back in an hour."

With sirens blaring, the police car left the once quiet neighborhood. Brolin, a devout Catholic and family man, had no patience for the devil or those he believed were spreading his message. From the backseat, Katie continued to declare her innocence.

"There's been a mistake."

"You can say that again," Brolin answered over his shoulder. "Killing innocent animals to placate the devil is certainly something I would call a mistake."

"I haven't killed anything. I don't even like to skin chickens."

"Disgusting," Brolin said with a shake of his head.

"I meant for cooking...the ones you get in the supermarket. I always buy boneless, skinless breasts," she shouted over the blare of the siren, but her message wasn't heard.

"Let's not start in about your breasts," Brolin declared. "Pornography involving youths is a federal offense. Lady, you're in real trouble and if I were you, I'd stop talking."

"You're not as nice as your partner," she sniffed into her tissue.

HODGSON'S NICE NATURE WAS GENERALLY AN ADVANTAGE, BUT today was not one of those times. He was raised by an English father and an American mother, and spent his formative years in Northern London. He attended the posh Radley School for Boys, and traveled extensively during summer holidays. It was on a trip to New York that his perspective of what he wanted to be when he grew up was forever changed.

A common street thief pick pocketed his father's wallet and the mishap was not discovered until the family had already ordered lunch from a local deli and proceeded to eat their sandwiches as tall as skyscrapers and ice cream sundaes dripping with syrups. The waitress took pity on them because she didn't want tourists...foreigners, to boot, to get a bad impression of the city and country she was so proud of.

She purposefully lost the check and then loaned them cab fare from her own wages so that they could get to a local police station. From that moment on, Miles Hodgson decided that he was going to help people as well and although the life of a police officer was not what his parents had intended for him, they gave their blessing under the condition that he work in a small, safe town, preferably as far from the pick pocketing incident as he could get. The choice landed him across the country facing the challenge of questioning the Pettigrew's neighbors about a sex scandal. How utterly embarrassing for him. You can take the boy out of England, but one certainly cannot take English Boarding School out of the boy. He just wasn't raised to do this sort of thing, police work or not.

Hodgson walked outside the Pettigrew home and thought for a moment about which way to turn. The next door neighbor would be eager to talk. She hadn't moved from her perch in the upstairs window since the ordeal began, but Hodgson decided to first pursue a more unbiased interview. He headed across the street to the house where two lawn chairs, a bottle of Evian, and a tube of sunscreen had been left by the front porch.

From the moment that Ireland opened the door, Officer Miles Hodgson knew he had chosen the wrong house. She was too beautiful to question about such delicate matters. There was no way he would ever be able to bring himself to do it, but with Ireland repeatedly asking if there was something she could do for him, there was no alternative.

"Just wondered if I could take a moment of your time, Madam, er Miss, uh, Mrs...," Hodgson faltered.

"Alexander. It's Mrs. Alexander, but please, call me Ireland," she beamed.

"Very well, Ireland. It's concerning your neighbors, the Pettigrews."

"Lovely people. Real neighborly, if you know what I mean," she said and winked.

"Not sure I do," Hodgson answered. "Have you ever witnessed anything inappropriate?"

"Inappropriate," she repeated, "Well that all depends on who you ask. I think the Pettigrews are just swell. And Dean has a certain sweetness for them, too."

"Dean? That would be your husband?"

"Yes, he and Rich have gotten real close."

"You mean they socialize?"

"Well, we see the Pettigrews at local community events and

parties, nothing out of the ordinary, although Dean would like to change that. Let's just say that he would like Rich to be one of his Poker buddies."

"So, nothing unusual here," Hodgson said satisfied.

"You're pretty cool, Officer Hodgson. I like a man in uniform who can look the other way."

"What do you mean? Is there something going on that you'd like to share?"

"Sharing is the opportune word, but unfortunately Katie seems to be a little selfish in that department. Keeps Rich all to herself, although Dean still hopes to change that, as I said."

"Oh, that's what you meant by Poker."

"I wasn't referring to cards, if that's what you meant."

"I see," Hodgson replied.

"Can I offer you a glass of wine?"

"No, I'm on duty, but you could answer one more question, although I must apologize for the nature of it." Hodgson adjusted his tie, cleared his throat and tried to avoid eye contact with the gorgeous Ireland. "Have you ever seen the Pettigrews...well, let me see, how do I put this delicately? They're accused of being part of something illicit. Have you ever noticed if Mr. Pettigrew, uh, pet the bunny, so to speak?"

And then, in response to Ireland's lack of response, Hodgson was forced to continue with the embarrassing line of questioning. "Have they ever given the bunny a carrot?"

"Amanda Exeter has accused them of just that," Ireland said thoughtfully. "I don't involve myself with neighborhood gossip, but I heard that her daughter lost her bunny to the Pettigrews."

"You're kidding," Hodgson said with shock. "How old is this girl?"

"Just a child. About ten, I'd say. That's why the Exeters were so angry. The girl was simply traumatized."

"And, why wasn't this crime reported? Surely, crimes of this nature involving minors would be prosecuted to the full extent of the law."

"I think they did tell the police. But, well you know how it is. Things like bunnies just get buried."

"Speaking of burying," Hodgson continued, "Have you ever noticed, you know..."

"What?"

"Has he ever buried his hose anywhere else?" Hodgson said with all the delicateness he could muster.

"God yes. He was up all night doing it when they first moved in."

"You don't say."

"Had Katie helping him with it by moonlight. Quite romantic, if you ask me."

Hodgson looked at Ireland with moral indignation. "I don't think public displays of that sort, particularly by people of this nature, can be considered romantic."

"You may be right." She shook her head as if the memories were flooding back to her, although her recollection of the incidents were not as she was conveying to Officer Hodgson. "Leaving the remains of their activities in plain view, someone was bound to wonder. And him, running for city council, I can't imagine what he was thinking."

"What do you mean?"

"Let's just say, if it wasn't the fact that Rich had such a *long* hose and he did away with the *bushes*, people might not have noticed," Ireland paused, recalling the incident. "Well, c'est la vie."

Hodgson's jaw had dropped nearly to his knees. "You say he trimmed the bushes in public? I assume you mean Katie's?"

"No, it belonged to their next door neighbors, Rachel and Paul Cox. Paul was really angry. He liked Rachel's bush just the way it was, really full and blossoming. It takes a lot of nerve to start in with the neighbor's property right from the get-go. Quite a bold move, if you ask me. Of course, I find that rather attractive in a man."

Ireland said this last line while edging closer to Officer

Hodgson. With every step forward that Ireland made, Hodgson took one backwards until he was safely outside her door, feeling the fresh air on his beefy neck, and the need for a shower to cleanse himself from the horrors he had just heard dissipated.

"Thank you, Mrs. Alexander. You've been quite helpful. I'm sorry to have put you through all this."

"No problem, Officer. As I said, the Pettigrews are really lovely people, just a little misunderstood."

Hodgson shook his head in disbelief, and muttered to himself as he made his way back to the Pettigrew home. "They're all a bunch of useless perverts."

Chapter 28

"I knew there was something funny about them the moment they moved in," Rachel said to the others gathered at the Neighborhood Watch meeting. It was the first meeting of the group, which had just been formed for the purpose of watching and discussing the Pettigrews, although truth be told none of the neighbors had needed a formal reason to discuss them before.

"If you were so sure then why didn't you say something?" Janet asked.

"Yes," Stacey agreed, "you should have let us know."

"Oh, like you're one to talk," Rachel objected. "You're the one who sold them the house in the first place. If it weren't for you, we wouldn't be in this position."

"How dare you," Stacey said. "I'll have you know that they paid top dollar for that house. I made a pretty penny in commission off them. You should thank me, really. Because of my manipulative abilities and scare tactics, they paid an inflated price, which will only serve to improve everyone's home value."

"Sure, like having convicted felons living among us will improve the value of our neighborhood," Rachel added sarcastically.

"Ladies," Dean interrupted with a suave growl. "You can't and shouldn't blame yourselves. I should have known something was up when they wouldn't sleep with us," he said motioning to himself and Ireland. "I mean, I can understand not wanting to sleep with you all, because you're all way too suburbia, but to turn down Ireland and me, that's just insanity. Maybe that's it!"

"What's it?" Rachel asked with disgust.

"Maybe they're not criminals, just criminally insane," Dean said with the joy that comes with making a discovery.

"I'll be the judge of that," Janet interjected. "I've volunteered to give the police a statement. They're interested in my professional opinion of the Pettigrews," she said with obvious pride.

"Maybe I should speak to them," Stacey interjected. "After all, in my line of work, one really has to know how to read people."

"Oh you sure did a good job of that," Amanda said, speaking for the first time all night.

"What do you mean by that?" Stacey asked.

"Again, if it weren't for you, we wouldn't be dealing with this mess. My daughter's rabbit wouldn't have been cruelly decapitated."

"I heard the rabbit was found," Janet wondered aloud. "Katie mentioned that she found it in the janitor's closet."

"Probably a plant," Amanda said. "The police found bones in her yard. Forensics are looking into it right now."

"Forensics. Gosh," Dean interrupted. "And, with all the sex stuff, it really is a made for T.V. movie. Cool!"

"Don't be so juvenile," Rachel admonished. "This is serious."

"Don't speak to my husband that way," Ireland said, standing up for Dean.

"Well someone should. If it weren't for the two of you, maybe Rich and Katie Pettigrew would have moved out by now.

I hear that Rich got quite an eyeful every time he looked out his kitchen window."

"Really?" Ireland said, seeming pleased. "That's interesting news."

"Speaking of news," Dean said. "Maybe we could sell our story to one of the gossip magazines. You know, something like, I lived next door to sex crazed murderers."

"They're not murderers," Janet reminded. "Although...the rabbit remains...well, those remain to be found."

Amanda surveyed the crowd in front of her. These were people she knew aspired to be like her. People not that dissimilar from the Pettigrews in some ways. Each and every one of them claimed to be each other's friend, neighbor, confidante. But they were all out for number one, whether that meant riding on someone's coat tails to gain wealth, power, or fame. Social climbers, all of them.

"Forget about that," Stacey voice floated in the air, bringing the attention back to the argument. "Now about my helping the police," she said turning to Janet.

"Oh, and what about me?" Rachel asked. "I knew there was something funny about them. I can help too."

"What did you notice?" Janet asked. "That business about the pouch?"

"Oh no, that's just good fashion sense. I was referring to her jello mold."

The conversation continued in the same vain for another hour with the neighbors discussing each other's merits for cashing in on their misfortune of having crossed paths with the Pettigrews.

Officer Brolin returned to the Pettigrew home after dropping Katie off at the station where she was to be held until her arraignment. Rich was being escorted home by two other police officers. When he arrived, he discovered Officers Brolin and Hodgson going through every inch of the home.

"This is outrageous," Rich declared. "You can't just sift through our private belongings. There are laws about this sort of thing."

"Mr. Pettigrew," Officer Brolin began easily, "the laws, as you have so aptly referred to require a search warrant, which we have obtained," he said producing a piece of paper. "I suggest you have a seat until we're finished."

"Haven't you heard of the Fourth Amendment?" he asked indignantly? "As a citizen, I am free from unreasonable searches and seizures. I don't want to have a seat," Rich said like a pouting child. "I don't. I don't," he repeated and plopped himself down on the couch and hit the cushions with his fists. As he did, a cloud of dust appeared. The three men looked at it in bewilderment.

"Katie never has been much of a housekeeper," Rich said by way of explanation.

"Uh yeah...the key word was 'unreasonable,' but I'd say we definitely have reason for this search...as well as the warrant," added Brolin, who then turned to Hodgson, "Check it out."

"More of the same," Hodgson confirmed and then began removing the covers to the cushions and splitting the seams of each.

"Hey!" Rich objected. Before he could protest further, he was cuffed and his rights were being stated just as had been done for Katie a mere hour earlier.

Chapter 29

The questioning began promptly when Rich joined Katie in the holding cell. Neither understood how they could have gotten themselves in such a fix. As far as the Pettigrews were concerned, the only things they were guilty of was the intention of stealing city water, a plan that fortunately had not yet come to fruition. As a result, they were not forthcoming with the information requested by the police.

"Mr. and Mrs. Pettigrew, I'll repeat the question," Brolin said. "How long have you been involved in pornography?" The Pettigrews stared at each other, unsure of what to say. "I'll repeat my initial instructions," Brolin said patiently. "If you cooperate, we will be lenient with you."

"Say something," Katie whispered.

"What?" Rich asked in a panic.

"I've always found my husband to be an incredibly sexy man. We partake regularly," Katie declared.

"I don't think that's what he meant," Rich said.

"Right again, Mr. Pettigrew," Brolin said. "Listen, I'm going to get a cup of coffee. When I come back, I expect some answers."

"Would you be a dear and fetch me a cup of tea?" Katie asked. "Cream and sugar, please." Brolin simply walked out of the room without answering.

"That was rather rude, don't you think?" Katie asked Rich.

"Yeah, I suppose."

"What's bothering you, honey?"

"Katie, we're in prison. Doesn't it bother you?"

"Of course not. It's all a big misunderstanding. If we're lucky, you'll become a victim of police brutality and we can use that in your campaign. It'll really make headlines."

"I think my chances of winning city council at this point are probably pretty slim."

"Don't you worry, Rich," Katie said patting his arm. "Things will get better. We still have each other."

"Oh my goodness. It's horrible. Please stop. Take them away!" Katie begged.

Officers Hodgson and Brolin had produced the photos that were downloaded off the Internet. The still shots showed Katie wearing thigh high stockings and a black peignoir.

"Rich, my thighs look so big. It's just terrible. Make them stop."

Rich leaned closer to the police. "Officers, would you please tell her she doesn't look fat. Trust me, she'll be a wreck if you don't."

"Mrs. Pettigrew, are you trying to tell us that your only concern is the appearance of your thighs? Doesn't your involvement in a site known to reel minors into a world of pornography concern you in the least?" Brolin asked with sheer disgust.

"Of course, but not because I've done any of that. My husband is running for city council. We always intended to run on a platform based on ridding our streets of crime. You can't possibly think we've done any of those terrible things you've accused us of?"

"Then who has?" Hodgson asked simply. "Your neighbor told me that you and your husband performed illicit acts on your body parts in public view, that you both engaged in relations under the clear vision of your neighbors, and perhaps worst still is the fact that you both had relations with a minor child."

"Who said that?" Rich said outraged.

"Mr. Pettigrew, we know about the incident you and your wife refer to as *the bunny*," Brolin said.

"But it was with a bunny, a rabbit," Katie said, "and I paid for that mistake. I left my position as a teacher."

"A teacher!" Brolin said with disgust. "How dare you abuse the trust our parents and children instill in you."

"But I found the rabbit. The janitor did it. He confessed and everything."

"He did?" the officers said in unison.

"So much fuss over a child's pet," Rich said shaking his head.

"Pet? As in animal?" Hodgson asked. "So you haven't been, you know."

"And that coke laced lemon cake?"

"I told you...I thought it was powdered sugar, not powder!" Katie answered, not able to hide her exasperation.

"You said a Harry Greene was staying with you for a while?" Brolin asked.

The officers looked at each other and then back at the Pettigrews. "We better get this Greene character in here pronto," Brolin said.

A QUICK BLOOD TEST FROM HARRY GREENE SHOWED LARGE traces of cocaine in his system. Followed by a search of his house and car, the police confirmed what the Pettigrews had suspected, Harry Greene was an addict who had hidden his stash in their home, unbeknownst to them. Once Harry was brought in for questioning and charged with illegal possession, he copped a plea by exposing Kyle Exeter's porn hobby, a scam that helped the boy to pay for Harry's goods. Harry hated to lose a good customer, but disliked the idea of prison even more.

The police decided to go easy on Kyle seeing that he was a minor and this was his first offense. Released into the custody of his parents, the Exeters quietly left for a trip around the Bahamas so they could recover from "the ordeal" in a style they were more accustomed to.

"Maybe we should go to the Bahamas, too? Or maybe Brentwood?" Rich asked, feeling the need to get out of town, even if it were only to the town next door.

"What about the city council? Your campaign is in full swing," Katie asked.

"There's always next term...or not. Somehow, it doesn't seem as important any more."

"I know what you mean," Katie said, taking his hand, and then holding it up and adding, "this is what's important. You and me."

"You mean that?"

"Of course I do. The only constant in our lives lately has been all the madness...and each other."

"You know, we do have *something* in common with the Exeters," Rich said, maneuvering Katie closer to him, so they were side by side, his arm protectively wrapped around her.

"What's that?"

Rich smiled at Katie. "Ahh Katie Cat, you know..." he formed their fingers into a heart. "It's called love and you can't buy that."

Katie beamed. "But somehow, I think ours is more real."

They stood that way for a moment, mimicking the now

famous Exeter pose that was the subject of countless paparazzi photographs. Staring at their home, a peace came over them.

"It's not the grandest house on the street," Rich finally commented.

"No, no it's not," Katie agreed. "But it's home, and that's all we need."

Katie leaned up and kissed Rich on the cheek, an important life lesson having finally been learned...perhaps.

"You know, I just got an idea," Katie thought aloud. "Why don't you get your real estate license? You could even start by selling this place. The commission is great when you list your own property. And besides, real estate agents always drive the best cars. I can just see us now..." she said dreamily.

Having escaped their brush with the law unscathed, the Pettigrews continued to plot the course of their lives, weathering the turns and maneuvering themselves into upward mobility.

About the Author

Mia Fox is a Los Angeles-based novelist who writes across varied genres including Contemporary and Paranormal Romance, Chick Lit, and Satire. She received her Bachelor of Arts Degree in Communications from U.S.C. and a Master's Degree in Professional Writing, also from U.S.C.

Before writing full time, she worked as an entertainment publicist, a career she chronicles in her novel, "Alert the Media." However, she is happy to leave that world behind her, preferring that any drama in her life is only that which she creates for her characters.

She lives in Los Angeles with her husband, three children, and their fur children, Oliver and Bean.

Stay in touch with Mia…
www.miafox.net